CROWMAN

DAVID RAE

Milton, Ontario
http://www.brain-lag.com/

Brain Lag Publishing
Milton, Ontario
http://www.brain-lag.com/

Cover artwork by Catherine Fitzsimmons

ISBN 978-1-928011-29-3

Library and Archives Canada Cataloguing in Publication

Title: Crowman / David Rae.
Names: Rae, David, 1962- author.
Identifiers: Canadiana (print) 20190199865 | Canadiana (ebook) 20190199873 | ISBN 9781928011293
 (softcover) | ISBN 9781928011309 (ebook)
Classification: LCC PR6118.A32 C76 2020 | DDC 823/.92—dc23

Dedicated to all the monsters in my life, big and small.

Chapter One
Meetings by the Roadside

Rain soaks the canvas of the wagon and drips spitefully down the back of my neck. Windy and wild, this rain is no blessing from the dark heavens. This is the weather for huddling up and enduring, for sitting indoors and listening to the pounding on roofs and gushing through gutters and drains. It is no weather for travel, but I must press on. I have long and far to go.

I may not sleep in an inn tonight. I am tired and sore, but old men are always tired and sore. It matters not where I lay my head tonight; tomorrow, I will be back in this wagon. Back in the rain. More tiredness and more pain.

I do not recall the way I came. I have pulled my wide cap low down over my brow. If you travel enough, all roads are the same. I am travelling through the forest—the dark forest—but the whole world is dark. It will be weeks before dawn. When will I see the Sun? Only moonlight lights my way.

On the wagon rolls. There, a man sits by the roadside, huddling beneath a tree, his ragged black clothing and wide straw hat soaked. He looks even more miserable than I feel. No one should be out in this rain.

The poet says that mercy is like rain. I do not see the similarity. Still, it would be a mercy—a simple mercy—to stop and offer the soaked man shelter and a lift. Small kindnesses are all the blessing I can give. I cannot stop the rain or make the Sun shine, but I can do this. I flick the reins and bring the horse to a halt.

"Hi, stranger!" I call, and the black-clad man looks up at me. "You look wet."

"Yes," comes the single, harsh reply.

"Can I offer you a lift?" I ask.

"Yes."

The black-clad man jumps with surprising grace up onto the wagon beside me. Now that he is closer and in the light of my lantern, I can see that he is tall and thin, as tall and thin as I am. The lower part of his face is covered with a dark neckerchief to keep out the damp, but above, two bright, black eyes shine out. Across his back, I see that he carries a black-bound blade. Is he a warrior? He does not look like one. A warrior would be broad-chested, muscled, and better armed. He looks like a scraggy old man. He looks like me.

"My name is Utas," I offer.

"Pleased to meet you, Utas," the dark man replies.

I wait a bit, but he does not offer his name, so I ask.

"What is your name?"

There seems to be a bit of a pause, as a stiffness or readiness comes over the dark man. He looks at me and then answers, "Erroi."

A single word; that is all he offers—nothing else.

"Pleased to meet you, Erroi," I say.

"Yes," replies Erroi. "Pleased to meet you."

For a while, we trek on through the gloom and rain in silence. No, that is not correct; it is not silent. We hear the flapping of the wind through the canvas of the wagon, the slap of the horse's hooves on the road, and the creaking of wooden wheels, but we do not share words—not for long miles. We do not sleep. Our eyes do not close. We gain no rest or peace. But we slumber, barely aware of the world passing around us.

I'd like to say I woke with a start, but I did not. A log—a fallen tree—lies across the road. I can see it stretching straight across the track. There is no way around it. The road is too narrow to turn around, and even if I could, there is no other way to go.

Two men step out from the forest and stand at the side of the road. They are armed. They are well armed, and one of them is very strong looking. They are bandits. The two bandits have rolled the log across the path. I consider charging the horse past them to escape, but there is no chance of that; the old horse is unlikely to break into a gallop and the cart would most likely crack an axle going over the log. I have no option. I pull the wagon to a stop and say a silent prayer.

"May I help you, sirs?" I ask. Fear is no excuse for abandoning courtesy.

The two bandits snigger.

"Shut your trap and get down out of your wagon!" demands the larger of the two bandits. These two do look like warriors… or at least one of them does; he is big-chested and muscled. He is armed with a sword and shield, and he is clad in studded leather armour. There are two daggers hanging from his belt, and a round, metal cap covers his head. The scrawny bandit is dressed in rags and is unarmed. He walks to the horse and holds it so it will not bolt. Slowly, I ease myself down from the wagon. In some ways, it is nice to stretch for bit. Perhaps I will get only a small beating.

"You too," demands the bigger thug, pointing at my passenger.

Erroi does not move. "Why?" he asks—a single, harsh question.

"Because I say so! Now move it, before I climb up there and drag you down by the bits!" snarls the bandit.

Erroi leans back with casual ease. "Yes," he says. "Come up here."

The bandit draws his sword and leaps to the wagon to pull himself up… or, at least, he tries to. I do not see clearly what happens. It is a blur of black cloth whipping, black blade swinging, bandit falling, red blood flowing, and bandit dying. It is so quick that I can barely gasp before it is over, and the air is tangy with the smell of blood… so much blood.

"Wha—" the small bandit and I stammer in unison, and before we can form a word, a black shadow flutters over me and over the bandit. There is no ringing of steel or clashing of swords. Instead, Erroi is now standing over the second prone bandit, and his black blade is pointed at the bandit's throat.

"Wait," I call, and Erroi turns to look at me, but keeps his blade against the bandit's throat.

"What?" Again, a single, harsh question.

"There's no need to kill him. You've bested him; just send him on his way."

"If I do not kill him, he will return with others and try to kill us again," says Erroi. "Better to kill him now. They would have killed us if they could have."

"No, no, sir," begs the bandit. "Stolen from you at least, perhaps beaten you a little, but not kill; we're not murderers."

"He was and would have," says Erroi, indicating the corpse of the other bandit, and we both know he is speaking the truth.

Still, to save a life is not a small kindness; it is a great one. I cannot make the Sun shine or stop the rain, but I can plead for a life.

"He's only a boy," I say.

"Boys grow," says Erroi, "and he will have friends."

"Please," begs the boy. "Kilhanga was no friend of mine. He used to beat me and made me come with him. I've never killed anyone, I swear." We both know he is speaking the truth.

"What is your name?" I ask.

"My name is Mukito," the boy replies.

A name is a magical thing, a special thing. Perhaps we could have killed a bandit in cold blood, perhaps we could have killed a boy in cold blood, but we could not kill him now. His name has made him real; it has made him one of us.

"My name is Utas, and this is Erroi," I say.

Erroi looks at me with his black eyes. During the scuffle, his neckerchief slipped down from his face, revealing thin features and a long, straight nose. He looks at me and sheathes his sword. Is he disapproving or relieved? I cannot tell.

"So you have decided," he says. "Boy, Mukito, you will come with us."

"Come with you?" Mukito splutters as he gets to his feet.

"Yes. If you will not come with us, then I will kill you," says Erroi.

"But—"

Before Mukito can say more, Erroi silences him with a glance. "Do not try to run away," says Erroi.

Now Mukito is standing up in his ragged, muddy clothes. He looks barely more than a child; he is barely more than a child. He is a child.

"Perhaps the boy has a mother," I suggest.

"Everyone has a mother," says Erroi and gestures towards the log blocking our path. He and Mukito lift the log and roll it out of our path, and then Erroi climbs back up onto the wagon.

"Wait," calls Mukito and runs over to the fallen body of his companion. He gathers up the dead bandit's weapons and gear and strips him naked. I can see the cruel cut from Erroi's sword tracing a line of gaping black-red down his chest. Mukito rolls the dead bandit out of the road and then, to my surprise, spits in the bandit's face and kicks him hard.

"That's for all the beatings you gave. I swore one day I would be even. I guess I'll just have to settle for this. I am well rid of you."

"Is there no kindnesses you would wish to repay also?" I ask, hoping to soften the boy's anger.

Mukito just snorts.

"This is a harsh world, sometimes people in it are harsher than they mean to be," I advise.

The boy does not reply.

"It seems that even though he beat you, he fed you and clothed you," I add. "Perhaps he meant to train you up to be a bandit. Perhaps that was the only life he knew and that was all he could think to give you. He must have kept you safe from beasts, or perhaps from the bigger and worse members of your band. Surely, he has done some small kindness that you cannot now recall. Offer a prayer on your companion's behalf. In that way, should his spirit cross your path, it will be in your debt."

"A prayer will cost you nothing," says Erroi. "Come with me and we will both say one. That way, should he come to haunt me tonight, he will be in my debt and then he will be merciful." Erroi walks over to the corpse.

Mukito stands over the prone corpse beside Erroi; his head is bowed and he mutters a few words that I cannot hear. I can see a single tear trace a line on his already wet and muddy check. He wipes his eyes with a ragged sleeve, then he moves to put the bandit's belongings in the back of the wagon.

"Wait," I cry. "I don't want that bloodied, flea ridden gear in with my cargo. If you want it, carry it in the front."

Erroi gives me another strange look. I wonder if he knows what I am thinking. Mukito puts the gear in the front of the wagon and then climbs up.

"Yes, that's right," I say. "Stay in the front where we can see you. I don't want you rifling through my wares."

Now there is nothing to do but to ride on. Throughout the disturbance, the horse has remained calm and undisturbed. I climb up and seat myself between the two passengers and flick the reins. The horse starts forward. I move closer to my destination.

At first, we travel in silence—the same silence we travelled in before, full of the sounds of the wagon and the rain. Mukito would like to talk, but he is afraid, afraid and excited. Erroi has pulled his neckerchief over his long nose and tugged his straw hat over his eyes. He is pretending to be asleep. But he is not; he is watchful and alert. I do not talk. I must think what to say. I have seen that Erroi is more than just a traveller, and I have acquired a boy. It seems it will be difficult to rid myself of my passengers.

The boy cannot stay silent for long. "Where are we going?" he asks.

Where indeed? I think.

"There is a town further on," I reply. "Can you see the lights? We will stop there and sleep."

Erroi breathes in, a little mock snore laced with laughter.

"From there, you and your new master can go where you will," I continue, irritated.

That gets Erroi's attention. He straightens up and pushes his straw hat back. "I am not his master; you are. The boy goes with you."

"You spared him. When we get to the town, you can either take him with you or let him go. He's not coming with me. I have far to travel and scarce enough to feed myself on the journey," I reply.

"You stayed my hand. The boy is your responsibility," Erroi states flatly.

"If he was my responsibility, we would have left him where he was," I respond.

"Killing him would have been more merciful than leaving him," Erroi replies. "If he had gone back to his band empty handed, without the fat bandit, they would have killed him, and not a swift death with a single sword stroke."

"Please," says Mukito, "the great swordsman is right. Don't send me back."

Erroi laughs. It is a good, clear, ringing laugh, full of pleasure and amusement.

"I'm not a swordsman," he says.

"I have never seen better," says Mukito, and truthfully neither have I.

"I am not a fighter," says Erroi.

"Are you a magician, then?" asks Mukito.

"No, I am not a magician," says Erroi and pulls his straw hat over his eyes; he will say no more for now.

At length, we arrive at the town. It is a poor town and food is poor and expensive. But every town is poor and food is always poor and expensive, except when the Sun comes out. We halt at an inn and after I have made the horse comfortable and secured the wagon, I send Mukito to sell the weapons and the gear he took from the dead bandit.

"He will not come back," says Erroi.

"If so, then may he prosper," I respond.

To be rid of the boy for the cost of the few coins he can raise from selling the bandit's gear will be a bargain. But Mukito does come back. Although he tries to hide it, Erroi is pleased the boy has returned. Perhaps he is a better man than I am. Who would wish a child to be cast adrift in this lawless place, with only a few coins to keep him?

"Will you bring your goods into the inn for safekeeping?" asks Mukito, and walks over to the wagon to help. But I shake my head and wave him away. Erroi laughs again.

We enter the inn. It is good to come in out of the darkness. There are lanterns and a bright fire. I turn to ask Erroi if he will eat with us, but he is gone. I feel a little sad. But Mukito and I sit at a table near enough to the fire to warm and dry us.

"It is like the Sun," says Mukito, reaching towards the fire to warm his fingers.

"Have you seen the Sun?" I ask.

"No," says Mukito. "I have just glimpsed it from a distance, but my mother always used to say the Sun is like a fire. One day, I hope I have enough gold to pay for a visit to the Sun."

"It takes a lot of gold to visit the Sun. It is a far journey to the City of the Sun, and even then, Vatu only unshrouds it on one day a year. Other than that, you must pay gold and tribute to Vatu. Even then, he is as likely to keep your gold and send you away without opening the box of the Sun as he is to show it."

"Have you seen the Sun?" asks Mukito.

I gesture to the innkeeper and he comes over.

"For both of us please," I ask.

The innkeeper returns later with two bowls and places them in front of us. The food is poor and meagre, but Mukito is glad of it. It is not difficult to see that he has had a hard life.

"So," I say. "You have a mother, at least?"

"Everyone has a mother," replies Mukito.

"Yes, but not everyone can remember them, especially not poor bandit boys."

"She's dead," Mukito says flatly, as if that explains everything. "She died when I was small."

What to do, I wonder to myself. Perhaps I can place the boy with a tradesman or a hunter. I surely can't take the boy with me. It is a pity that Erroi has deserted us. He could have taken him.

"Stay here," I say and go back out to check the wagon. As soon as I step outside, Erroi appears.

"I thought you were gone," I say. "I would have bought you a meal in gratitude." I realize that I have not thanked him for... For what? For killing a man? For loading me down with Mukito? For saving me from a beating or death? I could not be grateful for any of that.

"I was here," replies Erroi.

"Well, go and warm yourself by the fire. I have to check on a few things."

I turn to go to the wagon, but Erroi remains where he is. I try again.

"Mukito is in there; you should keep an eye on him," I say, but still Erroi remains. How can I get rid of him? "Here," I say, casting a coin over to him. "Go and rent us a room."

Erroi catches the coin with one swift, graceful, fluttering movement, but does not move. It is no use. I turn to go inside again and will come back later.

"I know," Erroi says.

That stops me.

"Know what?" I ask.

"What is in the wagon," replies Erroi.

"How can you know that?"

"I know," says Erroi.

I see there is nothing for it. I tend to things and then return to the inn. Mukito is still sitting at the table, but now his head is lying on his arms and he is asleep. It is a shame to wake him. I gently shake him and gesture upstairs.

Our room is not large. There are three beds and some dirty-looking blankets. It makes no difference which bed I take; they all look hard and uninviting and smell of urine. Perhaps we would have been better to have camped out of town in the rain. Mukito takes his worn boots off and climbs into the nearest one.

Erroi is here. How he got in, I don't know. I had locked the door behind us. He is sitting on the bed opposite me.

"You should bring her in," he says. "She will be safer here."

"Can I trust the boy? Can I trust you?" I ask.

Again, Erroi's eyes hold a mocking look. "I think you can trust the boy, at least."

"But not you?" I ask.

"No, not me," Erroi says, shaking his head, "but I already know."

Erroi helps me carry the bundle up to the room. We lock the door again and set the bundle on the floor. Carefully, we begin to unwrap it and there, lying in the blanket, frail and ill and beautiful, is my daughter.

I lay my daughter in the bed and I lie on the floor. I replace the dirty blankets with her soft, silken wrappings and she sleeps; her hand reaches out to me and her breath is soft. She sleeps through the night. It is a small kindness, for which I am grateful. I stay awake all night, looking at her glowing skin and pale, silvery hair. Even in this world, there are things too precious to lose; things a man will give his life for, things a man will give up anything for.

Erroi seems to sleep all night, but who can know for sure? Certainly there are soft snores from both him and Mukito. But perhaps he is also keeping watch. If so, I am grateful. I am grateful he saved the life of my daughter today also.

In the morning, it seems I slept after all. Erroi is awake and alert. Mukito is still asleep. He is barely bigger than my daughter. Perhaps we should wrap up Alaba before he wakes. I move to cover her with the silk wrappings, but as I do, Mukito wakes up. He rises up, snorting and stamping his feet and wiping his eyes. And then he stops.

"What…" he begins to say.

"Hush!" says Erroi. "No one must know she is here."

Mukito gathers himself. He is a quick thinker. He nods his head and says nothing. He helps us wrap Alaba in her silks, and then Erroi and Mukito carry her to the wagon.

At least it has stopped raining. I am ungrateful for the blessing of rain. We gently place Alaba in the back of the wagon amongst the other bales of silk. You would think that the wagon contained only cloth.

"Where will you go now?" asks Erroi.

"Further on," I reply. "To the next town, for now. That is enough for now."

"Why is that town better than this?" asks Erroi.

I do not know how to answer. Maybe he is right; maybe we should rest here, for a while at least. I have been travelling so long and so far. In the end, there will be no roads left to travel. In the end, every journey finishes. But my journey is not over, not yet. I can still run. I say nothing and just shrug. Then I turn and hitch the horse to the wagon. Mukito has climbed up onto the wagon seat. To my surprise, so has Erroi. He has huddled down and pulled his straw hat over his eyes.

What is the name of this town? I do not recall. It is like so many other towns; a wall, a gate, a market, an inn, and soldiers. Vatu's soldiers are everywhere. We wait to be allowed out of the gate. There is some kind of holdup. It looks as if the soldiers are checking for something. Perhaps my journey will end here.

Eventually, it is our turn. A soldier comes up to the cart.

"Where are you going?" he asks.

"Kota," I reply.

"That's a long way," replies the soldier cheerfully. "What are you taking there?"

I slip down from the wagon.

"Come, let me show you," I say. "Silk, some of the finest you'll ever see." And I open the canvas flap at the back of the wagon. "When I get there, I'll be able to sell this for a fortune. I'm getting old and this will be my last trip. When I sell this, I will have enough to settle down."

The soldier looks and runs a hand over a bolt of fine, sky blue shot silk.

"It's beautiful silk," he agrees, looking over the load. I know what he is thinking. He is imagining his lover dressed in blue silk. He wishes to do her a kindness. A soldier is not paid well; it is a poor life, yet every soldier has a lover. Why is that?

"Yes, it is beautiful," I agree. "I paid a good price for it. But I will get a better price when I sell it. There is a lot of it, though, and it took nearly all my coin to buy it. I had hoped to sell a little here to pay for our lodgings. I took that bolt to the market and the best offer I got was ten gold pieces for the whole bale. I'd rather starve than let someone steal from me."

The soldier is startled. Ten gold pieces is a lot of money, but not an awful lot of money. Certainly more than a soldier could afford to pay. He sighs. The picture of his lover in blue silk begins to fade from his mind. I must work quickly.

"He said he wanted a sample to show a customer, and like a fool, I cut him a length. Look here." And with that, I pull a length of cloth a yard long out from under the bolt of blue silk. A yard is not a lot of cloth, but it is enough for a chemise or bodice. "Totally worthless to me now."

I must be careful. I can tell the soldier has a good heart and that means he will be harder to fool. I cannot just give him the cloth. He would think I was trying to bribe him, and that would make him suspicious. I take the blue cloth and start to fold it away. I shake it out on to the wagon, and in the torchlight, the blue silk billows like the sky in sunlight and settles on the wagon like a blue ocean. Because the soldier is not greedy, he will not ask me for it or offer me a price.

"You would think the fool could have offered me a few shillings for it, at least," I grumble. The price is ridiculously low, but I know the soldier will not be able to afford more, and if he could, it would no longer be a small act of kindness to buy it for his lover.

"How many shillings would you want for it?" asks the soldier. I can hear hope in his voice.

"Why? Do you like it?" I ask. "Soldiers don't wear blue silk very often." My voice is laced with surprise.

The soldier blushes slightly; I forget that most of them are still children.

"It's not for me. It's for someone else," the soldier says and blushes more. Now he is thinking not of his lover in her dress, but of her grateful and happy eyes.

"Well…" I hesitate. If I ask too much, the deal is off; too little and I arouse his suspicions.

"Twelve, twelve shillings," the soldier says. "It's all I can afford. You'll need to wait here while I go and collect the money. Will you wait? Is it enough?"

The soldier is more honest than I thought. Twelve shillings is almost a fair price. I would rather he had offered less and let us on our way. I hesitate and the soldier misinterprets my pause.

"Fourteen shillings," he says. "The sergeant owes me two shillings. I'll get them from him."

I cannot let him talk to his sergeant about us. That could be disastrous.

"How much have you got on you now?" I ask. "I had hoped to make the next town today. I don't like to camp wild at my age; it hurts my bones. Give me what you've got and it's a deal."

Again, the soldier sighs. "Six shillings. But I'm off duty soon. I'll give you the six now and catch up with you and pay the rest."

"Yes, six shillings," I agree. "The thing is worthless to me anyhow."

I take the six shillings that the soldier has in his pouch. He offers me a few coppers that he has left over, but I wave them away. I hand him the folded silk, which he stuffs into his jerkin, and then he waves us on. We are through the gate.

How many lies did you tell today, old man? How many more lies will you tell?

Outside the walls, the glow of torches quickly fades as we follow the path onwards. There are torches along the pathway for the first few miles, but as we go on, they become fewer and finally stop. Soon, we are back in the gloom, lit only by our own lantern and by the stars. The moon has risen, but it is a bare fingernail of scarce light. As we leave the bare, withered fields, there is less and less company on the road. Eventually, we are trekking over desolate moorland. As far as I can see, there is only scrubby heath.

"Tell me now," says Mukito. "What is going on?"

"Can I trust you?" I ask.

"Yes, of course!" says Mukito, forgetting that he tried to rob me just yesterday.

Perhaps Mukito is right; perhaps the past is insignificant, perhaps we just have to trust those around us. I suppose I need to trust Mukito and Erroi.

"I have lived in the City of the Sun," I say.

Erroi interrupts. "You do not get brown skin like yours living anywhere else. Like I said, I know. You do not need to explain anything to me. I know."

"I didn't know that," says Mukito. "I suppose it makes sense. The Sun makes skin golden. My mother told me that, but I never thought about it. Yours is very golden. Now that I think about it, it's the most golden I've seen. Not that I've seen many with golden skin. My mother's skin was golden, but not as golden as yours. And she had spots of gold on her face and arms, like a sprinkling of gold dust. Her hair was golden too, not like mine."

"Freckles," says Erroi. "They are called freckles. I think if you lived in the City of the Sun, then you'd have them, too. And your hair would turn golden."

"Would I?" ponders Mukito. "Does everyone in the City of the Sun have freckles and golden hair?"

"No, indeed not." I laugh. "Very few. Freckles are kisses of the Sun. The Sun must have loved your mother very much, by the sounds of it."

"You don't have golden hair," says Mukito.

"No, very few people in the City of the Sun have golden hair. Most have dark hair and dark eyes, like mine. Dark skin, dark hair, dark eyes; they help shield you from the fierceness of the Sun. But golden skin and golden hair—they let you embrace the beauty of the Sun. You must not think we get to see the Sun every day in the City of the Sun. Only once a year will Vatu take the Sun to his highest tower and open the box of the Sun to shine on the city and the valley, for one day. Every other time, there are only cracks of sunlight coming through windows and under doors or glowing through the cracks in the stone walls of his palace."

"Why does Alaba not have dark skin?" asks Mukito.

I cannot bring myself to answer; instead, we trek on farther through the dark. When the moon slips below the horizon, we stop.

We have travelled far and now we are tired and hungry. We have not made the next town, but I did not really wish to. Mukito loosens the traces of the cart and rubs the old horse down. Then he leads the horse over to a clump of dry rushes. It is not much for the old horse to eat, but it is as good a meal as she will find in this desolate world. We will eat scarcely better. Erroi has collected a few dry twigs and lit a small fire using our lantern. We sit around the fire for warmth and I busy myself cooking a thin gruel. It will be poor fare, but scarcely worse than what we ate at the inn.

"How far from the Sun do you think we are?" asks Mukito.

Not far enough, I think, but just shrug and do not answer.

Erroi replies instead. "We are a long way from the Sun. On the day the Sun shines, it barely reaches here, I would guess. It must takes days, or weeks, possibly months to get to the City of the Sun from here. As you go further from the Sun, plants grow slower. In the Valley of the Sun, whole fields of corn sprout up and ripen, ready for harvest in a few hours, and apples burst into flower and fruit and flower and fruit over and over. Forests grow faster than a man can take an axe to them. Here, I'm guessing, the fields barely yield fruit."

Mukito looks at Erroi, wide-eyed. "I don't believe you," he says and looks at me for support.

"Erroi is correct," I tell him. "When the Sun is out in the Valley of the Sun, nature is bountiful and generous. It is a great blessing, but also hard work. Some will dance in the streets and celebrate the warmth and beauty of the Sun, but most of the people must harvest, and then harvest again and again, until the Sun goes away for another year. The Sun is glorious and fills your bones with strength and health. Even old men have the strength to chop and dig and plant and hoe and water and harvest."

Mukito looks up. "When the Sun came out, Kilhanga would make me gather nuts and berries, great big baskets of them. But no matter how big the baskets were, we were always short of food just before the dawn came. We were always hungry those last few weeks before sunup. All you could see was a bright glow coming from the Valley of the Sun, and then the warmth. Even if it was hard work, it was still the best day of the year. When the Sun went down, we knew we would not be going to bed hungry. When my mother was alive, she would buy corn seed and we would plant it and harvest it, but after she died, Kilhanga never seemed to have any coin. Even when he stole it, it did not last."

Erroi interrupts us again. "He is coming."

I turn and see a lamp moving in the dark. It is the honest soldier riding towards us.

"You should let me kill him," says Erroi.

"No, he is just an honest boy doing what he thinks is best," I say, horrified because of the cruelty of the suggestion and because I know he is right.

"True," agrees Erroi. "Still, it would be easier."

Eventually, the soldier catches up with us. His face is smiling and he is pleased to see us. "Hosta loved the silk! Thank you so much," he says. Hosta must be his lover. No, not his lover, his sister, a younger, favoured sister. The boy is kinder even than I had supposed. I cannot let Erroi kill him, no matter what.

The soldier dismounts and we pretend to make him welcome.

"You have come a long way," he says. "I thought you were going to Kota. You'd have been better sticking to the main road. I was going that way, but I asked some travellers and they said they had not seen you and suggested you must have come this way."

"You should not have troubled; this is a long ride for six shillings," I say.

"Eight shillings," corrects the soldier. "I said I would pay fourteen shillings. I got the two shillings the sergeant owed me. He grumbled a bit at first, but when I showed him the silk, he said even at fourteen shillings, it was a bargain."

Part of me is glad he has told his sergeant. Now I cannot let Erroi kill him, no matter what. If I did, they would be hunting for a cartload of silk and three travellers all over the dark lands. We would be stopped and taken at any town we visited.

"Come," I say. "Come and eat with us. Tell us your name."

"My name is Zintoa," says the soldier, "and I have to say, this is the worst gruel I've tasted in a long time. You should put some salt or honey in it, or berries. Don't you know there are edible berries growing on the heath? Here, let me show you. You need to get right down to the moss."

For a few minutes, he and Mukito take one of the lanterns and scrabble around in the heath. They return to the camp with a handful of dark red berries that look like drops of dried blood.

"Put them in the gruel and let them stew for a bit. They'll burst and let the flavour spread, and a little sweetness. Trust me, it will be worth it," says Zintoa. "But here, I'm forgetting to give you your money." He hands over eight shillings.

"I thank you for your kindness, large and small," I say, and I mean it. All kindness brings joy to the heart that receives them. I am touched to find such kindness in the dreary world.

In a few moments, the gruel is cooked, and I must say, much improved. Mukito carries a bowl over to the soldier and Erroi scoops up a large bowl for himself. Mukito is not much younger than Zintoa, a few years perhaps. A few years may seem like a long time to the young, but it is as nothing.

"Tell me, what was the holdup this morning?" asks Mukito. He is only trying to make conversation and means no harm, but I stiffen and Erroi shifts onto his feet.

"We were looking for a girl," says Zintoa. "Vatu is determined to find her. Why, I don't know. There are lots of girls in the world. How would we even know which one it is he's looking for? When I gave Hosta the silk, I said we could dress her up and send her to Vatu. She'd like to live in the City of the Sun, and so would I."

Mukito looks down at his feet guiltily. I hope that Zintoa does not notice and I curse Mukito for a fool under my breath, but it is not his fault. I should have trusted him. I should have told him. Erroi was right.

"Why would you like to live there?" I ask.

Zintoa laughs. "Why, because it is always warm and bright and there is lots to eat. Sometimes you can go up to Vatu's palace and he has big parties where he opens up the box of the Sun and you can all dance and sing in the sunlight for days and days on end."

"Really?" asks Mukito.

"Well, I don't know. I've never been there, but that's what they say," says Zintoa.

Is that what they say? Perhaps it is. Those that have never been there can imagine whatever they like. Certainly, there are parties at Vatu's palace, where girls must dance for days on end, and other things.

"I thank you again for your honesty and kindness," I say. "But you have a long ride home now. Perhaps you should be going."

I am bad mannered to suggest a guest should leave, but Zintoa is not offended.

"Yes, of course," he agrees and turns to mount his horse. Perhaps if he had ridden off then, all would have been well. Perhaps the Gods punish me for my rudeness. Perhaps all things are written and the Gods' will always prevails. But as he turns to leave, a great beast rears up from the moor. Where it has come from, I do not know. It must have been stalking us. Our horse rears and screams and Erroi leaps to his feet. Erroi moves to draw his sword, but Zintoa rushes forward towards the beast.

"Leave this to me!" he cries with the confidence of youth and draws his sword. Erroi ignores Zintoa's request and moves to intercept the beast before it can harm the soldier.

I stay him with a motion of my hand.

Erroi looks at me reproachfully. "You will not let me kill the soldier, but you will let him die thinking he is defending us?" he hisses.

Shamed, I nod, and Erroi leaps forward in blur of black cloth and shadow. The beast, a great cat, is dead instantly, but not before raking its claws across Zintoa's arm and chest. The soldier is wounded, not fatally, but severely. There is lots of blood. Mukito is first to Zintoa's side. He is the only one of us who is not thinking it might be better if the soldier dies.

"Hold still," says Mukito, and checks Zintoa's wounds. "You have ribs broken and you are losing blood. Quickly! We need to bind and clean these cuts. There are a couple of punctures that look worrying."

Erroi is looking at me. I know what he is thinking, but the soldier has done me small kindness and I owe him that at least.

"There is canvas in the wagon," I say. "It is stiffer than silk and more absorbent. It will give more support. Also, you will find oil; use it to wipe the wounds, then cut the canvas into strips and bind them."

Mukito runs to the wagon.

"Also," I continue, "bring out Alaba. She will need to be fed. The soldier will not be going anywhere now. We cannot wait for him to leave and we cannot hide her longer."

Zintoa seems not to hear. He is crying softly in pain. He is lucky to be alive; the cat would surely have killed him. We are also lucky to be alive. Once again, Erroi has saved my life. Even now, in despair, I live. The Gods have saved me; I am faithless.

Erroi tends Zintoa's wounds, and Mukito and I carry Alaba over to the fire. He feeds her what is left of the gruel and I watch. Alaba eats well. I did not think she would eat so much.

Zintoa struggles to sit up. "Will you kill me now?" he asks. He understands. He is quicker than I took him for.

"Of course not!" Mukito says. "Utas is not a murderer, and neither am I."

May the Gods bless you, Mukito, for reminding me of that.

"But you think I am?" asks Erroi, with amusement.

"No, not a murderer," says Mukito.

Zintoa sinks back and sighs. "Then what?" he asks. It is the question we all wish we could answer.

"We could leave you here after we've gone," suggests Mukito, but we all know that would be murder by another name.

"I could take him back to town," Erroi suggests, but can I trust the life of the honest boy to the dark man? Erroi told me I could not trust him.

"I'll take him," says Mukito. "On his horse. We can lash him to the horse and I'll lead it to the town."

"What happens to you, boy, when you turn up with a soldier's corpse?" sneers Erroi, and he is right. Even if Zintoa is not a corpse, Mukito will be locked up, or worse. It would be his death instead of the soldier's. How is that fair?

"We're going nowhere tonight. We need make no decisions now. Bring Zintoa closer to the fire. When you lose blood, you lose heat. We need to keep him warm. There are blankets in the wagon. Bring them. And make sure he drinks enough water," I say.

Once the soldier is settled, I carry Alaba close to the fire. She also needs to keep warm. I sit and watch the stars spin in the heavens. I cannot sleep. Mukito is sleeping and Erroi is at least pretending to sleep. But Zintoa lies all night with his eyes open, staring at Alaba and the soft glow that comes from her skin. I cannot see her face, but she does not turn away from him.

In the dark lands, there is only one dawn. Each day is signalled only by the singing of birds at the rising of the moon. The birds sing and Erroi and Mukito awaken. There can no longer be any delay. It is time to decide. No. I have already decided.

Mukito goes to wrap up Alaba.

"Leave her," I say, and I carry Alaba and set her carefully in the front of the wagon. She looks at me, saying nothing, but she smiles; perhaps she knows what I will do. Then I carry Zintoa and place him beside Alaba.

"So," says Erroi. "That is not what I would do."

"Thank you for your kindness, my friend," I say. "Please look after Mukito."

Then I turn the wagon and trek back to the town.

"Goodbye, friend," calls Erroi.

"Wait!" shouts Mukito, but Erroi is holding him back.

Chapter Two
Turning to the Light

It is a delight to see my daughter's face. Even just by the light of my lantern, it seems to glow brighter, brighter than any lamp. I think I could almost travel by the light of her face alone. But I know I cannot. Zintoa is still looking at her.

"Your daughter is very beautiful," he says.

"Yes," I say. "If I hide her again, will you let us go? It would be a kindness."

Zintoa shakes his head. I know he will not, but I had to ask.

"Why does she glow?" he asks.

"Because the Sun loves her," I reply truthfully. "His light is fading from her now, but once, she glowed like a beacon with his light."

"How is that possible?"

"I don't know. I only know it is possible. When the Sun shines on her, she gains strength, but as the light fades from her, so does her strength. Now, she can barely sit or talk. Once, she could dance and sing for days on end."

Alaba smiles, at me. They were happy days, at least some of them. Remembrance is a blessing, like rain and sunshine. Sometimes it is hard to be grateful for blessings.

Zintoa reaches over with his good arm and takes her hand in his. I am surprised. I know it is meant as kindness, but I feel anger rising within me. I say a silent prayer for the Gods to forgive me. Alaba does not push his hand away. Instead, her fingers curl around his. For a short instant, it seems she glows brighter. Zintoa gives a start. He has seen it too. I did not imagine it.

We left early and should arrive at the town by mid-moon. Nevertheless, I expect to meet Zintoa's comrades searching for him before then. I mention it to my passenger, but he shakes his head.

"No, the guards will not start looking for me until my shift starts. Even then, they will probably check the taverns and whorehouses first. Only then will they start to think to come out and look for me on the road."

"Is that where they would usually find you?" I ask the Gods to forgive me for my unkindness.

The soldier blushes. "No, usually I am on time for all my duty. But there are other soldiers who are not. That is where we check first, when someone is missing; usually that is where we find them. My mother will have gone to the sergeant last night, but he will think I am spending the two shillings he gave me elsewhere. I don't think he believed me when I said I was going to pay you the eight shillings."

How I wish he had not. Now we could be travelling farther from the City of the Sun with Erroi and Mukito. But in the end, what good would that have been? Eventually, either Alaba would have faded to nothing or Vatu's soldiers would have caught us. Every journey comes to an end eventually. I pray that my journey will end before Alaba's does. No father should see his child die.

"Forgive me. I have been unkind."

"Not at all," says Zintoa. "I owe you my life: first you save me from the great cat, now you let me live, even if it means ill for you. I am in your debt forever."

"But the debt is not enough to let us go," I reply, overlooking the fact that it was Erroi that saved him from the cat. My mind wanders again to Erroi. I have never seen anyone move so fast.

Zintoa seems to be getting stronger. By rights, he should still be gasping in pain with every jolt of the wagon, but he seems to be sitting up, sitting right up, and his breathing is normal, not laboured. He is playing with his bandages. I should tell him to leave them alone. His wounds itch, no doubt, but are best left. He takes his hand from my daughter's and looks down, puzzled. I want to ask him what is wrong, but before I do, he removes all of his bandages.

"I don't need these anymore," he says, and I see his wounds are completely healed, leaving not even a scar. I am amazed. I turn and look at my daughter, but she is sleeping prone along the bench. She has pulled her wrappings over her and her outline is glowing faintly through the silk.

Zintoa is right. No one is looking for him when we arrive. I look towards Zintoa, in hope, but he will not meet my eyes.

The sergeant spies him when we enter the gate and shouts out, "Where have you been? Your duty started an hour ago."

"I have a prisoner, Sergeant Borroka," says Zintoa. "Two prisoners."

"You do?" asks the sergeant, scratching his head.

"Yes, I have that girl we're looking for, and her father."

"Where? Let's see."

Zintoa lifts the covering from Alaba, and the sergeant can see my daughter sleeping peacefully and shining in the darkness.

"That's her, all right." The sergeant whistles. "Well done, Zinty. This is likely a promotion for you. How'd you know the traveller was carrying the girl?"

"I didn't. It's a long story," says Zintoa.

Strong arms pull me down from the cart. Zintoa lifts Alaba gently and covers her again in her silks. The sergeant takes us into the guard house. The guard house is strongly built, but small and low. There is a small, iron cell in one corner. I had expected us to be thrown into it and locked up, but they set Alaba carefully down on a rough cot, and I am allowed to sit by her. The sergeant, Borroka, looks through a pile of papers. He does not seem very pleased to have caught such important prisoners. Eventually, he finds what he is looking for and puts some eyeglasses on before he begins to read.

"You're to go to the City of the Sun, it says. We're to take you."

The sergeant sighs. He has never been to the City of the Sun. The thought of a long journey cannot be appealing. "You'll need to come too, Zinty. After all, you caught them."

"We'll need more than just the two of us," says Zintoa. "They were travelling with one of the finest swordsmen I have ever seen."

"Right, and then this swordsman just let you toddle off with the girl and the old man."

"It's true."

"Is it?" asks Borroka, addressing me for the first time.

"Yes," I agree. "He is the finest swordsman I have seen."

"Hmm, seen many?"

I have, but I just nod. That seems to be enough for the sergeant.

"So who is he?" asks the sergeant.

"I don't really know," I reply truthfully. "He is just a stranger I met by the roadside. I have seen him draw his sword twice."

"He killed a great cat," puts in Zintoa.

"A cat; he killed a great cat? Well, anything is possible. I suppose he just got lucky. If he's just a stranger, no doubt he'll just go on his way. Still, there are other things out there in the dark. The Sun does not come up every day, and it's a long way to go by torchlight."

They bring us food. It is better than the food we ate at the inn, but not as good as the gruel that Zintoa cooked for us. Zintoa helps Alaba to eat. He is very gentle.

Sergeant Borroka pushes a parchment in front of me. "Sign this," he says.

"What is it?"

"A receipt for your wagon and goods and for your coins. If you come back, you can reclaim it. Of course, I can't guarantee you will come back. Most likely you won't, and I can't guarantee that even if you do come back, it will still be here. Thieves everywhere these days." By which he means himself. He means to take the wagon and goods for himself. "Still, all signed, good and legal. I'd keep that with you, just in case. You might get lucky."

"Of course," I say and bow politely.

"No need to thank me," says the sergeant.

No, no indeed.

They do not lock us in the cell; not even later, when Zintoa has left. There is now just one guard. He is old and I think I could overpower him and escape. Perhaps they hope I will. But if I did, I would have to leave Alaba. So, I lie down on the mattress provided for me and sleep. I sleep well. I sleep better than I have for a long time. It is because I no longer have anything to fear. In my dreams, a man in black visits me. At first, I think he is death and move away from him, but he whispers to me, and I see he is wearing a straw hat. It is Erroi. He comes and sits by the edge of my mattress.

His eyes still hold mockery. "Well?" he asks.

"She is safe for now," I reply. "They will not harm her."

He turns towards my daughter. In my dream, she glows brighter than before. She is sleeping and looks well. She turns slightly and seems to murmur in her sleep.

"What will they do?" he asks.

"Return us to the City of the Sun," I reply. "At least she will be stronger there, if they let her live till dawn."

"Is she strong enough for the journey?"

"I don't know."

I sit up and look around. In my dream, the guard house is almost exactly like it is in real life.

Erroi stands up. "I will go now, but you should sleep more; sleep is good." Then he is gone.

I lie down and sleep, but I do not have any more dreams.

In prison, the day starts early. We are not awakened, but the old guard rises from his watch and is replaced by a younger man. The younger man sits scribbling at the desk. The noise of his pen and the light from his lantern is enough to awaken me.

The young man turns and looks at me. "You should go back to sleep," he says.

I know he is right, but I cannot sleep. Instead, I lie awake in the half light and remember. I think of the most beautiful thing I ever saw: Alaba's mother. She is dead now. It is a few years since she left us, since she was taken. Like Alaba, the Sun loved her, though not so deeply. Her hair was golden and her skin speckled. I loved to sit and look at her.

"What are you looking at?" she would ask.

"I'm looking at you," I would reply, and she would flush pink and rose by the torchlight.

"Well, don't," she would say, teasing, but then she would come and kiss me lightly on my brow.

What is the good of this? She is dead and I will never look at her again, or feel her kiss upon my brow, at least not in this life. Gods be good to me; let me know her kindness again in the next.

I wait a long time. The sergeant returns later, after we have eaten and refreshed ourselves.

"Tomorrow," he says, "we will set out. You and the girl will be in a coach. There will be a small escort: not too big, we can't spare the men. We will escort you to the next town. Hopefully, the garrison there will take over your journey."

Why he is telling me this? How many soldiers are there in the town? Not many, judging by the size of the guard house. There cannot be much to do so far from the City of the Sun. Just keep the tribute coming; just keep the town quiet enough and safe enough to attract no attention. The door opens and the sergeant jumps to attention.

The Lord Mayor enters. He waves the sergeant at ease. A chair is provided for him and he sits and looks at me. His robes are fine, but not magnificent, and he is middle aged and portly. Even in his prime, he would have looked unimpressive. I see he has dark skin. He has lived in the Valley of the Sun, if not in the city. How did he end up in this cold and distant spot? He has come to look at the important prisoners.

"Why does the Great Dark Lord Vatu, keeper of the Sun, wish to see you and your daughter?"

I ask myself the same question. I know the answer. "You must ask him, Lord," I reply and bow.

The Lord Mayor grimaces. It is unlikely that he has ever seen Vatu, much less that he will have the chance to question his commands. I expect him to instruct a guard to strike me, but he does not.

"The Great Lord is not here to ask, so I ask you. Why does Lord Vatu wish to see you?"

"I cannot know the Dark One's mind. I am just a humble traveller and this is my daughter. Great thoughts do not come to one such as I."

The Lord Mayor shifts. I can see him considering asking the guard to strike me after all. But he does not.

"You cannot know his mind, but you must guess. And your guess will be better than mine, for all your humility. Share your guess with me."

It is courteous; perhaps he has lived in the City of the Sun. I wish I could return his courtesy. I understand his concern. He has been posted here, far from the Sun. It is a mean and miserable place, but it is also far from the gaze of Vatu. He sends tribute—not enough tribute, the treasurers tell him, but it is enough to keep Vatu's attention elsewhere. Now that will change. Now the town has been harbouring fugitives. Why did the fugitive run here? Does he have friends in the town? Will Vatu send emissaries to investigate? Will he seek to punish the town and the Lord Mayor? What can I say that will put him at ease?

"I am loyal to the Sun," I say, and that is not a lie.

"We are all loyal to the Sun," agrees the Lord Mayor, "but loyalty is not enough. We must please him as well."

"If I do not please him, then I shall live in darkness when he turns his face," I reply.

He nods his head; neither of us say that we all live in darkness, no matter how we try to please him. I can see I have been of little use to him. But I cannot help him. He wishes for guidance, for clues to how he may please Vatu. I do not know how to please Vatu, and I have tried.

The Lord Mayor sits. He hopes I will speak more. I do not.

"Very well, then," he says. "I shall accompany you to the City of the Sun."

It is a wise choice. If it is better to be far from us, then he can return. If he stays, he will learn nothing. He is not pleased with his choice. No doubt he has a wife and children, and perhaps a mistress, but it is the right choice.

"You honour us with your presence; it will be a great kindness."

The Lord Mayor talks longer with the sergeant and then leaves. He will have goodbyes to say. Now that he has left, I must wait again; so much waiting.

When the torches are doused, it is hard to sleep. Alaba is lying on her cot; she seems to be drowning in her sleep and each breath is heavy and tortured. How can she suffer so and live? And yet she does, and even in her suffering, she can sleep. I turn to face the wall. Perhaps I have done wrong. I tried to save her, but I could not. Only the Sun can save her. Was I wrong? Gods forgive me if I have wronged my daughter and made her suffering greater.

I cannot sleep. There are memories—not dreams nor phantoms that parade before me. It is as if I am back in the City of the Sun, back in the Palace of Vatu, back in the presence of the keeper of the Sun. I am kneeling prone, my face is hard to the floor. I can feel the cool stone against my cheek. Vatu has opened the black box of the Sun and the brightness is blinding. The heat drills through my clothes and through my flesh. My eyes are closed tight. Vatu is laughing.

"Dance," he commands. "Dance." And the girls who were brought as tribute, who are stripped naked and decked with necklaces and bracelets of gold, enter. They begin to turn and gyrate, twist into shapes of seduction and desire. And as they dance, hooded men play instruments of gold. Horns and trumpets and clavicles and cornets blast out. And as they play, and as they dance, Vatu is laughing. And as Vatu laughs and as the girls dance, the glory of the Sun comes upon them and consumes them. Flesh chars and blisters and burns, skin shrivels, hair smoulders, bones blacken, and one by one, the girls flare up like torches, spinning and turning a dance of fire and flame and death. Vatu is laughing.

The gold of the necklaces and bracelets melts and runs in pools on the floor, a floor paved with gold. How many times have I seen that dance? How many times have I told the tribute girls that they must dance for Vatu? How many times did I tell them that perhaps if they danced well, they might attract his gaze? I am a liar and a murderer. No wonder the Gods have cursed me and mine. Alaba, I have done this to you. You should hate me.

I cannot sleep. It is a wonder that I have ever slept. When I close my eyes, I see the brightness of the Sun. It is the fire of justice.

Once, I lived as close to the Sun as it was possible to be. Once, I saw the Sun in all its glory every day. Now, I cannot get far enough from its vengeful glare. Even in the deepest darkness, I see its all-consuming light. Now, I must return to the light. It will have its vengeance.

I cannot sleep. I look at my daughter. I hoped to save her, yet she lies sick and dying, far from the light. The glow she carries is fading. Every day, she is weaker. She cannot live in darkness. She will fade to nothing and die. Was I wrong to try to save her from the light?

I cannot sleep. I think about Erroi and the boy. What a strange creature Erroi is. What chance brought us to meet? I know nothing about him. Did he really come to me in my dreams last night? It seems impossible. Mukito is strange also. I know nothing about him either. Now, because of me, they are together. Where will they go? Mukito could go back to his hovel, the one he lived in with his stepfather. It will be a hard life. Perhaps Erroi will join him? I doubt it. I cannot see Erroi living as a bandit. I pray the Gods are good to them. My prayer, for what it's worth, is all I can give them for their kindness.

I cannot sleep. Tomorrow, I will be travelling back to the City of the Sun. There is only death waiting there for me. Perhaps I can find a way to take my life before I am taken to Vatu. I have watched Vatu kill. He is not merciful. There is no kindness in him. They do not call him the Dark One for no reason. Perhaps I deserve to die in such a way, after all the men I have brought to the Dark One with my own hands. How will Vatu kill me? I have seen him kill in so many ways. He will find a new way to kill, just for me. I am selfish, I think of my own death and not of the death of my daughter. He will not be merciful to her either.

I cannot sleep. Now my body will not rest; it knows it must rise soon. I know tomorrow I will suffer for lack of sleep. It is a small suffering. It is nothing. Am I so weak that the pains of the flesh are greater than the pains of my heart and mind? Are my pains greater than those of Alaba? Are they greater than those of murdered men and girls and starved workers in the dark? What is fatigue next to that?

I cannot sleep. The guard is restless and there is a moth fluttering around the lantern. The rain has started again, falling softly. There is a noise outside. Not a loud noise; it is the sound of awakening. Soon the torches will be lit and it will be moonrise. I look around. My daughter breathes easier. She has a soft smile and her silver hair has fallen over her face. She wakes. It is as if she has risen up out of the deep. She sees me and smiles. What does she think? Does she know the fate I tried to save her from?

"Papa," she says, and for a moment the world is less bitter.

We are taken to a coach. It is a fine one, much finer than I had expected. Perhaps the Lord Mayor is richer than I thought. It is much finer than my wagon and is enclosed. There are cushions on all the seats and lanterns in each corner. We are led in. Alaba is placed on one of the benches, propped up with pillows and covered with quilts. I will sit on the seat opposite. The guards leave and the door is locked. There is more waiting. For prisoners, there is always more waiting. I hear the noise of horses being hitched to the coach. The window is closed and I cannot look out, but I can hear only coach horses. The guards will walk or else take turns to ride on the coach. The Lord Mayor cannot afford to give all ten guardsmen each a horse. They would never be returned if he did. I am glad. Men march slower than horses gallop. I am in no rush to finish this journey.

The door of the coach is unlocked. The Lord Mayor enters, but the guards stay outside. Is he so certain that I will not try to kill him? He will travel with us in the coach. It is the safest and most comfortable thing to do. We look not like a gallows wagon, but like the train of a wealthy provincial lord with his escort, on his way to visit friends or perhaps to visit the City of the Sun. I wish he had brought a guard in with him. It would help excuse my cowardice for not killing him.

"Let us be comfortable," he says, as if we are old friends going on a journey. "I have not introduced myself, I know that is rude of me. My name is Gutiza. As you have guessed, I am the Lord Mayor of this town. It will be my pleasure to accompany you on this trip. We shall have a long time together. It will be a pleasure to become better acquainted." He proffers his hand, and to my shame, I take it.

I hear the driver crack the reins and urge the horses forward. The carriage lurches on its springs. We nod and bob and sway. The journey has begun. Gutiza has the decency to remain silent, or at least not to speak. We have long to go and there is no need to use all our words at once. Instead, he settles in his seat and rocks back and forth to the same rhythm as the carriage. We travel for about an hour and then we stop. Gutiza gets up and taps on the carriage door. The door is opened and he gets out, leaving us. I peer through the door; they do not close it. I can see guardsmen standing around. They look bored. I am pleased to see Zintoa. He looks in through the door and smiles. He looks brave and foolish in his uniform. The guardsmen are alert, but not alarmed. We wait a long time. I hear the sound of a horse approaching, two horses. They have been waiting on someone. The horses are riding fast, but not very fast. They stop and I hear girlish giggles. I hear Gutiza welcome the guest. Are there kisses? Can you hear kisses? It seems you can. There is the sound of joviality, of excitement. Then Gutiza returns to the carriage and on his arm is a young lady. She may be young enough to be his daughter, but she is not his daughter. She is not finely dressed and her bearing is common. I can see that the cloth is cheap; it is brightly coloured and cut lower than is decent. Her figure is not a fine figure, but it is well displayed. She hides her features behind a scarf, as if to conceal her identity; it is just a game. Any that know her would recognize her instantly. And those who do not would recognize her type. It seems that the Lord Mayor will bring his mistress to the city of gold. He has indeed made himself comfortable.

When the couple enter the coach, she sits between myself and Gutiza. She lets the weight of her breast press against my arm and looks slyly at me. Does she imagine that I would be aroused by such a thing? Does she think to make Gutiza jealous? Does she think all men will desire her? She is not fit company for my daughter.

"Let me introduce my wife, Juana," says Gutiza. "She has persuaded me that it is better that she accompanies us."

His companion giggles. She is not his wife; his wife would not need to meet some hours distant from the town, away from prying eyes, away from his wife's eyes. I can imagine how she persuaded him to bring her. If I had such a mistress, I would not trust her while I was gone either. She is looking around curiously. No doubt she has heard all about the apprehended fugitives, about me and about Alaba.

"Why does your daughter glow?" she asks.

I would like to ignore her, but a prisoner must be more courteous even than a free man. It would do no good to insult my host, my jailer, or to insult his mistress.

"I do not know." I try to keep contempt from my voice.

"Is that why Vatu wants to see her?" she asks.

"Again, I do not know," I reply.

Gutiza comes to my rescue. "My dear, you cannot interrogate our guests. They are not criminals."

But if we are not criminals, what are we? I, at least, have done criminal things. My daughter is innocent, but it is she who is suffering, not I; she who will suffer. He slips his hand inside her bodice. He is no gentleman. His mistress makes a mild protest, but he does not remove his hand. She leans into him. I do not know what she whispers to him, but by the subsequent laughter, I know it is indecent. We travel on. I sit while Alaba sleeps and the two lovers whisper and giggle.

Eventually, it is time to make camp. Gutiza and his mistress go out and stretch; they are stiff and sore from riding in the coach. I am used to travelling, but I would also like to stretch. The door of the coach is locked when Gutiza leaves. I pace and stretch, but it would be nice to have more air. After a while, the door opens. Zintoa enters. He is pleased to see us, but is uncertain of his welcome.

"I have prepared a sleeping place for you," he says. He picks up Alaba and I follow him to a tent. It is modest, but no more modest than the tents the soldiers will sleep in. There are two cots, and best of all, a charcoal brazier. We will not be cold. The cots are made up. I notice there are extra blankets on Alaba's bed. Has Zintoa put them there? He places Alaba in her bed and covers her delicately. She is looking at him, but does not speak. Zintoa turns to me.

"I will be back with food," he says.

"Thank you," I reply.

Gutiza and his lover will sleep in the coach. At least we will be spared their company for the night. We are left alone in the tent. The soldiers think they are doing us a kindness. Certainly, we will not run away. I will not and Alaba cannot. Zintoa returns with two plates of white beans.

"Here," he says. "I made these. It's nothing fancy, but they are good." He hands me one of the plates and takes the other to Alaba. He begins to feed her. The food is good. Simple, lightly flavoured and well cooked. The boy is wasted as a soldier if he can make white beans taste so fine. I clear the plate. I was hungry. Alaba has eaten, not a full plate, but more than I have seen her eat in days, perhaps weeks. In the tent, the only light is from the brazier, a dull red glow, and from Alaba, a pale, silvery glow. Zintoa is kneeling on the ground beside Alaba.

"May I sit with you a while?" he asks. I reply that I am his prisoner and that he may do as he wishes. He blushes. If he is to become a soldier, he must become less sensitive.

"You may sit with us," I say. It is better to sit with a friend than to sit alone. It is better to sit with an enemy than to sit alone. He is pleased.

"I want to thank you again for saving my life," he says. "I am in your debt."

"But not enough in our debt to let us go free?"

"Would that I could, but I have my duty."

I want to strike him for his foolishness, and yet I cannot condemn him. I have done far worse things for the same small word. Duty is such a small word, such a big responsibility. Eventually, I saw I had a duty too; not to Vatu, but to myself, to my daughter, to the world and to everyone in it. Hopefully, one day he will see this too.

"I will do everything I can to help you."

I let it pass; everything but free us. I smile. What assistance does he imagine that a common soldier and a naive boy can give against the wrath of Vatu?

"I want to ask you something, if it is all right." I nod, and he continues. "Have you been to the City of the Sun before?"

"Yes, yes," I reply. "I have been there many times. It is why my skin is dark. The Sun causes skin to darken."

"I thought so," replied Zintoa. "So will my skin darken?"

"Perhaps," I agree. "But only if you are there in sunlight. For most of the time, the city has no more sunlight than anywhere else. Vatu keeps the Sun in his box and in some ways, that is a mercy. We are not made to live close to the Sun, at least not for long."

"How many times have you seen the Sun?" He can hardly keep the excitement from his voice.

"Hundreds and hundreds of times," I say and bow my head in shame.

Zintoa does not notice my shame. He looks at me in awe.

"I have seen it twenty times," he says. "I cannot remember all of them, of course, but my father held me up so I could see the glow coming from over the hills. When I got older, we would go and climb up the hill behind the town. The glow was brighter there. We had to climb up in darkness and then rush back to get to the harvest. We only have one harvest here, so we don't have to start on it straight away, but it must be done by sundown."

I cannot contain a chuckle. "I am not hundreds of years old. I have seen the Sun in Vatu's palace. Sometimes he opens the box just to stare at it."

"It must be very beautiful."

It is, beautiful and deadly.

Someone shouts outside, perhaps the sergeant. Zintoa gathers our plates and dashes out of the tent. He leaves me with Alaba and with my thoughts. He does not return that night.

I am tired, more so than I thought. To sit all day is exhausting. I sleep as soon as I lie down on my cot, or at least that is how it seems to me. I dream of Erroi again. He is standing at the tent flap. He enters and warms himself by the charcoal fire. I want to speak, but I am afraid the soldier will come.

"Why are you here?" I ask.

"I am not here," Erroi replies.

I have no time for his games.

"Ten soldiers," he continues and then, when I do not speak, he says, "I could kill them all."

"I doubt it," I reply. Erroi is a fine bladesman, but to kill ten soldiers is an empty boast.

"What will you do then?" he asks.

"Nothing," I say. "Nothing for now."

Erroi nods. "That is a good plan." There is the sound of fluttering and when I turn, Erroi is gone. What a strange dream.

Morning comes sooner than I think. I am shaken awake and I look up to see the old guard who watched us on the first night standing over me.

"You must arise, sir," he says. I am allowed to relieve myself before breakfast. The old guard stands close, but not too close. "How did you sleep?" he asks.

"Well," I reply, "and you?"

The old guard looks at me as if he will speak. But the sergeant calls us and he says nothing. Instead, he motions us to return.

Breakfast is quick and plain. Alaba does not eat. Zintoa carries her into the coach. He hands me some dry bread.

"She must eat," he says. "Perhaps she will eat for you."

I promise to try, but I know she will not.

When I enter the coach, she is covered almost completely with blankets. She is barely glowing.

Gutiza and his companion are sitting on the other seat. There is a strong smell of wine and spirits from them. Gutiza is somewhat dishevelled, but his mistress is wearing a new dress. It is finer than her old dress and more modest, although it is too tight around her bosom. Gutiza has taken it from his wife's wardrobe. He is a bigger fool than I thought.

"Good morning," I say as I sit.

Gutiza mumbles; clearly, he wishes he was at home in his villa. His mistress smiles, but it is not a pleasant smile. What I have done to earn her ill will? The coach starts and we continue on our way to the next town.

"We should reach there by midday or late afternoon," Gutiza informs me. The governor of the town is a friend, he insists. We will pay our respects. It seems that Gutiza will display me like a trophy as we journey to the City of the Sun. Gutiza sleeps; no doubt he slept little last night. It is a kindness not to have to hear his voice. I try to make Alaba take some bread, but she will not. It is as if she cannot even see me. Gutiza is snoring.

His mistress looks bored. "Do you know the next town?" she asks.

I do not. It is slightly nearer the Sun, but still very distant. "No, I don't, my lady. Do you know the town?" I ask.

It is a long way to the City of the Sun. I will have to share the coach with this woman. I should try to be polite. She can make trouble for me if she wishes.

She smiles when I call her 'my lady,' enjoying the pretense that she is not a whore. "No," she says. "I have lived all my life in Riga, but my husband says it is a much finer place. He says he will show me around and buy me earrings made of silver."

Had she really been the wife of the Lord Mayor, she would have wanted finer than silver earrings.

"I must look my best when we arrive at the City of the Sun," she continues, imagining that silver earrings will be counted as finery there, or that the mistress of some minor provincial dignitary would be of interest to anyone except the slave market and brothel keepers. Will Gutiza let his mistress return to Riga or sell her? I feel sorry for her. If Gutiza is cruel, then her fate will be barely better than ours. I look more closely at her. She will not fetch the best price at market, but she is passable and will sell easily enough. Selling her could pay Gutiza enough to cover the losses he is making on this trip, assuming that he survives it.

"You should go back to Riga," I say.

"Why?" she replies. "If I go back, his wife will have me whipped, perhaps murdered. She is spiteful and hateful. Gutiza is afraid of her; otherwise he would have left her and married me. You think when I say I am his wife I am a liar, but I am the wife of his heart. I give him the love she will not."

Not for the first time, I think how cruel men are, and how foolish are women, and for the first time, I realize how young she is. Behind her bravado and brazenness, she is a child, a mistreated child. I realize I have been unkind and feel ashamed.

"What is your name?" I ask.

"Juana." There is defiance in her voice, and tears.

"How old are you?" I ask.

"Old enough, just. I wasn't the first time, but it was all right. He looked after me, and he loved me, so that was good. It was better than starving. I was able to give food to my mother. She's dead. Now there is just me. He is kind to me. You have seen it with your own eyes. What else is there for me?"

After that, she will say no more. Gutiza continues to snore, unaware and uncaring.

We stop to eat. It is not much farther to the next town, but Gutiza is hungry. The old guard leads us out of the carriage and Zintoa brings us food.

"It's nothing much," he says apologetically and hands me bread and cheese. He has a flask of water and tries to get Alaba to drink. I think she drinks some, but not much. She does not open her eyes. She is surely dying.

"I must ask you something." Zintoa turns to me. "That dark man you travelled with?"

"You mean Erroi?"

"I suppose so; is that his name? Who is he?"

"I told you I don't know. We only travelled some days together."

Zintoa frowns and then continues, "I saw him last night—no, not saw him—I mean, I had a dream and he was in it. It was strange. He walked right through the camp. I could see him, even though I was in the other tent.

"He came in and said, 'Get up, I want to talk to you,' just like that, telling me what to do, even though he was in a tent full of soldiers.

"I was worried, in case he woke the others, so I told him to be quiet. I got up and went out of the tent and he followed me. I asked him what he wanted and he told me he wanted to save me. He said he saved me twice already, and so he felt he had to keep me safe. He said I should beware. I asked him of what? 'Lots of things,' he said. 'Like what?' I asked. 'The Sun,' he said. I should beware of the Sun. Well, I've only ever seen the Sun twenty times, and only really from a long way away, not up close. So I said, I've never seen the Sun, not the way he meant it. He said I will, unless I want to run away. I told him I can't do that. Then I'd be a deserter. He told me that being loyal was all very well, but we needed to be careful what we are loyal to. I am loyal to the Sun, I told him. 'Yes,' he said, 'but who is the Sun loyal to?' And then he said, I was to look after you and Alaba. After that, he just disappeared, vanished. That is how I knew it was a dream and when I woke up, I was still in the tent with the other soldiers. What is it? What can it mean?"

"It is Erroi," I reply.

Chapter Three
A Journey in Darkness

We are taken to the mansion of the Governor. Although this town is barely finer than the last, the Governor of the town is very rich. He is older than Gutiza, although his skin is almost white. Clearly, he has never visited the Valley of the Sun. His mansion is very fine, lit with many lanterns of coloured crystal. When we dine, he serves us fish. It is a great delicacy, although Alaba will not eat it. Juana is not with us. The Lord Mayor of a small town does not present his mistress to his superior.

The Governor sits very upright. I suspect he has problems with his bones. He is dressed plainly in white, but it is fine cloth, much finer than Gutiza's robe. They are not friends; the Governor make a great effort to keep his distaste from his face. Some people would not notice it. Gutiza is fawning over the Governor.

"Let me show you my companions," he says, and withdraws the coverlets from my daughter so that her glowing face is clearly visible.

The Governor has heard about this girl. Vatu has instructed that we be found. His face displays no emotion.

"Is it not amazing?" gloats Gutiza. "I have never seen such a thing."

The Governor turns and looks at my daughter. Do I catch pity in his eye? It is gone quickly and instead I see him calculating and considering. He is wiser than Gutiza and more dangerous. He is wondering if he should take charge of the prisoners. Gutiza is in his domain; the guards would obey his orders. But then what? He would have to take us to the City of the Sun and then he would be in the gaze of Vatu. And as he got closer to the City of the Sun, the likelihood that he would be killed and the prisoners taken by a superior would become greater. Gutiza is gambling that he can make it to the City of the Sun, or at least turn us over to some grandee for a small reward, rather than end up murdered and buried in the dark with no lantern to mark his grave. The Governor has no wish to make that gamble, and he knows that Gutiza may well lose everything, but it is galling to think that his hated rival may get some benefit and could rise above him. It is not a decision to make quickly.

"It is good to have you here, my friend," the Governor remarks. "We will talk of this at length and between us, we will make wise decisions."

The fat Lord Mayor's face turns pale. He hoped only to gloat and show his good fortune to his enemy and then go. Now, he realizes that it will not be as simple. He is wishing he had brought his guardsmen with him. But that would have been foolish. They are not his guardsmen; they are Vatu's guardsmen, and they will obey the Governor before they will obey him. He is caught, and he fears his prize will be stolen from him. He has been too long from the Sun and has forgotten how jealous the servants of Vatu are of each other.

The Governor lets the pleasure he feels at Gutiza's discomfort show on his face. He will toy with him some more.

"So, tell me, my friend, what have you learned from our prisoners?"

Gutiza lets "our" pass. He is shamed. He has learned nothing. "I have travelled with them for two days, but they have let nothing slip. The girl does not talk and I think she cannot. In spite of her glowing countenance, she is very ill. I fear she may die before she reaches the City of the Sun."

Again the Governor smiles. "What will the Great Dark One, keeper of the Sun, think if your prisoner should die? I hope for your sake that she lives. The Great Dark One is merciful, but perhaps not too merciful."

Gutiza bows his head. It is too much. The Governor forgets that Gutiza once resided in the Valley of the Sun; he hopes he still has some friends there. Once, he had powerful friends, he boasts, friends who visited both the City and even the Palace of Vatu. They will not have forgotten him. He has written to them and he has hopes of meeting them on the road. He wishes to share his meagre success with his friends. It is a good thing to have friends and to share good things with them. All this and more, Gutiza reminds the Governor.

The Governor is pleased. His barbs have hit home.

"There is much wisdom in what you say," the Governor interrupts. "I must think on this, but not tonight. You must excuse an old man his ill health. It is my habit to retire around this hour and at my age, I cannot afford to disrupt my routine further. So forgive my rudeness, my friend, but I will happily discuss these matters more with you tomorrow."

Gutiza is flushed with displeasure, but says nothing. He rises. He motions me to my feet and waves a guard over to Alaba to carry her.

"Ah, no, I think not," says the Governor. "They will be safer with me than in your carriage or whatever inn you will pass the night in." Clearly, Gutiza is not invited to lodge with the Governor. "And I can keep them in better comfort." While this is undoubtedly true, it is also a great insult: to invite Gutiza to the mansion and then make him stay in the town like a merchant or traveller.

Once Gutiza is gone, the Governor motions and wine is brought; a goblet is placed before me. It is not good wine; there is no good wine this far from the Sun, but I drink it anyway. Not to drink it would be impolite. If he hopes to loosen my tongue with strong drink, he will be disappointed. However, he asks me nothing.

"I will not ask," he says, "but I can guess much: you have flown too close to the Sun."

He leaves and we are taken to our quarters. They are fine quarters draped with fine cloth that lets air pass in to cool the room but prevents the ingress of flying insects. There are many cushions and divans to repose upon. There are ewers of silver to wash in. It is long since I have had such comfort.

The maids lay Alaba on a divan. "Is there anything we can do for her?" they ask. I shake my head and they bow and leave.

The maids return early next moonrise; as soon as the first birds sing, they arrive. They assist us to wash and dress us in clean clothes. I am grateful for this kindness. We are taken back to the cool marble hall we were presented in the previous night. The Governor is there. When I see him by moonlight, it is clear he is very ill, but he is smiling; he has enjoyed his game. Gutiza is there. He looks worried and he has not changed clothes since last night.

The Governor turns towards us. "I hope you slept well?" he inquires.

"My friend," interrupts Gutiza, but the Governor waves him to silence.

"I have slept well, thanks to your generosity. I thank you for your kindness."

"I ask only that you remember me fondly," replied the Governor. "Those who will be corrected, Vatu loves best. Those who will not be corrected, Vatu destroys."

He turns to Gutiza. "I have thought long on what you have told me. You are wise to seek my counsel. Alas, I am too frail to accompany or assist you. It falls to you this task and you must do it for both of us. You should seek out these friends of whom you speak; perhaps they may remember you. It is possible."

His servants lift him from his chair and he turns to go. He cannot resist hitting Gutiza with one last goad. "It is more likely they will remember him," he says and points at me.

Gutiza motions to his guards to escort us to his coach. Zintoa comes forward to lift Alaba, and she puts a hand on his shoulder.

In the coach, Juana is present. She is not wearing silver earrings, nor is she wearing the fine dress of before. She smiles at Gutiza, but it is a smile with fear behind it. Gutiza has shared his anger. I do not think we will visit many more dignitaries. The mood of our party is sombre. Gutiza glares angrily at me. I think it best to remain quiet.

"I could kill you," he says. "I could have you killed. One word from me and the guardsmen will run you through."

He is mistaken, but I do not contradict him. Although the guardsmen would not suffer Gutiza to kill us for fear of Vatu, they would not stop him from punishing us in other ways. He could have us whipped or beaten. He could have us starved or tortured.

"I have been good to you," he yells. "I have treated you with respect. Remember that."

I prostrate myself. It is undignified, but I have done this many times. "Yes, Lord," I say, with practised ease, "I am grateful for your kindness. It will live long in my memory and I will praise the day we met."

Juana is cowering beside Alaba, as if my daughter could protect her. Alaba is glowing more brightly than before. She is glowing bright enough to light the whole coach. Juana takes her hand. I do not grudge her that; it seems to give her comfort. Gutiza does not seem to notice; perhaps I just imagined it.

The fat Lord Mayor sits down, and scowls. I wish Juana would go to him and calm him. It is shameful that I should wish such a thing. I remain prone and Juana remains with Alaba. Gutiza remains seated and scowling, threatening. We remain thus until the coach stops. Zintoa opens the coach. He seems not to notice how afraid we look. I think he sees only Alaba; he goes to her and lifts her. Juana helps him, or tries to. She follows Zintoa out of the coach. Gutiza does not seem to notice. He is still glaring at me with hatred and loathing.

Juana will not sleep with Gutiza; she will sleep by Alaba's bed in our tent. She says she is concerned for my daughter. Perhaps she is. I am concerned for Alaba. The sergeant is here too. I cannot remember his name. I remember he has stolen my horse and goods. I remove the receipt he gave me from my belt. In the dark, it is difficult to read. Borroka, his name is Borroka. It is he who brings us food; he does not talk, but simply passes it to us. Juana smiles at him. He is too wise to draw Gutiza's anger.

When I sleep, Erroi is there. He drifts in from the trees around the camp and walks past the guards' fire. He points at Juana. "You have found another one for me."

"She is a danger to herself," I reply.

Erroi nods his head. "Of course."

He asks me if I am well. What can I say? I am fed, I am clothed, and I am not beaten.

"Yes," I say. "I am well." And then I tell him of Gutiza's humiliation and anger.

"It is madness," he says, and then he is gone.

When the moon rises, Gutiza sends for Juana. She is taken to the coach while the guards break camp and pack the tents onto the wagon. Sometime later, we are also taken to the coach. Gutiza looks pleased and welcomes us with words of kindness. Juana is smiling. She looks relieved, but her dress is torn and I can see bite marks on her flesh.

We do not travel far. Gutiza explains that we will travel slowly until we meet his friend from the Valley of the Sun. When we meet his friend, things will be better, he tells us. We will travel with the protection of his friend.

"My friend is a very important man," he says. "He owes me a great deal."

Important men do not like to be reminded of a debt, still less to repay it. He has been foolish.

We stop at a large town; perhaps you could call it a city. We do not introduce ourselves to the ruler; instead, we camp outside. After last time, that is no surprise. I think Gutiza will wait here for word from his friend. The soldiers pitch the tents in a clearing, and we are led to our tent. Two guards wait outside.

It is a good campsite. There is plenty of firewood to collect and there is running water down at the edge of the trees. It seems we will stay here for a while. It's good to be spared from travel, even for a few moon turns.

Gutiza leaves us and goes into town. He does not take Juana with him. Later, two guardsmen carry him back, one on either side. He is very drunk. The guards help him into the carriage, where he will sleep. Again, Juana will sleep in the tent with Alaba.

Juana has helped with the food. It is her who brings it to us in our tent. She helps Alaba to eat, but my daughter will take only a few mouthfuls.

The soldiers have lit a fire for warmth and cooking. Now they sit around. They are restless. They call to me to join them. It would be impolite to refuse. I sit on a folding stool by the fire and warm myself.

"Come on, old man," they say. "You must entertain us if you will share our fire." It is meant kindly. They have been telling each other implausible tales such as rough men tell each other everywhere. They are tales of their triumphs and disasters with women; they are funny because they are true, they are sad because they are true.

"I have no such tales," I reply. Is it true? Is my life not also a comedy? Am I just too proud to be the butt of my own jokes?

"Can you sing?" asks the old guard.

I can. I have not sung for a long time. There is no music to accompany me and I sing poorly, but I sing. I realize that my song is not so different from their tales. The men applaud my singing with more kindness than it deserves.

Juana has crept to the edge of the fire.

"What of you?" asks Borroka. "Can you sing?"

Juana shakes her head.

"Then what? You think you can share our fire for free?"

Juana stands up. Once again, she is the proud mistress of a lord. "I will dance," she says.

Her hips begin to sway slowly back and forth. The men smile and she smiles back at them. She taps one foot to a slow rhythm and the men start to clap to the same beat. It has started slow, but gathers and builds. Juana brings her hands forward then to her side. Her head tilts backwards. She is graceful and skilled. She turns in the firelight and as she does, the eyes of the soldiers are fixed on her. Is there magic in dance? She twists and turns around the circle of the fire, pausing briefly before each soldier in turn. She lingers in front of Zintoa.

"Leave him and come and dance for a real man," calls Borroka.

The next moonrise, Gutiza is ill. We will not travel that day. Juana is called to nurse him. He is carried out of the carriage and sits on a pile of furs and cushions by the fire, surrounded by lanterns. He is demanding. Juana is sent to the town for eggs and honey. It will make him better. Borroka will accompany Juana to ensure she is safe, and that she does not run away.

Zintoa calls to me. He is bright eyed with excitement.

"That man was here again last night," he says.

I ask what Erroi told him.

"He told me to beware again. I asked him what I should beware of, and he told me to beware of Juana."

"That is good advice," I say.

Zintoa laughs. "She is only a girl. What harm can she do me?"

What harm indeed?

Juana has returned from the town. She has mixed the eggs and honey in a wide bowl and is spooning it into Gutiza. He looks the worse for wear. He is making loud belching noises and shivering. He is brought close to the fire. Juana is wearing earrings. They are not real silver, but of a cheaper white metal such as a sergeant could afford. Later, Gutiza instructs Juana to dance. Again, she dances to the rhythm of her feet and snapping fingers. But the men do not look at her, except for Borroka. Later still, Gutiza is helped to the carriage, where he will sleep. Juana helps him. She enters the carriage and closes the door.

Today, Gutiza is better and we will travel on. Zintoa carries Alaba into the coach. Juana smiles at him, but he does not notice. He is looking at Alaba and the light glowing from her face. He reaches forward as if to smooth her hair, but then draws back. Gutiza has noticed and is scowling.

The carriage smells of sickness. A small, wooden hatch is opened, but the smell persists. Gutiza looks pale. He breaks wind and belches frequently. Juana is not wearing earrings. But she is smiling and leaning into Gutiza. He pays little attention.

"You," he says, pointing at me, "are the cause of my misfortune." He is too weak for anger, but there is hatred in his eyes.

Again Gutiza is sick. We are camped, just by the roadside.

"How long will we camp?" I ask Borroka.

He shrugs. "Who knows?"

Juana has eyes for Zintoa; I can see why. He is tall and slim; his features are comely. He is young and kind.

The men are bored. They will stage practice bouts, swinging swords and quarterstaffs. It is the job of a soldier to fight.

Gutiza watches. "Come," he says. He points at Zintoa. "You shall fight Borroka."

Borroka and Zintoa have practised all day. "My Lord, perhaps later, when we have rested."

Gutiza scowls, but agrees. Again, I see hate in his eyes. But it is not hate for me. Zintoa brings the food to our tent that night. He has cooked it and it is good. I have not watched the fighting closely today, but I believe Zintoa is a better cook than he is a fighter. I caution him to be careful tomorrow.

"Why?" he says. "It is just a practice. We have practised together many times."

"So you will fight Borroka for Juana?"

"Juana is not Borroka's girl," says Zintoa.

"No?" I ask. "Whose girl is she?"

"He is welcome to her," Zintoa says. "Although he should treat her better."

I am not sure if he means Borroka or Gutiza.

Later, we gather around the fire. Borroka and Zintoa have stripped to the waist. They each hold thin rapiers, which they swish to and fro, making whistling sounds. Borroka's face is serious. He is well muscled and broad. I can see many scars on his arms, but none on his body. Zintoa is too young and un-practised for scars. Four rods and a rope mark out the arena in front of the fire, and there are lanterns around the edge, hanging from poles. Gutiza is sitting with Juana next to him. I cannot see his face, but I can see fear in Juana's eyes.

The fight begins. It is closer than I expected. Zintoa is quick and nimble; Borroka is experienced and practised. They fence around each other much as they must have done many times in the past. I can see Zintoa has done this many times before. He is expecting this to go as all the other practice fights. But this is not a practice. Steadily, the momentum of the fight builds. Borroka's attacks become faster and more pressing. There is a new rhythm. It is like the magic of a dance. Zintoa is defending himself well, but I can see he is surprised at Borroka's determination. They are still evenly matched. Zintoa is cool headed as well as quick. Gutiza is leaning forward. I can see his face now; Juana is right to be afraid. Borroka is pushing Zintoa back. He is pressing hard. This is no practice. I see concern on Zintoa's face. The sergeant has never attacked him like this before. There are openings in Borroka's defence, but Zintoa will not exploit them; he has no wish to injure his friend. The men shift uneasily. It is enough, they think. This is a game, not war; we are friends and comrades.

Borroka continues with his reckless push. Again and again, Zintoa counters. In the firelight, sweat glistens and the steel catches glints like sparks of daylight. I have seen many swordsmen. Neither Borroka nor Zintoa are among the finest I have seen, but they are competent swordsmen. I had not expected to find two such competent swordsmen in the provincial garrison of a squalid town such as Gutiza rules over. Both men are tiring. Zintoa is younger, but has had to work harder.

Suddenly, Zintoa takes two steps back and lowers his sword. "I yield, Sergeant. Well fought. I could not live with that much longer."

Gutiza calls out, "Finish him! I told you to kill him."

But Borroka has cast his sword aside and has stalked off into the darkness, into the trees. Juana goes to follow him, but Gutiza grabs her by the wrist. The old soldier, I do not know his name, goes after Borroka. The rest of the men swarm around Zintoa protectively. They are proud that he fought so well, and angry that Borroka would think to betray one of them. Angry glances are cast towards Gutiza and Juana. Gutiza retires to his coach, pulling Juana and slapping her once.

I am taken back to my tent. I hear loud and angry voices for most of the night. The men are angry and confused.

I look around; Erroi is there.

"Your plan is a good one," he says.

"This was not my plan," I say.

"No?" asks Erroi. "Then what was it?" Then he is gone.

I am taken to the coach the next day. I can see neither Borroka nor Zintoa. I hope both are well. Gutiza is in the coach, as is Juana. She smiles gaily. She is brave.

Gutiza is not ill today. He smiles and bids us welcome. I sit beside him as he instructs. He smells bad. He is glaring at me and grabs my arm. "This is your fault," he says. "I know what you are up to."

Juana is looking away.

Erroi is here, sitting beside Gutiza.

"Should I kill him now?" Erroi asks.

"How did you get here?" Gutiza asks.

"I walked," says Erroi. "It is not far to walk."

"Who are you?" Gutiza wants to know.

"To you, I am death," says Erroi.

"You think you can kill me," screams Gutiza. "I have guards."

"They cannot help you," says Erroi, "and they would not if they could. Perhaps they will kill you. Or perhaps she will. Or perhaps I will, but you will die. It is time for you to die. Past time."

Gutiza grabs a short, curved dagger from his belt and lunges at Erroi, but Erroi is gone. The curved dagger slices through shadow.

Gutiza vomits black blood.

"You," he says and grabs Juana. "You are poisoning me. You are doing this!"

Juana screams and tries to push the fat man away. The guards do not come. They have heard Juana scream before and know not to interfere. Juana scuffles with Gutiza and I try to come to her aid.

Then Gutiza is on the floor. He has collapsed. He is vomiting more blood. The smell is very bad. He begins to shake and then his eyes begin to bulge. He is making retching and choking noises. Juana is still screaming. I sit beside him. He reaches for the dagger, which has dropped to the floor. He tries to stab me with slow, clumsy thrusts that I move away from easily. Still the guards do not come. There is no one to help him. He will not let me help him.

Juana is banging on the door. She has found the key and is unlocking the door. She opens it and runs out. I am alone in the coach with the dying man and my sleeping daughter. There is no wound or injury on him that I can see. I do not know why he is dying, except that Erroi has said he must.

He is gasping for breath and in pain. His dagger is now in my hand. I have taken it from him to stop him from trying to kill me. He is glaring at me with hate. He cannot speak. I see his great pain. I could stop the pain with a single push from his dagger. One quick, sharp push into the base of his neck and it would all be over for him. It would be a mercy. It is a mercy I deny him.

Juana returns. Borroka and the older guard are with her. Tito: I remember the older guard's name is Tito. I heard one of the other men call him that. Borroka looks alarmed. Gutiza points at him and then, with a final convulsion, is dead.

"Bring the body outside," he says to Tito.

Tito shakes his head. "It may carry disease," he says. "I will not touch it."

Borroka can see that Tito is wise and nods. "You," he says to me. "Bring the body outside." So quickly has Gutiza become just a corpse.

I, too, am afraid that Gutiza has some disease, but I know that Borroka does not care. If I do not carry out the body, he will beat me or perhaps kill me. He can report that I died of the same disease as Gutiza. He thinks no one will care. I try and lift the fat man, but he is too heavy.

"Just drag him out," says Tito. "He's not going to care now."

I pull the corpse by the legs and he bounces down the steps of the coach.

"Over there," says Tito, pointing. "Away from the camp."

Borroka is ordering two of his men to dig a grave in amongst the trees. "Make it deep," he says. "If this is plague, then let's bury it deep. And make it wide. Remember, he is fat."

Zintoa is one of the diggers. I am glad to see him alive and unharmed.

"We should burn the coach," says Tito.

Borroka agrees. He shouts to some men to let the horses loose and unpack the coach. They loosen the two horses and transfer the supplies from the coach to their wagon. The coach is on fire. Flames of white and red reach up to the sky, casting shadows around the camp. I remember Mukito warming his hands by the mean fire of the inn.

"It is like the Sun," he said, but it was not like the Sun and neither is this. It is only a fire, no matter how brightly it burns.

Borroka motions for me to search the corpse. I collect some letters, keys and money. His clothes are stripped and thrown on the fire to burn. He is wrapped in a sheet. I push him into the hole. Zintoa and his friend fill it in behind me. The men gather around the hole. I realize they are looking at me. They are expecting me to say something. Borroka calls the men to silence.

"Who will light his lantern?" he asks. Tito nods and goes forward to place a lantern over the head of the grave.

I realize that I must speak. "Gutiza, I have known you for the shortest time of all us gathered here. I have less cause for grievance at your hand than some here, but those grievances I freely forgive and consign to darkness. May the light not be shone upon them. Much of your life is unknown to me, and like all of us, you will have some merits. To me, you were often courteous. For that, I thank you and ask the light to shine upon your good deeds, whatever they were."

I look around and the soldiers are nodding; in death, they are merciful. But Juana is not; she has anger in her heart. I cannot blame her; she has suffered much at Gutiza's hands.

After I have spoken, the soldiers seem to relax. They start to drift back to the camp. Zintoa looks as if he would speak with me, but Borroka is waiting to talk to me and so he leaves. Juana also stays.

"I will not pretend to be sad he is dead," says Borroka. "But you must tell me how he died."

"I cannot tell you," I reply. "He seemed to just convulse and die. You were there."

"Tito has said it could be plague, but it could also be poison, or a thin blade pushed in the right place. We did not look too closely. Did you kill him? Do you know of any others that might have?" And with this, he indicates Juana.

"Did I have cause to wish him dead? Some, but I can think of others that might have greater cause, including yourself. Did I kill him? No. There were only myself and Juana in the carriage, and my daughter. Juana and Gutiza were scuffling and I'm sure she had good reason to wish him dead, but I do not believe she killed him. As you saw, there was no wound when we stripped the body."

"There are other ways to kill than with a blade: you can snap his neck, or smother him, or poison him. Blood has come out his mouth; if you strike hard to the body, that can happen."

I do not doubt that Borroka is correct in what he says. I shudder to think how he knows such things, how I know such things.

"Juana says there was a man, another man, in the carriage."

"How could that be?" I ask.

Juana turns and looks at me. She is afraid. "There was a man, tall and dark. He said to Gutiza, 'Die,' and he did. It was magic, dark magic, to kill with a word, to come into locked places. Gutiza tried to kill the dark man, but he vanished: more magic."

I want to remind Juana that the dark man had probably saved her life. It was surely only a matter of time before Gutiza would have killed her.

Borroka sneers. "Magic. Yes, that sounds better than poison. You and Zinty poisoned him; that's why you were fawning over the boy, so he'd poison the boss. Zinty made all the food for the boss."

Juana flinches at his words. "It was not poison, and if it was, I would not have needed the boy's help. Gutiza drank much. If I wished to poison him, I would have poisoned his wine. He drank more than he ate. It would have been easy. You should drink less," she says.

Borroka is startled by Juana's threat. He has taken it for granted that she would come to him now that Gutiza is dead. Juana laughs.

"Do not be afraid, not of me. I will not poison you, my love. I will not leave you for the boy. He has no eyes for me, anyway. You should have killed Gutiza."

"I would have," snaps Borroka. "I said I would."

"Yes, sure, I believe it," replies Juana. "Till then, he beat me and raped me and kept us apart. Such passion, such love, I am lucky."

Borroka moves as if to strike her, but Juana does not flinch. Borroka holds back.

"She did not kill Gutiza. I am sure of it," I say. "When Gutiza started to bleed from the mouth, she started screaming and ran from the coach for help. If she had been poisoning him, she would not have been surprised. Also, I think she would have stayed and gloated over his dying. I know why you ask this now. You fear that having killed one lover, she will kill the next. If you strike her, then that would be possible, even if she did not kill Gutiza. If you are good to her, then it is unlikely she will kill you, even if she did. You fear she will cheat on you. I cannot say if she will or not. It is possible. But it is possible for any woman to cheat, and any man."

"I will not cheat on you," says Juana. "Not as long as you don't strike me."

The two lovers look at each other. I am intruding and withdraw. I walk back to the camp. The coach is still burning bright and the heat of it is strong. I have to skirt around the fire to stop from scorching myself. I walk into the main knot of soldiers and sit on the ground. There only about five sitting there. I do not know any of their names. They are looking at me. I have nothing to tell them.

Tito arrives. "What are you all sitting about for?" he asks. "Make camp; we'll be here for a bit until the sergeant decides what's next."

"What about the prisoners?" asks one of the men.

"What about them? They ain't going anywhere. Let's get this straight: it was us that was taking them to the City of the Sun. Fatso being dead don't make any difference. I'm loyal to the Sun and so is Borroka. Any that ain't are likely to find things hard for them."

"Well, where we heading, then?" asks another of the men. "And don't say the City of the Sun; we need to know where we're heading next. Does Borroka even know where we're supposed to go?"

"Course he does. You think that fat fool was running things? Best thing that could happen, him dropping dead. Now we can get on and do our job."

"Well, where next, then? Where're we heading?"

"Gutiza was headed for Fadu. He was going to meet some high

up one there. So that's where we'll be going, unless Borroka has other ideas."

Borroka and Juana return. Juana looks pleased, but there is still worry in Borroka's eyes.

Will they be happy? I wonder and hope. Now I go back to the tent. Alaba is there and Zintoa is with her. "Why are you here?" I say.

"I want to talk to you."

"Do you?"

"Juana says he killed him; the dark man killed him, she says. I think she means Erroi."

"Yes, I think he did."

"Did you call him? Is he a demon?"

"I have no power over him," I say. "I do not know what he is. Perhaps he is just a man."

"A man that can do such wonderful things?" says Zintoa doubtfully.

"All men can do wonderful things," I reply, "if they try."

"Could you do these things? Could I?"

"Yes, if we knew how, perhaps."

"Do you know how?"

"No," I say and shrug. I expect Zintoa to leave, but he does not. He is still looking at me as if I can answer his questions. He thinks I know more than I have said. He thinks I can answer his questions.

He turns to Alaba again. He puts his hand on her head. She is glowing, but does not seem to notice us. She is mute.

"You are a strange man."

"How so?"

"You have a friend that is a demon and a daughter that glows. Is that not strange?"

"The world is strange," I reply.

"Will she ever speak?" he asks.

"I cannot say," I reply. "I do not know why she does not speak. I do not know how to make her speak."

"Perhaps your demon can make her speak."

"Perhaps. You must ask him."

"Will he come after moonfall?"

Again, I shrug.

When the moon falls, and the world is lit only by stars, Erroi comes again. Zintoa is here in my dream, or perhaps I am in his. He looks to me, but I have nothing to say. Zintoa bows before him.

"Great demon," he says, "I ask one favour from you. Heal Alaba;

remove whatever curse sits upon her and bring her to a fullness of life."

Erroi's eyes glitter with amusement. "I am no demon. I am a man. No, not even a man. I am just a dream. You are dreaming. Alaba is under no curse. She will rise to a fullness of life, but not by my doing."

"Then whose doing? How can I bring her to health and wellness?"

"You cannot, and neither can I."

"What brings you here, friend?" I say. "Have you more mischief to spread?"

"You call me friend and then accuse me of mischief. It is not I who spreads mischief. There is mischief enough in the world without me adding more. You blame me for Gutiza's death. That makes less mischief, not more. Less mischief for you, at any rate; more for him, I admit."

"What is your purpose?" I repeat.

"To do good," Erroi says. "To do mischief."

"What mischief will you do?" I ask.

"What seems good to me," he replies.

When the moon rises, the soldiers prepare to leave. There is no coach for us, so Alaba lies in the back of the cart. It is not a fine cart like my wagon and has no canvas awning. She is wrapped up to keep her warm. Only her face is showing, glowing in the moonlight. I will walk. I would rather ride on the wagon, but there is no room. The two horses freed from the coach have been saddled. Borroka is riding one of the horses. A man I do not know is riding the other horse. Juana will walk too.

To march is hard work for someone not used to it. Juana and I struggle to keep up; Zintoa marches at the head of the column and we do not speak to him. Tito drops back to urge us on. Once, Borroka drops back and lifts Juana onto his horse. She rides behind him for a bit and then he drops her from his saddle near the head of the column. We are travelling much slower than before, I imagine. We do not reach Fadu by moonset. When we stop, I am glad. I almost wish I was back in the coach with Gutiza. My feet are sore and I remove my shoes.

Zintoa comes to meet me. He is carrying a small bag. "Here," he says and hands it to me.

"What is this for?" I ask. It is a small flat bag of cotton, filled loosely with dried beans or peas.

"It is for your feet," he says. He takes off his shoe and puts one of his feet on the bag. He slides his foot backwards and forwards. Then he passes it to me.

"You try," he says.

I rub my foot back and forwards; the beans or peas roll back and forth, massaging my foot.

"Thank you," I say. "This is much better."

"Tomorrow, we should reach Fadu," says Zintoa. "Borroka is likely to get a carriage for you there."

"That would be good," I say.

When the tents are up and the fire lit, Zintoa starts to cook, but I am too tired to eat. I sleep and do not dream.

We reach Fadu by midmoon. The moon is once again just a sliver of light. The march is easier than yesterday. Fadu is a great city. There is much black coal here that is dug out of the earth. There is also much ore, which they also dig. In the city, there are huge furnaces, which are lit all the time. They smelt the ore and make metal. The furnaces are a source of great wealth, for some. There is black smoke everywhere. You cannot see the stars for the smoke and the glow of furnaces. It is very hot.

When we enter the city, a great crowd gathers. People point at Alaba. They can see her glowing face. They have heard of the girl who Vatu seeks. The soldiers pretend to ignore the crowd. They straighten up and march in good order, with Borroka on his horse at the head and the wagon just behind. Juana is at the back. She would have liked to ride in on Borroka's horse, but he would not have it. She is surly and does not speak to me. I look at the crowd. There are a great many people there. We stop in an open space in front of the Great Hall of Fadu. The ruler of the city comes to meet us. There is another man with him. The soldiers of Fadu step forward to take Alaba and myself away. Borroka is talking with the two men, but I cannot hear what they say. The ruler of the city looks angry, but the other man lifts a hand. He points to the Great Hall, and the ruler nods. They turn and walk back to the Great Hall. Borroka follows, and gestures to Tito to bring Alaba and myself.

"Come on," says Zintoa, and lifts Alaba. I follow after them and enter the Great Hall. The hall is very fine; the city must be very rich. Borroka is called forward and I see him talk with the two lords. I cannot hear what they are saying. The tall one motions and I am brought forward.

"I hear Gutiza is dead."

"Yes, lord," I say. I think the tall one must be the friend that Gutiza wrote to. He does not look very upset to hear of his friend's death.

"How did he die?"

"I believe from sickness, lord. That is why the soldiers burned his coach."

"But you are not sick, nor is your daughter."

"My daughter is very sick, lord."

"But no one else is sick."

"That is correct, lord."

We are waved away. I am taken to a cell and locked in. There is barely enough room for me to stretch out on the hard floor, where I make my bed. In the dark, I lie alone, thinking. Alaba is not taken to my cell. I do not know where they have taken her. I hope they are taking better care of her than they are of me.

In the darkness, I do not see him come, but I know he is here. I can hear him settle beside me, but I can see nothing. How can he come into my cell? I wait for him to speak.

"What now?" he asks.

I am angry. What does he want from me? What does he think I can do? I cannot walk in and out of locked cells. I cannot leave my daughter. Does he mock me?

"I have brought you food," he says, and he hands me two apples.

I eat and realize I am hungry. The sweetness of the apples is better than wine. I thank him for his kindness. "Why are you here?" I ask.

"Because I am needed. I will go soon."

"I saw a face in the crowd today."

"Yes," he says. "The boy is here too; I told him to run away. No one listens to me."

Then he is gone. I do not hear him go. He is gone. The cell is empty.

It must be moonup when I am awakened. A guard comes and shakes me. I am given no food, but I am told to follow him. I am taken to the Great Hall. The two lords arrive. The smaller one looks tired, as if he would still sleep, but the tall one is alert.

"Who are you?" he asks.

I do not know how to answer. "My name is Utas," I say.

"Lies," says the tall one. "Tell me now. Who are you?"

"I am Utas," I continue. "It is my name." It is my name, for now. The tall one motions, and a guard strikes me from behind.

"I am the father of Alaba," I say. "The one who glows in

sunlight."

The tall one nods. I am not struck.

"Why does she glow?"

Why indeed? How can I answer? I know only that she does. I pause and think. I do not wish to be struck again. I shrug. It seems that is enough for the tall one.

"Vatu wishes to see you," he says. "Alive. If you will not answer me, you will answer him."

I do not speak. There is nothing I can say. I cannot answer questions that I do not know the answer to. I bow my head.

The tall one turns away. The shorter one waves and a bier is carried in, draped in cloth. It is a body.

"Your daughter is dead," says the tall one and draws the cloth down from over her face.

Chapter Four
In Town

I want to run after him and stop him. I want to shout. What are you doing? You're just going to go and hand yourself over to the guards? Why do they want you anyway? How is this going to help your daughter? Why don't you at least leave her with us? But I don't. I am held back. The cart travels down the track and eventually I can no longer see the shine of its lantern. I am released and I sink to the ground. I dig my fingers into the dark soil. I should have gone after them. I should have done something.

"What?" says Erroi. He is right, what? I look around at the camp. Our fire is still lit and most of our gear is lying around. Zintoa's horse is tethered to a peg. Erroi asks if I can ride a horse; I have never ridden a horse. Kilhanga had one that he stole from a traveller, but it was bad tempered and would kick and buck. I tried to ride it once and was thrown badly. The horse also threw Kilhanga. Eventually, he got angry. I thought he was going to kill it; I'm sure he wanted to. Instead, he took it and sold it. I don't know how much he got for the horse, but it was enough for him to be drunk many days. Sometimes it was all right when Kilhanga was drunk. He would just lie around and do nothing or sing stupid songs I'd never heard. Dirty songs, he would not have sung them if my mother had been alive.

Anyway, I ask Erroi if he can ride a horse; he says he has no need to. I take it that means no. Seems he cannot do everything after all. I realize that I am alone with a man who wanted to kill me just two days ago. I wonder if he will try to kill me now that Utas is not here to stop him, and then I notice that Zintoa's sword is also lying on the ground, beside the corpse of the great cat. I walk over to it and pick it up. If Erroi will kill me, then at least I will die trying to defend myself.

"Do you know how to use that?" he asks.

"Kilhanga showed me how to use one a little. I know you killed him easily, but that was when he was trying to climb onto the wagon. He was a decent swordsman and you'd have found it harder in a fair fight. He used to sell everything for drink, but never his sword. When I took his sword to the market, I was surprised at how well he had kept it and how much it was worth. It was worth enough to keep him drunk for a month at least."

"So," he says, all dark and full of himself, "you know nothing. There are no fair fights. If I fight you, how is that fair? I would kill you easily. If you sneak up on me in the dark and stab me while I sleep, is that fair? You could kill me easily, if you were lucky."

I will not be afraid of him. If he will kill me, then let him do it now. I turn towards him and brandish the sword in front of me and sink into the crouching stance that Kilhanga taught me. Erroi does not draw his sword.

"Will you kill me?" I ask. "If so, then get on with it and try me."

The dark man is thinking.

"No," he says, "I will not kill you. I spared your life and you owe me for that. But I owe you also. I can teach you how to use that sword, and a great many other things. All I ask in return is that you do not come sneaking up on me in the dark."

What a stupid thing to say. He owes me nothing. And I am not a coward who would stab a sleeping man. If I was, then Kilhanga would have been dead long ago with a dagger through his eye. I put the sword back on the ground. There is no sheath. I sit down and put my head in my hands.

"What choice do I have?"

"None," agrees Erroi, "at least none that are good choices."

"And this is a good choice?" I ask.

"Yes," says Erroi. "Now come over here and bring that sword. We will skin the cat and sell the hide when we reach the next town. We will need money."

"There is a bag with money over there," I say and point. "I

heard it jingle as Utas threw it from the coach. I guess he thought he would have no need for it where he was going."

Erroi looks both surprised and pleased. He walks over to the small sack, picks it up and throws it to me.

"This must be for you," he says. "Count it."

I open the bag and it is full of money, more money than I have ever seen. More money than when I go to market and the traders open their purses to pay for whatever wares we have stolen. Utas must be very rich, richer by far than a travelling cloth seller.

"I don't think we will need money," I say and pour the coins into my lap. I will not count them now.

"We will," says Erroi. "Poor travellers always need money, and that is what we are, or what we must appear to be. If we have money, we attract attention. We will skin the cat and sell the pelt, it will bring enough."

"Then why has Utas given us this money?"

"He is trying to pay you off. Go and settle down and forget about him. Here's some gold to make it easy. Buy a farm or a shop. It would not be quite as easy as that, people will try and trick you out of the money, but it will be easier than coming with me."

It seems I do have a choice.

"What will you choose?" Erroi asks.

I do not think. I throw the bag over to Erroi.

"Take it," I say. "Bury it. Perhaps one day we can return it to Utas. I will not forget him or Alaba."

Erroi crouches and starts to dig. He puts the gold into the ground and buries it. Afterwards, he rolls a big stone over the hole. Then he takes his sword and draws it lightly across the stone. I look and I see three lines scored into the stone like claw marks. What kind of a sword can cut stone?

"It is better to have done it right away," explains Erroi. "Gold has a power; the longer you have it, the more you are in its power. Utas must be very powerful to have had this gold and still be free of it."

"It has no power," I say. "It is just men's weakness."

Erroi looks at me, startled, but he does not argue.

"Come, then," he says. "Let's get the cat skinned."

The cat is very big and very heavy. It smells bad. It is hard work to skin the beast, and Erroi does not help. When I have cut the last of the hide free, he comes and throws salt over the rawhide. Then he rolls it up and ties it with string.

"The meat of a cat is not good to eat," he tells me, although I already knew, "but the teeth and claws are also of value. Pull them out."

It is even harder work to remove the teeth. They are fixed hard into the jaws and must be drawn back and forth to loosen them. There are many teeth. The claws are severed and are less work. I look at the hide and the teeth and claws. Erroi is right. We will make good money selling them. I hope Erroi does not spend the money on drink.

"Now make dinner," says Erroi.

I am tired and hungry. Could he not have made dinner while I laboured? I make dinner, weak gruel. There is no salt for it, as Erroi has used it all on his hide.

"The gruel is good," says Erroi. But it tastes bad to me.

"Should we not be going?" I ask.

"No," he replies. "You are young and eager, but we wish to follow, not catch up, not yet anyway. If we ride into town today, the soldier might notice us. 'Look,' he will say, 'these are the men who were with the prisoners yesterday.' That would not be good for us."

"But how will we find them if we do not keep up?"

"Prisoners move slowly, there is always much talk about what to do and where to go. They will not travel fast. Besides, we know where they will be taken."

"Where?" I ask.

"To the City of the Sun," says Erroi.

"How do you know this?" I ask.

"Utas and his daughter are wanted by Vatu. They will be brought to him. He will not come to them."

I can see the logic in his remarks and nod agreement.

"But why does he want them?"

"Because Alaba glows."

"But why does she glow, and why would that make Vatu want her? He has the Sun, what difference does it make to him if she glows a little? Even at her brightest, she is fainter than starlight. What will he do with them?"

Erroi looks at me. I think he will speak and then he stops. He does not know any more than me. He has only been travelling with Utas half a day longer than I have. He pretends to be so wise and mysterious. He's no different than me at all. I tell him that he does not know.

"You may be right," he says, "perhaps I do not know, perhaps I do not tell. Either way, you do not know and I will not tell you. Are you loyal to the Sun?"

"Yes, of course," I say.

"Good," says Erroi, "but think on what that means."

"Are you loyal to the Sun?" I ask.

Erroi stares at me as if I am mad. "No, of course not, I am loyal only to myself."

We wait for two moon rounds. I can see that Erroi is right. If we go and are spotted, we would be arrested; that will not help anyone. Still, it is difficult to sit and do nothing when I know that Utas and Alaba are in danger.

Towards the end of the second moon round, I say, "You said you would teach me."

"I am teaching you to be patient," says Erroi. He sees me scowl. Is he mocking me? But then he continues, "Patience is important. But perhaps it is enough of that lesson for now."

"So what will you teach me? Will you teach me to fight like you?"

"No," says Erroi, "not like me, but I will teach you the proper use of a sword."

I stand up and pick up the sword. I crouch down and balance on the balls of my feet just like Kilhanga taught me and bring the sword up in front of me. Erroi walks around, inspecting my stance.

"Will you draw your sword?" I ask.

"No," he replies. "I only draw my sword to kill."

I know that is a lie; he used his sword to score the flat stone just a few yards away. I let it pass.

"Attack me," he says calmly.

"But you have no sword."

"It does not matter, attack me."

I lunge at him and he slips away easily. He shakes his head.

"Attack me properly, as if you wish to kill me."

"But you are unarmed," I say. "What if I do kill you?"

Erroi looks mockingly at me. "If you can kill me, then you will have no need of me as a teacher. Come, a proper lun—"

I thrust the sword at him before he can finish speaking, but he slips easily out of my reach. He nods. "Better, but still not enough. I will tell you a secret. It is a great secret. Each of us is connected. When one of us dies, a bit of all of us dies. Because of this, to kill another man is a hard thing. To kill another person is to kill a part of yourself. Few men can kill, fewer can kill easily; those that do, and those that can, are diminished. What is the point of fighting, if not to kill? What is the point of killing, if you are killing yourself?"

Is he looking for me to answer these questions? Is he trying to confuse me?

"I have seen you kill," I answer, "and you would have killed me."

"Yes," he replies, "and you have seen that clumsy bandit kill too, I guess, but you have never killed."

It is not a question, it is a statement.

"Did being a killer make the clumsy bandit a better man or a worse one? Did killing him make me a better man or worse man? I have killed many men, more than your bandit, many more. Does that make me a worse man or a better man than him?"

I have seen Kilhanga kill many times. I have seen him run his blade through merchants and travellers that would rather fight and die than lose their belongings. I have seen their breath stop and eyes dim. I have seen blood flow and stain both ground and cloth. I have seen people turned into corpses. Each time, I wince and close my eyes. Each time, Kilhanga would shout with triumph, or what I thought was triumph; perhaps it was despair.

I turn and throw the sword away.

"Good," says Erroi, "now I have taught you the proper use for a sword."

"I am defenceless," I say.

"Yes," agrees Erroi. "We are all defenceless, that is wisdom."

I have been humiliated. I had thought that I would travel with the dark swordsman and we would rescue Utas and beautiful Alaba. Now I see that is not to be. What use am I if I cannot kill?

"What use am I?" I say, bitterly.

"Very useful," says Erroi. "Now go and pack up. It is time for more lessons."

The moon has dropped behind the horizon and there is only starlight. I go to light a torch, but Erroi stops me. We will travel in the dark.

"We cannot see without light," I say.

"Then we must travel without seeing."

I have packed everything onto Zintoa's horse. It occurs to me that we might be taken for horse thieves. But then, I might have been taken for a horse thief and a bandit at any time in the last ten dawns. I lead the horse forward. Even with just the starlight, it is bright enough to see the road, just the road in front and no more. We travel slowly and I worry that we will get lost. From time to time, I stumble on rocks lying on the path; even the horse stumbles occasionally. Erroi does not stumble. How can he be so surefooted? He is not walking slower than I am. In fact, sometimes he is far ahead and then waits for me to catch up. I want to ask him how, but I fear that if I do, he will say something like, 'because I do not,' or 'my steps are sure,' or some such nonsense.

"If so few men are killers," I ask when I catch up with Erroi, "why is there so much death?"

In the darkness, I cannot see his face, but I hear his breathing take a sad note. We walk on in the darkness and silence.

"Well?" I ask again. "Why?"

"You think I know the answers to all the world's questions," says Erroi shortly. "But I do not. Consider a lord in his castle. Someone has offended him and they must die. He does not ride out and cut the offender down. No, he sends guards who arrest him, he is sent before judges that try him, witnesses will be called that will testify against him. He is held by jailers. Eventually, he is sent to a headman that will take his life. Of all these, which is the killer?"

"If it is just, then there is no killer," I reply.

"What is just?" says Erroi. "Everything and nothing. Consider a farmer who grows rice, many bowls. A poor man comes, the farmer will not feed him; that is just. The poor man dies; is that just? What of your friend? I killed him with a single blow. He would have killed me. Is that just?"

"I don't know," I say.

"Neither do I," replies Erroi.

We walk on and we reach the town gates well before moon up. We will have to wait outside. It is cold and I wish to start a fire for warmth. Erroi stops me. We huddle beside the horse and its warm, moist breath is all the heat we have. Eventually, the moon rises. The gates are opened and we go to enter. A guard stops us and asks us our business.

Erroi points to the hide on the horse's back and says, "We have come to sell that. We have its teeth and claws too."

"Skin from a great cat," says the guard; he sounds impressed.

"Yes," says Erroi. "We have had poor hunting and now we

know why. This brute has been raiding our traps. He was caught in the last one and we were able to kill it, but it was something I never want to see again. A great cat in a trap is not something to play with."

The guard waves us on. He is not interested. We go directly to the market. It is too early still, but we are able to buy some warm food while we wait. Eventually, the stalls open one by one. Erroi has taken the hide and unrolled it. He has draped it around him. It still smells bad, but passers-by look at it with interest. It is an impressive sight. In the moonlight, you can see the silver and black stripes. It will bring a lot of money. We do not go to any merchant. Erroi is waiting for one to come to us. He does not have to wait long. A little man in yellow silk comes and tells us his master wishes to speak with us. We follow him to a booth and we are led into a room at the back. The merchant is finely dressed, but not too finely; he does not wish to make his clients envious of his wealth.

"My friends," he says, "I have heard about this wonderful cat skin. I see now that I have not been deceived."

Erroi says nothing, but places the skin on the table. The merchant inspects it, and runs his fingers through the fur. He turns it over and holds the hide up to the light of his lantern. There are no holes in the hide.

"Impressive, no arrow holes. It must have been a clean kill. You must be a very great hunter."

"I am," says Erroi, "and one with little time."

The merchant smiles, but it is a false smile.

"Thirty gold pieces," he says.

Erroi says nothing, but reaches over and starts to roll up the hide.

"Wait, wait, what am I saying," says the merchant, and puts a hand on the hide. "Tell me what you want for this fine hide."

Erroi does not respond.

"Very well, sixty," says the merchant.

"Closer," says Erroi, "but I can drink sixty gold pieces in a night. I would want more than one night of pleasure for this."

"You want a hundred and twenty for this," says the merchant in amazement.

Erroi shrugs. "I can sell it for triple that," he says, "and you will sell it for much more. See, here are the claws and teeth."

Again the merchant looks at them. "None of the teeth are broken, and the claws are intact; very well, one hundred and twenty. Wait here while my man goes and fetches the coin."

Erroi's lips narrow, but he nods. The little man in yellow silk is sent scurrying off.

"Can I offer you refreshment?" asks the merchant.

"Perhaps for the boy," Erroi replies, "but not for me, I do not want to ruin my thirst."

The merchant grunts; he does not offer me any refreshment. A short time later, the man in yellow returns. The merchant steps out. A figure in black silk enters, a woman. Behind her are two men. They are not in any uniform, but it is clear they are fighters. Erroi draws his sword.

"Wait," commands the figure in black. It is a command, not to Erroi, but to the two men. The figure draws back her hood. She is of middle age. She may once have been beautiful and no doubt older men would still find her so.

Erroi has put his sword away.

"What do you want?" he asks.

"I have come to see this cat skin," says the woman. "They are very rare. I heard about a great cat being killed just days ago. It is unusual to hear of another great cat so soon after."

"Not so unusual," says Erroi. "Perhaps this is the mate of the other you heard of."

"Great cats do not mate," says the woman, "at least not for love and do not stay together long."

"But long enough," replies Erroi.

"Yes," says the woman. "Perhaps too long. Let me tell you how the first cat died. He was killed by a great swordsman, who killed it with a single thrust. Or so I heard. I heard he was the greatest swordsman that the soldier had seen. You perhaps know this swordsman. He was travelling with some fugitives that were seeking to escape Vatu's judgment. At least, that is what my husband told me."

"Who is your husband and where is he now?"

"My husband is the Lord Mayor of this town. We were exiled here because he could not keep his stuff in his trousers. Not that he has much stuff, to be honest. He's gone on a journey to the City of the Sun. It would be sad if he never returned."

"No doubt you would weep for him if that were the case."

"No doubt, a woman's life is full of tears."

The woman is running her fingers through the fur of the cat skin.

"I would like to buy this, it must be very valuable. Would five hundred gold be enough?"

I almost choke. That is a fortune indeed.

"For the skin perhaps," says Erroi. "Tell me, where is your husband headed?"

"He is going to Fadu. There he will meet his friend, or one who he thinks is his friend, but is not. Still, I think this friend will keep him safe. It is a long journey to Fadu."

"And what of his companions?"

"He has ten soldiers with him. We could not afford for more to go. It would make things difficult here. Also, he is travelling with his whore. I care not about that. He thinks I do not know. And two other companions, they may be known to you."

Erroi scratches his nose. "I'm just a hunter that wants to go and drink."

"Of course," says the lady. She drops a bag onto the table and one of the men steps forward to pick up the hide.

"Wait," says Erroi. He has emptied the bag on the table and is counting it.

"Do you not trust me?" says the woman. "Very wise."

After they have left, the merchant returns to his room. He seems to want us gone. It amuses Erroi to stay and talk, small talk about the weather and which inn he should go to. The merchant tries to be polite, but is clearly desperate for us to leave.

Eventually, Erroi is bored and we move on, leaving the merchant in peace. He hands me the gold. I wonder what he will do with it. We do not go to the modest inn we stayed in only a few nights earlier. Instead, we stay somewhere much grander, the sort of inn Kilhanga would have stayed in when he had money. But he would have been thrown out after one night. Our room there is large, and there is a fire in it. Erroi tosses me a coin, a whole gold piece.

"Go and entertain yourself," he says.

I go out into the town. There is not much entertainment. I sit by the square and watch aimlessly. Eventually, I am hungry. I buy some skewers of meat. They are hot and greasy and not very good. As I sit eating, I feel the change in my pocket. It is enough to feed a family for a week at least. My mother never had so much money. Kilhanga did, but all he used it for was to buy drink. I get up and return to the inn. The door to our room is locked and I bang on it loudly. Erroi opens the door and welcomes me in. He has been sleeping. The room is warm from the fire and brightly lit. His bed is unmade, and he is partially undressed. He smiles when I enter. There is a sickly smell, like lilies. He seems pleased with himself.

"Will you kill the woman's husband?" I ask.

"He is a cruel and greedy ruler and a bad husband," says Erroi. "Tell me, would it be just to kill him?"

"Does it matter?" I ask. "I do not know the answers to all the questions in the world."

"You are right," says Erroi, "it does not matter. Yes, I will kill him."

"And the others?"

"I will spare them if I can. Are you hungry?"

"No, I have eaten. What will you do with the gold?" I ask. "Will you bury it too?"

"No, it is much easier to get rid of gold in a place like this."

I follow him downstairs. He is ushered to a table and starts to buy drink. Soon, men and women gather around him. He buys them drinks, too. He laughs and jokes with his new friends. His friends laugh with him. I have seen this before with Kilhanga. The laughter is brittle and false. Behind the smiles, Erroi's new friends have greedy, desperate eyes. One of Erroi's new friends suggests a game of cards, for small stakes. Erroi agrees willingly. He is right, it is easy to lose gold here. Kilhanga lost lots of gold in places like this. After he had lost the gold, he would be angry and want to fight with his so-called friends. His false friends would call on the innkeeper, who would call on the guards and out we would go. But then I see Erroi look at me and wink. I notice he buys more drink for the others than he does for himself. He loses small amounts. He is cautious in his gambling. His friends encourage him. It is a shame he has such bad luck. Perhaps he can win his money back if he is bolder, they say. After all, luck will even itself out.

I have sat and watched Kilhanga play cards many times. He was not a good player, but he was not a cheat. I can see that one of the card players is cheating. He is hiding cards and his friend is signalling what is in Erroi's hand. He's not even very good at it. Surely Erroi must have noticed. Even stupid Kilhanga would have noticed by now and would have started a fight. Is this how he will get rid of his gold, give it to thieves? The stakes are getting higher, and the pot is getting bigger. Erroi has not brought all his money to the table, but he has brought enough. The pot must hold three hundred gold pieces; about half of them have come from Erroi's purse. The gambler is confident he will win. I don't know what is in his hand. Erroi has kept his cards face down. No one knows what they are, not even him. He has not looked at them. The gambler puts his cards down and shows them. He has slipped a card into his hand to make a run. It is a good hand. I think he should win. He reaches over to take the pot. Erroi is drumming the table with his fingers.

"Wait," he says, "let's see what my hand is anyway."

"If you like," concedes the gambler, who continues to gather the gold.

Erroi starts to turn the cards. I am watching him and I cannot see him change cards. He did not deal the hand, he has not looked at them. He has a run also, but his is higher. He has won. How?

The gambler stops. He is amazed. How can Erroi have won? This was not a game of chance. He looks at Erroi; I can see he is convinced that Erroi has cheated. I think for a moment that there will be a fight. The gambler is not alone, but I have seen Erroi fight. There would only be one winner. The gambler is not a fool, he knows this too. He can hardly accuse Erroi of cheating when he has cards hidden on him. He leans back in his chair.

"Well," says Erroi, "I have been lucky. Come now, I'll give you the chance to win it back. That is only fair. You gave me the same chance."

The gambler shakes his head. He has no money and will be beaten badly when his backers find he has lost so much.

"Well, let me pay for a drink," says Erroi; he tosses him maybe ten gold pieces. It is more than enough for a drink. It is enough to pay for a horse and to run from the town. Erroi's friends seem subdued.

"Time to go," says Erroi. "Boy, come and help a drunk man up the stairs."

I go, collect his gold, and help him stand. He is very light for a man his size. I can see he is not as drunk as he pretends, but his breath smells of brandy and he leans heavily on me. I help him stagger up the stairs. I get him into the room and instantly he straightens up. He pushes me gently away.

"Go and sleep."

He lies down and is asleep almost instantly, or appears to be sleeping. Erroi is never what he seems. He is lying on his back. He has not bothered to undress, and he is snoring gently. There is nothing to do but to sleep. I douse the light and fire, and then

I lie down and close my eyes.

The door must not be locked. I was certain I had locked it, but when I wake to relieve myself during moondown, the room is empty. I check the door and it is still locked; the key is still in the door. That is some trick to disappear and leave the key in the lock. I check the windows and they are also locked. It appears I must sleep alone. That is no hardship. I will ask him about it in the morning. In the meantime, it is time to sleep. I roll over and am sleeping quickly. In the morning, he has returned.

"Where did you go last night?"

"Many places."

I know better than to waste time prying. I get up and dress.

"Will we leave today?" I ask.

"Maybe."

A late breakfast is served in our room.

"What will you do today?"

"Wait."

"Have you recovered from last night?"

"Yes, and I will have to do the same tonight."

"Why?"

"People expect it. If you do not do what people expect, they notice. We do not wish to be noticed. Don't worry, there will be no trouble. I will drink alone and no one will play cards with me. Afterwards, we will leave. You should make sure we are ready to go tomorrow. We need salt and you should buy oats for the horse and for gruel."

"You could have let the gambler win, then you could play again tonight."

"Yes, I thought about letting him win. I wanted to lose the money. Would it have been fair to let him win? He has cheated many people. Should I let him cheat me?"

"No, it would not have been fair, but was it fair to cheat him?"

"I did not cheat him. I was lucky."

I cannot believe that, and I tell him.

"So you saw me cheat?" he asks.

"No," I admit.

"So you don't know if I am a cheat or if I am lucky. You choose to believe that I am a cheat."

"I have never seen anyone be as lucky as that. I have seen many people cheat. I have seen it before; just because you are better at cheating than others does not make you less of a cheat."

"I did not cheat, I was lucky."

"You must have cheated; no one is that lucky."

"I am."

I do not argue, instead I head off to the market to buy provisions. There is a shortcut to the market through an alleyway. It is badly lit and quiet. It runs crooked and as I turn a corner, I realize I am being followed. A boy steps up in front of me. He is bigger than me, but not by much.

"Give me your purse."

I look at him. He is stocky, but still looks ill fed. He is dressed in cheap, ragged clothing, but it is clean. Someone has washed them for him, perhaps a mother or a sister, a mother or sister who needs fed. If he had asked, I would have given him a few shillings. I could just give him the money. There is plenty more in our room. But if I do, then I am helping him become a robber, a thief, a bully. Why should I just give him the money? Perhaps it is pride that stops me from handing over the money, but I know I will not give it to him. If we fight, he will not win easily; perhaps I will win. I have no sword or dagger, but I have my fists. I have spent ten dawns being hit by Kilhanga, I know how to grapple and dodge. I could fight him and take his money from him. It would teach him not to pick on others. That would make me a robber, a thief, a bully.

"Come with me," I say, and to my surprise, the boy follows me. We go to a stall and I buy oats and salt, two bags. I hand them to the boy. "Come," I say. He follows me back to the inn and helps me stash the oats with our gear. I hand him four shillings. It is generous. He would not have thought I had more when he tried to steal from me. He looks at the coins.

"The horse will need loaded tomorrow; if you are here to help, there will be more."

"How much more?" asks the boy, as if he might have a better offer.

"The same," I say.

The boy nods. "Is there anything else I can get for you?"

I say no. He leaves and I will see him tomorrow. His family will eat tonight. I brush the horse, and decide he is called Cavall. Utas is right, there is a magic in names. I should have asked the boy's name. "My name is Mukito," I tell the horse. "We're going to be friends."

The horse nuzzles my hand. He is looking for food; still, it is nice to have a friend, even if it is just a horse. It is not even my horse. I have never had a friend. When I was small, it was just me and my mother. Then, for a short time, there was me, my mother and Kilhanga, then just me and Kilhanga. Kilhanga is dead now. He was not my friend. Is Utas? Is Alaba? Is Erroi? What is a friend? Erroi says we are all connected, but I feel alone. I feel as if there is nowhere I belong. What nonsense; in the end, we are all alone. I have learned that the only one I can depend on is me. Erroi would have killed me just a few days ago. Now I am his servant. Utas left me without even turning back. Alaba cannot speak; did she even know I was there? Is this what life is: loneliness, needing? Does everyone feel empty? Cavall nuzzles me again. I stroke his head. I have one friend at least.

Erroi joins me in the stable.

"I see you have the oats and salt."

"Yes, it should be plenty."

Erroi lifts the bags. "Yes, plenty," he agrees.

"Should we not go now?" I ask.

"No, not today, tomorrow."

We go into the inn and Erroi orders a large meal. I eat some of it, but there is too much for me to eat it all. Then Erroi goes back upstairs. I head back to the stable to check our gear.

Later, I return, and the door is locked again. When he opens it, Erroi is again in a state of partial dress. We go down to the inn. He orders drinks, but tonight, no one gathers around him. The gambler from last night is not to be seen. Perhaps he has left the town. It is as Erroi said it would be; he sits quietly drinking, left alone.

After we sleep and eat, it's time to go. I am glad to be going. I head down to the stable to pack up. I do not really expect the boy from yesterday to be there and I am right, he is not. There is another boy, smaller and more ragged. I notice he is wearing the same jacket as the other boy.

"Are you the man with the horse?" he asks. "Hasera said that you would pay me to help load it."

Hasera must be the boy I met yesterday. I should have asked his name.

"What is your name?"

"Pobre," says the boy. "Hasera cannot come, so he sent me."

"I see," I say. Hasera has sent this boy to do the work and

then he will take the money from him, I think. Anyway, the horse needs loaded.

"Yes. Here is the horse, help me load him. His name is Cavall."

The boy is a good worker and the horse is loaded quickly. I give him four shillings as I had agreed, then I hand him another two.

"What are these for?" asks Pobre.

"Hasera will take the four shillings from you when you go back. He will make you hand them over. Give them to him, but keep the other two. It is not right that you should work and he should take your money."

Pobre bows his head. "It is not like that," he says.

"No?" I ask. "Then what is it like?"

"Hasera is sick; no, not sick, injured. When he came home last night, he was stopped by two capos, two gangsters, they knew he had money and wanted it. He would not give it to them, so they beat him. They beat him very bad and took the money anyway. They took all of it."

"Will they beat you?" I ask.

"Perhaps," says Pobre, "if they catch me. They know where we live. They take all our money. They take everyone's money. They are big capos."

I go to the horse and gather the bandages and salves that I had used on Zintoa. It is my fault that Hasera is injured. I can see to his wounds.

"Come," I say, "take me to him."

"Take you to who?" asks Erroi. He has entered the stable and is standing behind me. I tell him about the boy, Hasera. I tell him he has been beaten because of me. I tell him I will help him.

Erroi shakes his head. "You are not responsible, and we must leave."

"No," I say and move to go past him. For a minute, I think Erroi will force me to stay, or worse, tell me to go and that he will leave. But he does not, he moves to let me pass.

Pobre leads me out into the town. We go through the market and then down an alley leading to a group of poor-looking shacks that are built hard against the town wall. Two large men walk up beside us. I notice one has a bruise on his face and the other a slight limp. Hasera has fought hard. They have angry, hard faces, and Pobre cowers from them.

"What have we here?" says one of the capos. "Introduce us to your friend, Pobre. Is this your rich friend?"

I wonder if Pobre has led me to a trap. But I can see the fear in his face, and he could not have thought that I would come to help Hasera. I know I cannot fight them, and if I did, I cannot look for help from Pobre.

"What do you want?" I ask.

"What is in the bag?"

I take a handful of bandages from the bag. They are of no value. The capo looks disappointed.

"What else do you have?"

"Nothing," I say.

"We'll see," says the second capo and moves towards me, grabbing my wrist. I struggle, but he is strong. I do not struggle too hard. I do not want to fight. He reaches into my waistband and lifts my purse. There is still forty shillings.

"And you," says the capo, moving towards Pobre, "what do you have?"

Pobre holds his hand out and offers six shillings. There is fear in his eyes.

"Is that all?" says the capo. "Not enough." And he cuffs Pobre hard, sending him spinning to the cobbles.

The capos have drawn knives. Why? They have taken our money. What else do they want?

"Stop," I say, but they do not listen.

I think they will kill me. I think they will kill Pobre. Why?

The two capos pause and look startled. Then I see that Erroi is beside us. He walks forward. He looks frail and weak compared to the two big capos. It is comical, like a child that will bait a bear, or a twig that will hold back a torrent. The two capos laugh. They should not. Erroi could kill them both in an instant.

"I think you should give the boys back their money," he says.

Again the capos laugh. They are being threatened by a skinny man in black rags and a straw hat.

The first capo points his knife at Erroi. "I think you should give me your money," he says.

"No," says Erroi, "I will not. Now will you give the boys their money or do I have to take it from you?"

More laughter comes from the capos, and then short cries of amazement and then shouts of pain and anger. One capo is lying on the ground. His arm is at a strange angle; it must be broken, and it must be very painful. The other capo is pinned against the wall. Erroi has his hand at his throat. He has taken back my purse and tosses it to me. Pobre's shillings have fallen to the ground and he darts forward to collect them.

Erroi lets the capo go. He watches as the capo helps the other from the ground and then they leave, walking at first and then running.

"You should have killed them," I say.

"This is better," says Erroi. "They will leave the boy alone in case I come back. If I killed them, there would be others coming. Perhaps they would kill the boy in revenge."

"They still might," I say.

"Who knows?" says Erroi. "We cannot always know."

Pobre takes us to a hovel near the wall. It is made of mud brick and is very low. There is no fire and no light. In the hovel, there is an old woman and a young girl. The woman is very old and has no teeth. The girl is still a child. There is a pile of rags on the floor and lying on it is Hasera. The capos have beaten him very badly. I can see that his face is badly bruised and he has broken teeth. He has a broken leg which will not heal quickly. I wash the cuts. Two of his teeth will need to be pulled. I tie a cord around them and give the other end to Erroi. He tugs hard and they come out more easily than I had thought they would. Then I try to set the leg. Hasera squirms in pain, but does not cry out. It will not set. Or if it will, it is beyond my skill. We could call a bonesetter, but I doubt one will come to such a place for fear of being robbed or killed. If the leg cannot be set, Hasera will be a cripple.

"Can you set his leg?" I ask Erroi.

"No," says Erroi, "but perhaps I can help him."

I wonder what kind of help the dark man will offer, but he pushes past me and sits beside Hasera. He inspects the leg. He is frowning. It is a very bad break. I think it is broken in more than one place, probably many places. Erroi is holding a small knife. What will he do? I wonder. Does he think Hasera is better dead than a cripple? It is a hard truth. Erroi lifts the boy's hand. He takes his knife and cuts a finger from Hasera's hand.

"What are you doing?" I shout in anger and rush forward. But Erroi just pushes me away.

Hasera starts with pain. This time, he does cry out.

The old woman comes forward and holds his hand. "What have you done?"

"What was necessary," says Erroi, and leaves the hovel. I turn around and Hasera is standing, holding his bleeding hand. I take his hand and bind it. It will heal. It is the smallest joint of his smallest finger that is gone.

"How can you stand?" I ask.

"My leg is not broken," says Hasera. "Thank you, and please thank the dark man too."

I go outside and Erroi is waiting for me. What can I say? I tell him the boy is grateful.

Chapter Five
To Fadu

We leave the town later that day, and pass through the gate without any further mishap. Erroi has a piece of paper from the Lord Mayor's wife that he shows the guard, but the guard is bored and just waves us through. He does not even look at it. He pays more attention to the horse. It is Zintoa's horse and I worry that he might recognize it. If they were friends, then perhaps he has seen Zintoa on it. The horse does not look much like a pack animal. We should have sold him and bought a mule. But it does not matter. We are not stopped. We set off, heading towards Fadu. I have never been there before, but Erroi seems to know the way.

"How long will it take?" I ask.

"A few days, perhaps a week. We will get there before Utas and Alaba."

"What will we do when we get there?" I ask. Rescuing Alaba from an armed guard will be difficult, but rescuing her from a fortress will be harder still, if not impossible. I say this to Erroi. I want to know what he plans. Are we just going to follow them all the way to the City of the Sun? What would the point of that be? Perhaps if Alaba is taken to Vatu, he can make her well. The dark spirit is very powerful. Perhaps we should let her go.

"You will see," he says.

Just that and no more, he will not say anything else about his plans. Why is he so secretive? Does he even have a plan? Still, I will not give up. If I can help Alaba and Utas in any way, I will. There is nothing else for me to do. So I follow after Erroi, leading the horse. He is a good horse, or so I think. I am no judge of horses. He is calm and patient and gentle. He nuzzles me for food, and likes it when I groom him. He does not kick or shy or bite. Not like the bad tempered horse Kilhanga stole. It would kick and shy when I tried to feed it or to load it up with gear. I was glad when he sold that horse. I wonder if I could ride this horse. I think he would let me. We seem to be friends, so I think it would be all right. But he is heavily loaded with oats and apples and salt and stuff. It would be too much for him to carry me too. Also, we have no saddle. Perhaps he would let me ride him when we stop and I have unloaded him. They say riding a horse is like flying. How can they say that when they have never flown? I don't think Erroi can ride a horse. I ask him if he can, and he says yes, of course he can. So I ask if he will teach me to ride Cavall; that is what I have called Zintoa's horse.

"We have no saddle," he says.

"Do we need one? Could I not sit on him without a saddle?"

"You could, but it would be more difficult."

I think that Erroi cannot ride a horse, and he is making excuses.

"Is riding a horse really like flying?" I ask.

"No," says Erroi.

"How can you tell?" I ask.

"Then why do you ask?"

It is cold. There is a lot of cloud. You cannot see the moon, which is a shame, as it is almost full. It would have been nice to walk by moonlight rather than to stumble along by the light of our lantern. I travel in the light of the lantern, but Erroi walks ahead, out of the pool of light it spreads on the ground. How can he see the road in the dark? Does he have cat's eyes? When we came to town, he made us both walk in the dark. He seemed to manage that fine, too.

"Why don't you come and walk in the light?" I ask.

"I have no need of it," he replies. "I can see. There is enough light."

Later, it starts to rain, big heavy drops of rain falling. I stop and unpack an oilskin, which I wrap around me to keep the rain off. I wrap another one over the baggage, and it will keep some of the rain off Cavall, too.

"Do you want something to keep the rain off?" I ask.

"I have a hat."

"Yes, but that won't keep you dry. I have another oilskin. You could put it over your head and shoulders. You don't want to get ill."

I'm a bit surprised when Erroi takes the oilskin and wraps it over his head. It is very wet, but I expected him to say something like 'It is only raining in your head.' But he does not, instead he says thank you.

For the rest of the day, we travel. The moon sets and we get a glimpse of pearly white through the cloud and rain. It is a pretty moonset. Sometimes the colours white, blue and purple are truly spectacular.

"What a beautiful moonset," I say. "Is there anything more beautiful?"

"Yes, many things are more beautiful."

"You have no soul," I say, laughing.

The rain is still coming down hard. Now that the moon is gone, it is very dark and even colder.

"We should camp," I say. "We can light a fire and string up these tarpaulins. It won't be a comfortable night."

"There is a better place up ahead," says Erroi.

"Really? How do you know? Have you been here before?"

"I can see it," says Erroi. His eyesight must be very good.

He leads us off the road and into the woods. Soon, we come to a clearing. There is a house there. No one lives in it. You can tell right away. The house is low and small. The door is broken and the two windows are hollow. From the light of the lantern, I see that the clearing was once a garden. There are hummocks where vegetables once grew, now briers and brambles grow there. We have to cut some briers away from the door to get in, and break down what is left of the door. We go inside, and I bring in the lantern. Inside, there are two rooms. The floor is wooden, but has rotted. In places, it has been pulled up. I worry about bringing Cavall into the house in case he stumbles on the floor, but Erroi says he will be better inside. I lead Cavall in and unload him. I give him a small bag of oats and rub him down. He is glad to be out of the rain. Erroi has pulled up some of the floor and made a small fire. I make some oatmeal. When I am finished, I hand over a small bowl to Erroi and we eat.

After I have eaten, I start to look around. I wonder who could have lived here, and why they left. The house must once have been stout and well built, but now it is well on the way to being a ruin. The house is far from any town, and the garden is too small to be a farm. I wonder how the people lived.

The house has two rooms. The front room where we have put the horse and lit the fire is little more than a shell with a fireplace and roof. The single window is gone, but there are boards across it. The other room has two beds in it. One is very small; it must have been a child's. By the light of the lantern, I can see it is painted. I am not sure what is painted on the bed. I ask Erroi if he knows.

"They are roses," he says.

"What are roses?" I ask.

"They only grow close to the Sun. They are grown to look at and for their smell."

"Really? You can grow something just to look at?"

"Yes. Near the Sun, things grow quickly in the dawn. Some people do not have to grow everything for food. Have you ever seen apple blossom?"

I told him I had.

"Well then, apple blossom is pretty to look at and has a pleasant smell. A rose is like an apple blossom that sets no fruit but instead gets prettier and more fragrant."

"I would like to see a rose," I say.

"Perhaps you will."

"So," I ask, "why would these people paint roses? They must have come from the Valley of the Sun."

"Maybe," agrees Erroi, "or perhaps just the cot; maybe they bought it from a traveller, or maybe a traveller painted it for them. Although why such a thing should be in such a poor home, I do not know."

The other bed is much plainer and bigger. It is the sort of bed that I shared with my mother when I was small, then she shared with Kilhanga, and then Kilhanga slept in alone. Now no one sleeps in it. My house, Kilhanga's house, is deserted, just like this one. Will travellers stop and wonder about who lived there? Will they light fires in our small house, and pry up the floorboards for firewood? Was the child here happy? Were the people that shared the big bed happy? If they were happy, why did they leave? Or did they stay here and die? First the mother, then the father, and last the child, then there was no one left. Then the house was empty.

"I hope there are no ghosts here," I say, partially in jest.

"Of course there are ghosts," says Erroi.

"Really! Well, I hope they will not harm us."

"Of course they will not harm us."

"How do you know that?" I ask.

"Because they are dead, the dead cannot harm us."

I wonder if that is true.

The bed is damp and dirty and rotten. We will not sleep there. Instead we put blankets down around the fire and lie down. I fall asleep quickly.

There is a boy standing next to me. He is very young, and he looks very healthy. Who are you, he asks me. I tell him my name and he nods. Will you play with me, he asks, and takes my hand. I say I will, and he leads me outside. It is very bright, brighter than any full moon or even dawn. The garden is full of growing things. I ask him what they are, and he looks at me. He tells me they are sunflowers. They are tall and yellow and round. Is that what the Sun looks like? I must ask Erroi. We play in the garden for a while, and then a voice calls from the house. When I turn around, the house is no longer a ruin. It is still small, but is neat and painted white. The roof is yellow straw. There is a woman standing in the doorway. She calls us in. She has made food. There is a table and chairs, and we sit there. There is no fire or lantern, and yet the room is bright. Light is coming into the room through the window. On the table, there is bread and also round balls the colour of the sunflowers. The boy hands me one. I look at it. Don't you know what to do, he asks me, and then takes a knife and cuts it into four pieces. Each piece has yellow flesh, and it bleeds yellow blood. The boy eats each piece in turn. Then I cut mine. The blood is like acid. When I eat, the blood flows into my mouth and is sweeter than wine. The blood is very good, I tell the boy. Not blood, juice, he tells me.

Then it is dark, and I am alone. Or perhaps I have gone blind. I call out, "Are you there?" There is no answer, or perhaps I have gone deaf. I reach out and start to crawl. My hand touches something hot, and I draw it back. It is the ashes of the fire. It must be time to awaken. I can hear the breathing of Cavall, and now I can see. The room is dark and our lantern is out, but the moon has risen, and some light has come through the open doorway.

Erroi is up and dressed.

"There are ghosts," I say.

"Yes," agrees Erroi, "but they will not harm us."

"No," I agree, and I find my eyes are crying. "At least, they do not mean to harm us."

I ask Erroi if he will let me try and ride Cavall before we head out.

"You may do as you wish," he says.

So I take Cavall out into the moonlight. I speak gently to him and then ease up onto his back. He stands quietly and makes no attempt to throw me. It is a strange feeling to sit on top of a horse.

"You must tell him to walk. Hold on to his reins and grip with your knees."

I urge Cavall forward, but he ignores me. He leans forward and starts to graze on the thin turf.

"Urge him on," says Erroi.

I pull up his reins and drum his ribs. Cavall takes a few steps forward, then a few more.

"Don't go too fast. Remember, you have no saddle."

But I am not listening. I am urging Cavall on, and he picks up speed. He is cantering around the clearing. I am light as a feather and do not need to grip hard. Or so I think. Cavall is moving smoothly and quickly. Cavall turns quickly, too quickly for me, and I am falling and land hard on the ground. I land flat on my face.

"Perhaps horse riding is like flying," says Erroi.

I pick myself up. I cannot be angry with Cavall. I should have gripped tighter like Erroi told me. Why didn't I?

"Enough," says Erroi. "You did well, but we need to get going."

"Can we buy a saddle, when we get to Fadu?" I ask.

"Why?" asks Erroi. "You will not be able to ride him there. We will have other things to do."

I know that Erroi is right, but still, I have ridden a horse, and it is like flying.

Once I have packed the baggage onto Cavall, we head back to the road. It is still early, and the road is quiet.

It is still cold, but at least it is not raining. The moon is almost full. There are birds singing in the trees, and moths are fluttering around us. One tries to fly into the lantern. I am still tired, in spite of my sleep. I walk with my head down and eyes closed. We still have a long way to go.

About high moon, we fall in with some travellers. I ask them where they are going, and they look at me with empty eyes. A tall man tells me they are going to the Sun. He drops back from the others and walks beside us.

"Is that allowed?" I ask. "I thought you needed passes to get to the Valley of the Sun. Do you have passes?"

The tall man shakes his head. He does not. He is desperate and poor. He can think of no other way to live.

"What if Vatu will not let you live there?" I say.

"Then let him kill me quickly instead of slowly."

I turn away, muttering that I am loyal to the Sun. Surely Vatu will be kind to those in need. If the man is so poor, why does he not clear land from the forest, like my mother had, or like the cottage we stayed at last night? But I remember how often I went hungry at home, and that now the cottage is abandoned. I hope Vatu will be merciful.

Erroi tells me we must move on.

"We cannot stay," he says.

"He is hungry," I say. "Can we not share with him?"

"Do you think we have enough?"

"For one meal, yes."

"Very well," he agrees, "for one meal."

We stop and I cook. The man eats with relish, not looking up from his bowl until it is finished.

"Give me more," he says.

I scrape what is left in the pot into his bowl, and he eats this, too.

"More," he says again.

"There is no more," I say and continue to pack.

The man gets angry.

"Make more," he says.

"No. There is no more."

He moves to threaten me. It is laughable, he is weak and is no match for me. I push him away. Then we move on. The man makes no effort to follow. I am angry that the man has been ungrateful. What did he think I would do, give him all our food? I could have left him without feeding him. I did not need to feed him. Why should I have given him more?

"What will happen to him?" I ask Erroi.

"He will die," Erroi replies. "He will die soon. Either Vatu's guards will break his head, or he will starve or he will die some other way."

I look back at the man as we move on. He is sitting at the road side. I thought he would follow us. If he had, I would have fed him tonight. We have enough food to get us to the next town. There we could get more.

We do not reach the town that day. Instead, we camp by the road.

"Is there nowhere else we can camp?" I ask.

"We could stop at a farm house, I suppose," says Erroi. "But we may not be welcome. It is darkest just before the dawn, and that is when people are hungriest."

I had forgotten that dawn was just over a week away. How could I forget? Dawn, the day of rosy glow and sunlight.

"How many dawns have you seen?" I ask Erroi.

He snorts. "None of your business."

I would guess thirty. Erroi is not young, but neither is he old. He has no grey hair, but his hair is thin and worn looking. He is thin and worn looking. He walks briskly, but stiffly.

"Will we reach Fadu tomorrow?" I ask.

"Perhaps. If not tomorrow, then we will get there the next day. Like I say, we will get to Fadu before Utas."

"How can you be so sure?" I ask. "In any case, we need to get to Fadu, and think what to do before they arrive."

"I know what we will do."

"Then tell me. I should know. I thought we were partners."

"Partners?" says Erroi. He thinks for a bit and then says, "No, we are not partners."

"Well, what if something happens? What if we get separated, or if you get lost?"

"Nothing will happen."

Why is he so adamant that he will not tell me what we are doing?

"I am not afraid," I say. "Whatever you plan on doing, I will not back down."

"You are very loyal to your friends," says Erroi.

Friends. I had not thought of them as that. I had just thought of them as people whom I owed something to, people who had been kind to me and whom I wanted to pay back.

"That is a friend," says Erroi.

"Does that make you my friend?" I ask. "You have been kind to me. Are you their friends, too? Have they been kind to you, too?"

"I do not owe them anything, and you do not owe me anything."

"Then why are you helping them? Are you their friend? You can say what you like, but you've been a friend to me. Even when you were drunk, you were kind. When Kilhanga was drunk, he was mean. He shouted at me and would say 'stop looking at me,' and then beat me. I used to never look at him, but it made no difference. 'Just like your mother,' he'd say."

"It must have been hard."

"No, not really. Once you get used to it, you know it is best to cry and roll about. That way, he stops quicker. Sometimes it was not even that sore. He'd be drunk, and although he was strong, it was not that bad, as he'd keep missing his blows. I could run away from him, but that just made him madder. Then he would beat me when he was sober; that was worse. After he beat me, he would be crying and saying sorry. It was a bit pathetic, really. I'm glad you're not like that."

"You could have left."

"Yes, I could have. I probably should have. When my mother died, I was too young to leave. And anyway, he hadn't been like that when she was alive. I was not his son, but he treated me fairly. When she died, he started to drink, and then that was all he wanted to do. Still, it was home. I suppose I was afraid to leave. Then I would have no one. Does that sound a bit pathetic, too?"

"No."

"I would have left eventually. Or have killed him."

"Ghosts are all around us," says Erroi.

After a bit, I ask him what he means. But he will not reply.

"Did you see the ghosts last night?" I ask.

Erroi looks startled. "Did you?"

"Yes, a small boy and his mother. The house and clearing were bathed with light. I think it might have been the Sun. We played together and then they gave me something to eat. It was round and golden in colour. It was sweeter than any apple I've ever eaten. What does it mean? Is that what life is like when we die? Do we go from the dark to the light?"

Erroi shakes his head. "I do not know. I have not died, but I have seen many ghosts. Not all live in the light, many are in darkness."

"When I die, I'd like to go back to the cottage and play there. It was a bit childish, we played children's games, but it was fun. I thought ghosts would be more frightening than that. I thought they would be cold and cheerless."

"Many are," says Erroi. "You were fortunate that they were not. They cannot harm us, but still, it can be unpleasant to be with them."

"Did you see them?" I ask.

"No, not the two you describe. There are many ghosts. These are not the ones I saw."

"I call them ghosts, but I could just have dreamed the whole thing."

"No, you did not," says Erroi. "You are learning."

"What am I learning?"

"You are learning now."

Later, I am asleep. Erroi shakes me by the shoulder.

"Come," he says.

I get up. It is still many hours to moonrise, and I would rather sleep.

"What is it?" I ask.

"Come," Erroi repeats.

I do not want to come, it is warm in my blanket beside the fire. But he is insistent. I follow him. We walk along the road a short distance and then we stop.

"What is it?" I ask. "Where are we going?"

"We have walked far enough," says Erroi. "Turn back."

I turn around and start walking back.

"Stop," says Erroi. And I stop.

"Look," says Erroi.

"What am I looking for?" I ask.

"Look," says Erroi, and I look.

Although it is dark, I can see as clearly as if it were moon up, as clear as if it were dawn. I can see the camp and the fire, now doused. I can see our baggage, and bits of gear. I can see Cavall lying in some ferns I gathered for him. And I can see two figures lying, sleeping in blankets. One is a tall, thin, dark man, who has a straw hat pulled over his head. The other is a young boy with fair skin and hair. He is very small and cannot be more than fifteen dawns old. He is lying on his back. I can hear him snoring gently.

"What is this?" I ask. "Who are they?" But I know who the two figures are. How can this be? How can I be there and here? How can Erroi be there and here? I look at Erroi. His face is masked by shadows.

"Is this magic?"

"No, there is no such thing. It is the beginning."

In the morning, I am very tired and sleep late. When I awaken, Erroi has packed the horse. There is a bowl of gruel beside me. I realize I am very hungry and eat. It is very bad, he has burnt it and it has no salt in it. No wonder he thinks my gruel is good. I get up and put my boots on, roll up my blanket and stuff it in with the rest of the baggage. I wonder if I dreamed last night, or if I really moved out of my body. How is that possible? If it was not magic, how was I able to do it?

We start off down the road.

"Did it really happen?" I ask.

"Yes."

"How?"

"Because I brought you with me, away from the fire, away from your body."

"Could I do that on my own?"

"Yes, everyone can do it."

"No, they can't. People don't go around leaving their bodies around and heading off in their... what would you call it, spirit?"

"Yes, they can. I did not say that everyone does it or even that many do it, but they can."

"So I can do it again?"

"Yes and no."

"What does that mean?"

"It means you can do it again, but I will have to help you."

"So I can only do it with your help?"

"No. To begin with, yes, but you will be able to do it without me. It's like teaching a child to walk. At first you need to hold its hand, but in the end, it will walk alone."

"So I am like a child then?" I ask.

"Yes, like a child."

"So when can I do it?"

"Eventually, anytime. To begin with, it will be easier at moon down, when you are asleep. But later, you will be able to do it anytime."

"So you could do it now? You could just slip out of your body and walk away?"

"That's not quite how it works, but yes."

"If you did, would you just fall down asleep?"

"No, not necessarily. Perhaps. Like I said, it does not work that way, or at least it does not have to."

"Is that how you found that house then?" I ask. "Did you slip out of your body and walk ahead?"

"No, not entirely. Partially, it is part of it. It is the beginning, like I said. This is the start of things, not the end. You have much more to learn."

"Good, I like learning this. What will you teach me now?" I ask.

"To be silent," says Erroi.

It is difficult to be silent. I am silent for a while, but I have too many questions. I try to be silent, I try to blot them out, but eventually, they fill my head and then fill my mouth.

"Why do I need to learn to be silent?"

"There are things to know and things to be unknown. To be unknown, you must be silent. To be un-silent is to be known. Silence is not just about the mouth or the body. It is about the mind. You must have a silent mind."

I did not understand any of that, silence, un-silence, known, unknown. It sounds like rubbish.

"I have never heard a mind make any noise. Not even my own and it is right next to my ears." I stop and listen, but I cannot hear anything. "Do people's minds really make a noise when they are thinking? If you could hear what they are thinking, then that would be a good trick. Is that how you won at cards? Could you hear what the other players were thinking? I'd say that was cheating a bit."

"I told you already, I did not cheat, I was lucky. But yes, you can hear people think. Not by listening to their heads, but other ways. Take rain, for example. Can you hear rain fall?"

"No, you can't. Well, yes, you can, sometimes. It depends."

"Yes," agrees Erroi. "What does it depend on?"

I think for a minute. I can see he is watching and waiting for me to answer. I can think of many things. How heavy the rain is, how much wind there is, how fast the rain falls, what the rain falls on.

"Well?" says Erroi.

"It depends if you are listening," I say.

"Good. Can you hear a moth's wings flutter?"

"Yes, if you are listening."

"Can you hear a candle flicker?"

"Yes, if you are listening."

"Can you hear leaves falling, or birds flying or snow blowing or trees growing or moonlight shining?"

"I can hear some of them. Not all the time. I can't hear trees growing or the moon shining."

"No," says Erroi, "not yet."

I think he is stretching his point a bit. Yes, I get that you need to listen to hear something, and that for some things, you need to listen harder, but there are some things that make no noise, and people thinking is one of these things. I don't say this to Erroi.

"So how do I learn to listen to these things?" I ask.

"By learning not to listen to other things," says Erroi.

I try. First, I stop listening to the sound of our feet on the road, and Cavall's falling hooves. Then, I stop listening to our panting breath and snorting. I stop listening to the birds in the trees singing. I stop listening to a cicada. I stop listening to branches creaking in the wind. I stop listening to the sound of our clothes rubbing against our skin, and of our hair swaying as we walk. I stop listening to the sound of grass rubbing together. I stop listening to the sound of voles walking. I stop listening to the sound of owls flying. I stop listening to the sound of horses riding full pelt.

"What is that?" I say, and look around. In the moonlight, I cannot see far, but I can hear that there are horses coming up the road to meet us. They are travelling fast and will come upon us soon.

"Horses are coming," I say.

"Good," says Erroi. "How many?"

I stop listening to one horse, then another, then another.

"Three," I say, "one horse in front and two behind."

I stop listening to the sound of silver bridles jangling.

"They are richly dressed, perhaps it is a lord and two guards. They are travelling fast and come far."

I stop listening to laboured breathing. I stop listening to the creak of leather riding gear and the jangle of chain mail. I stop listening to swords flapping back and forth.

I can see three pricks of light bobbing up and down. The lights are lanterns held high by the riders. As the riders get closer, we move to the side, out of the way. They come nearer and I can see that the first rider is slight and small. He is dressed finely and is labouring his horse. The other two riders are bigger and ride about half a measure behind. They are not accompanying the first rider, they are pursuing him. We have moved to let the first rider past. The rider turns and shouts at us.

"Help me! I can't outrun them much longer."

The rider is young. I see that his horse is nearly spent. It is unlikely that the horse will be able to last much longer.

I step out into the road, hoping to stop the pursuers, but the two riders charge straight towards me. The first pursuer shouts at me to step out of the way. He lashes at me with his reins and cuts me across the face. I fall down and the other pursuer almost tramples me. The riders are now milling around. The first rider is knocked off his horse. As they spin, their lanterns dazzle and then pass. I shut my eyes and stand up. The flashing of the lights no longer dazzles me, so I step forward.

"What is this?" I ask. I am kicked by a booted foot and sent spinning. The two pursuing riders have dismounted and are grappling with the first rider. He is screaming, and I realize he is not a man, but a woman. No, not a woman, a girl.

"Stop that. What has she done?" I ask. One of the riders swears at me and the other tells me to mind my own business.

"When someone is attacked in front of me, then that is my business," I reply, but they just ignore me. I reach forward and grab one of the riders by the shoulder. He spins around and I see he has drawn his sword.

He comes at me. I think he is going to kill me. Before he can kill me, Erroi steps forward. He slides in beside the rider and places his hand on the rider's arm. He brings his hand to his side, and the rider is sent sprawling to the ground.

The girl has broken free and has moved towards us. The two riders are now standing together.

"Get out of our way, and hand the girl over," they say.

The girl has now moved behind me.

"Why?" I ask. "What do you want with her?"

"Just get out of the way, boy; this has nothing to do with you."

"The girl says it does," I reply. "She has asked for my help."

The two riders do not answer, instead they lunge forwards again. Again Erroi steps forward into the dancing light spilling from their lanterns.

The two riders are more cautious. They look at each other. They have an air of confidence, but I stop hearing cautious footsteps and the sound of a knife being loosened in its sheath. I stop hearing breathing that is heavy and deep. I stop hearing voices that are pretending to be calm, but are tense. I hear their minds. They think they will circle around Erroi. They think that one will attack from the back and the other from the side. They think this will be easy and they will kill Erroi. They think that I will be no threat to them. The larger rider thinks he will tease the other rider about this when they are done. They think they will kill me too. But they also wonder why Erroi does not look afraid. They wonder why does he not shrink or run or pull out his sword. They move slowly. They move with caution.

Erroi is not moving. I cannot hear his mind. He is silent.

The riders attack, but they hit nothing. Erroi has slipped behind them out of their light. Again, I can hear their thoughts. They are worried, how did he do that, they think.

"You should ride on," says Erroi, but they do not listen. They are angry and want to prove they are strong. They want to beat us, then kill us. They circle around Erroi and then charge. Again Erroi slips out of their range, just beyond the pool of light that falls from their lanterns.

"This is wasting your time," Erroi says. "Move on." But they do not listen.

I listen to their minds. I can hear only anger. They are hasty and attack at once. Erroi does not move out of the circle, but turns around it. He leads each rider like a dancer and when the dance stops, they are lying on the ground.

"Is it enough?" he asks, but he knows it is not enough. He knows they are not going to stop. They wait until they are both standing, but attack one after the other. He turns once, twice, three times and again they are in the dirt.

"Please, this is wasting my time. No one is hurt, leave now." But they cannot hear.

This time, when they attack, Erroi moves with more purpose. The riders are now in a heap together. Erroi is walking back to Cavall. He is finished. The riders rise up. They do not attack. I hear their minds. They have better things to do. Who is this man anyway? They can come back and sort this out later. They will remember him. She will not escape. They ride back the way they came. Eventually, I stop hearing the fall of horses' hooves and men swearing and panting. Eventually, I stop seeing pricks of light bobbing up and down.

I still cannot hear Erroi's mind. He looks calm and unruffled. I realize my heart has been racing; now that it is all over, I am shaking. The girl is calming her horse. She is holding its head and telling it to be calm. I can hear that she is as agitated as the horse, as agitated as I am.

"What was that about?" I ask.

The girl does not answer. She is soothing her horse.

"Are you all right?" I ask.

"Yes, yes, of course," she says and continues to soothe her horse.

"What did they want?" I ask.

"What do all men want?" the girl snaps back. "And don't you get any ideas."

"Don't flatter yourself," I reply.

The girl is walking her horse. She does not want it to run lame. She is trying to help it cool and is cleaning foam from its flanks. Erroi is standing beside Cavall.

"Perhaps we should stop here tonight," he says. "We will not reach the town before moonfall."

He is right. I unload Cavall and rig up a lean-to. Erroi has lit a fire, and I hurry over to cook. I do not want to eat burnt oatmeal again. The girl is still settling her horse.

"Do you wish to share our meal?" asks Erroi.

The girl has no baggage. She has no food with her. She must either share our meal or go hungry. The girl brings her horse and tethers it near Cavall.

Erroi fills a bowl with gruel and hands it to her.

"Here," he says. "It is good gruel, Mukito is a good cook."

The girl takes the bowl and starts to eat. I realize she is very young, no older than me. After she has eaten, I offer to take the bowl, but she starts back and draws a knife.

"Mukito is only taking the bowl," says Erroi. "You do not need to worry."

The girl grimaces, and I notice a dark stain in her fine riding jerkin.

"You're hurt," I say. "One of those brutes has cut you. Let me see."

Again the knife flashes.

"You'd like that, wouldn't you?" she sneers. "Just you keep your filthy hands to yourself. This is just a scratch."

"Men like those two do not scratch," I say. "If you don't want me to look at it, that's fine, but I have some bandages and padding you can use to bind it up. Let me get them for you."

"I said I am fine," she snarls. "Why can't you just leave me?"

"All right, as you wish," I agree and back off towards the campfire.

Erroi and I sit by the fire. The moon is down and it is cool. The heat of the fire is pleasant on our faces. The girl remains at some distance. She has put her lantern out and is sitting in darkness.

"You are welcome to share our fire," I say, and in response she edges closer. Erroi and I sit on one side of the fire, and she sits on the other. She keeps the flames between us. She is glaring at us and does not speak. I wonder why she is so angry with us. We have helped her already and mean her no harm. If we wanted to harm her, we could have done so easily. Perhaps she thinks we are beneath her. I can see from her attire that she is the daughter of a wealthy man. When I look at her, I see that she is not beautiful. She has lots of dark hair, which is unruly and wild. Her eyes are dark, but her nose is large and her mouth crooked. She is not beautiful at all, but she carries herself with a pride that makes her desirable.

"You could tell us your name, at least," I say. "I am Mukito and this is Erroi. We are travelling to Fadu. There we will look for work. People say it is easy to get work at Fadu, and it is closer to the dawn when it comes. Do you know how far it is to Fadu? Erroi says he knows the way, but I don't think he's ever been there. He thinks he knows everything."

Erroi pretends to be offended at the last remark, and replies, "No, not everything, just more than you."

The girl still looks angry, but she says, "You are not far from Fadu, perhaps another day. I am going there, too."

"Really?" I say. "Then you can come with us."

"I have a horse, I will be quicker alone. You would not be able to keep up."

"No," I admit, "but your horse is almost spent. You would be better to walk her for a bit tomorrow. You must have ridden hard to escape those capos."

"They are not capos," she says, but will not say more.

"Well, anyway, what is your name?"

"My name is none of your business," she snaps.

"Her name is Eskanza," says Erroi.

Eskanza looks at Erroi in amazement. "How did you know that?" she asks. "Are you some kind of trickster that can tell things?"

"No," says Erroi. "But one of the capos called you Eskanza when you struggled with them. 'Hold still, Eskanza,' he said."

"Yes," she says. "My name is Eskanza, what of it? It is a common enough name."

Eskanza will say no more. Eventually, we roll out blankets by the fire. I offer one to Eskanza.

"Throw it over," she says, and I do. She retreats back from

the fire and from us, and lies down.

"Remember," she says, "I have my knife and I sleep light."

I roll over and go to sleep.

In the morning when we wake, she has gone. She has taken her horse and ridden on. I am not sorry. She has taken the blanket with her. I say to Erroi she must have been in a great hurry, but he says no, she is just very afraid. Why is she afraid, I ask. But Erroi says he does not know.

We come across Eskanza's horse just before moon high. It is walking calmly around, grazing moss and fern. I look around, but I cannot see Eskanza.

"The capos must have got her," I say.

"No. If they had taken her, they would have taken her horse."

"Then she has fallen from the horse. She must have been hurt worse than she would admit. She must be lying in the darkness. She could be lying dead, and we have walked right past her. We should go back and look. She might still be alive. Perhaps we can save her."

"I would have noticed if she was lying by our path," says Erroi. "Besides, the horse could have walked back up the road as well as further on. It is most likely she is here. Perhaps she stopped to rest. Look over there."

I follow where Erroi is pointing and I see a faint glow. Eskanza is lying down, facing away from the road. The light from her lantern is shining on some ferns, making them reflect pale green. It is hardly noticeable in the moonlight.

I rush over and turn her over. She is breathing, but her breath is ragged. She is pale, and her lips are blue. Her eyes roll in her head. I can see the dark stain of blood on her jerkin and when I open it, the cut is deep. It has mostly dried, but some blood is still welling from the wound. I bind the wound.

"Start a fire," I say. "We must keep her warm if she is to live."

Erroi has already started a fire and is standing beside me. "Here," he says, and hands me a flask of water. "She will need this. See if you can get her to drink some."

I dribble a few drops into her mouth and then we move her to the fire. And then we wait. I do not know if she will live.

"Can you help her?" I ask Erroi, remembering how he aided Hasera, but Erroi shakes his head.

"She has nothing to give," he says.

Eskanza does not die. I thought she would, but she does not.

We wait there until next moonrise. She is still weak and will not or cannot speak. We tie her onto her horse like a sack of corn. It is not dignified, but she is too weak to complain.

By midday, we reach Fadu.

Chapter Six
In Fadu

Fadu has no walls. Instead, great heaps of ash and cinder surround the city. They loom up, great black and grey silhouettes against the starry sky. There is no gate, but there is a check point. We are stopped.

"What is wrong with her?"

"She had a fall," I tell them and the guard waves us on.

Eskanza is still ill. We need to get her to a surgeon. I ask where to find one, and I am directed to a large house. I knock on the door and a maid answers. I am ushered into a room and told to wait. Eventually, a small man enters. He is dressed in yellow silk. He does not look at Eskanza, instead he asks for payment. I find two silver coins and hand them over. He pockets them and leaves. Later, he returns and turns up the lantern.

"Bring her over here," he says and I carry Eskanza over to a low couch. He loosens her clothing and inspects the wound. It is red and weeping. He removes the bandages and wipes the wound with some lotion. He pokes and prods the wound, but it does not open. Then he looks in her eyes, ears and mouth.

"The wound is healing," he says. "She is weak, but should recover. She lost much blood, but the lung is not punctured. I will give you some tonic. It will help with the blood loss. You should make sure she eats."

After that, he rebinds the wound and ushers us out. Erroi has taken the horses, and so we must walk. Eskanza can walk slowly with my help. Erroi comes to meet us and leads us to a tall, dark tenement. It has been made of cinder block and is leaning to one side, where it is propped up by wooden supports. We help Eskanza up the stairs to our rented room. The room has a fireplace, but smoke is coming back into the room from the chimney. The room is grimy and sooty. Erroi has put our baggage in the middle of the floor. I place Eskanza on the bed nearest the fire.

"What have you done with my horse?" she asks.

I start to cook some lentils. When they are ready, I try to get Eskanza to eat. Again she asks about her horse.

"Erroi has stabled him," I say.

After she has eaten, she sleeps.

"You must get a job, otherwise people will wonder why you are here," says Erroi. "There is always work at the furnaces, go there. Utas and Alaba will arrive here soon."

"Will you get a job?" I ask.

"I have other things to do." He gets up and leaves. I follow him, but he has gone. What does he have to do that is so important?

I head to the furnace. It is a huge building with a great fire and crucibles on cables moving from one place to another. I get a job loading up crucibles with ore. The crucibles are taken to the furnace and heated until the ore is liquid and glowing. Then it is taken, and slag is raked off. The metal is poured into moulds. It is very hot, and there are sparks and smoke flying. There is a great deal of noise. The work is very hard, and I have to shovel ore into the crucible all day. It is hard, hard work. My back is hurting, and my hands are blistered. I have stripped to the waist due to the heat. Some men are naked. They are coated in grime and sweat. The furnace and molten ore give off a brilliant light. It is like being close to the Sun. Or so I think. I have never been close to the Sun. There is a boy bringing water to us, which we drink when we can. The water is stagnant and tastes brackish and is gritty with ash. It quenches my thirst, but no more. At the end of my shift, I am glad to leave. Like the rest of the crew, I head to the baths. I stand under the tepid shower for long enough to clean the dirt off me. The sweat and grime runs like mud off my body. I turn my face up to the shower and let the water run over my face and through my hair. Then I take a small towel and dress. I must remember to bring clean clothes to change into tomorrow, instead of having to put on the same dirty clothes I wore in the foundry.

After work, I stop and buy some bread. It is expensive and seems hard and heavy. Still, it is as much as I can afford. When I reach the house, Eskanza is waiting. She is sitting up, but still weak.

"I'm hungry," she says, and I offer her some bread. She takes some and grimaces.

"This is the worst bread I have ever tasted. Have you no fruit or wine?"

I tell her we have neither of these things and offer to cook some lentils, but she shakes her head.

"I have money in my saddle bag. Go and buy apples and wine."

But there are no stalls open in the market. If she wants wine or fruit, she will have to wait till tomorrow. I cook up the lentils and serve them to her. She eats them without a word of thanks and then hands the plate back to me.

"If I was at my father's house, I would have wine and meat. Then we would have confections."

"Sorry to disappoint you," I say. "Perhaps you can go to your father's house when you are better. Does he live in Fadu? Is that where you were going when you were attacked?"

"No. My father is dead. I cannot go there, not now at any rate."

I am too tired to talk more. I bank down the fire and pull out one of the pallets to sleep on. The mattress is hard, and the blanket is thin and scratchy. How I wished I had not left my blanket with the horses. I will fetch it when I go and visit Cavall. Nevertheless, I am happy to sink into sleep. I am tired after all I have done today.

"Do not forget I carry a knife," says Eskanza. I ignore her and go to sleep.

There is a horn blow at moonrise. It is the signal that I must rise and head to the foundry. I get up and dress in the dark and take the bread I bought yesterday. Eskanza is right, it is poor bread, but there will be nothing else for me to eat at the foundry. I walk through the dark streets. The lamps are still dimmed. But I can see the glare of the foundry and walk towards it. The furnace is still glowing. They do not let it go out. It takes a long time to heat up, and if it were to need relit every day, there would be much less smelting done. Besides, one of the men explains, when the furnace cools and is reheated, it starts to crack. If we let the furnace cool every day, then it would need to be rebuilt often.

Like yesterday, I am set on a gantry next to a great heap of ore, which I shovel into each crucible as it is wheeled below me. Once it is filled, then the crucible is wheeled away and another takes its place. I am far from the furnace, but I am still hot, and sparks sometimes fly even to where I stand. Some of the men wear face masks of leather and mica, but mostly these are the men who work near the furnace or with the molten metal. Over the whole day, I fill about ten crucibles. Or ten crucibles are filled; I am not the only one filling them. I have a short break to eat my bread, but other than that, I am working the whole time. The roar of the furnace, the hiss of hot metal, the clang of crucibles and the rumble of coal and ore in chutes; it is too loud to speak or to hear.

I am glad when one of the men gestures that it is time to stop. I go and wash and then go to the market. At the market, I buy apples, oil and wine. I hope it will please Eskanza. When I get back, she is up and dressed. The fire is lit, but she has not made anything to eat. I throw her one of the apples and start to make small meal cakes, which I will cook over the fire. Eskanza eats the apple. It is old and wrinkled, but it is as good as I can get until dawn comes. She leaves the core, like a rich woman. When the cakes are ready, I bring her a small plate and some wine. We eat in silence, and again, no thanks are offered. Eskanza is used to being cared for by servants. You do not thank servants, or so it would seem.

"Tomorrow I will get my horse," she says.

"You are not well enough to ride," I reply, "at least not yet. Besides, where will you ride to? You say your father is dead."

"What?" sneers Eskanza. "You think I will stay here? In this place and eat lentils every night? Where is the dark man, and where is my horse stabled? I will go and see my horse."

"I don't know where Erroi is, or where he stabled the horses. He has not been back here since he paid the landlord. That is three days now. Perhaps he is drinking. I don't know."

"I don't believe you. You must know where the horses are."

"I can try and find out," I say. "There cannot be that many stables in Fadu. I would think that he would put them in the nearest stables."

"I will get my horse tomorrow," she replies.

After that, we say nothing, and I sleep again on the hard

pallet. Again Eskanza reminds me she has a knife.

When the horn goes at moonrise, I wake up and light the lantern. Erroi is sleeping in the other pallet.

"Where have you been?" I ask.

"Around," he says in that cryptic way that he uses when he does not want to answer me. Eskanza wakens.

"Where is my horse?" she says.

"Stay away from the horses," says Erroi blankly.

Eskanza is taken aback. For a moment, she is silent, but then she starts. Erroi does not interrupt, instead he sits and listens while she calls him a thief and a robber. He listens to a tirade of abuse without interest. Then she starts on me.

"Hold on, I have nothing to do with this. Besides, if Erroi says stay away from the horses, then he has a reason."

"What reason? I bet he sold them."

"No, they are stabled nearby."

"Then why can't I see my horse?"

"It is being watched. I think by friends of the two capos that attacked you. Your horse is very fine. A horse like that is noticeable, especially with those fine trimmings. No doubt they are waiting for you to return. Perhaps you would like to meet up with them again."

Eskanza scowls. "They are not capos."

"If you say so. They still tried to kill you. I think you should try and avoid them."

"Why did they try to kill you?" I ask.

"They were not trying to kill me," she says.

"Well, trying or not, they nearly did kill you. If we had not stopped, you would have died."

I have no time for more talk because I need to get to the foundry. I head off through the city. Although Fadu is a great city and there is work to be had, it is also full of poor people. Many of them are crippled or injured. Some worked in the foundry or mines and then became too sick to work. The constant smoke is bad for lungs and skin. There are many beggars and thieves. It is said there are many who camp in the ash and spoil heaps. There are many who die from disease or from starvation, and violence. Today the city is busy. The streets are full, and it is difficult to get through them. I have to push hard through the crowd. I get to the foundry only just on time. I start to work filling the crucibles with ore. At break time, I sit and eat apples. One of the men comes up and asks me where

I'm from.

"Riga," I say.

"Never heard of it," the man replies, shaking his head. "It must be far. What brings you here? Work, I suppose, there is always work at the foundries or at the mines."

"Yes," I reply, "work is better than starving."

The man nods his head. "Yes, that's true, but not much better."

He is right, the smoke and heat and hard labour are not pleasant. Even in the few days I have worked here, I can feel the ash work into my skin and eyes, and the smoke fills my lungs. This is better than starving, but the pay is barely enough to do more than stay alive, for a while. Eventually, the smoke, the ash, the heat will kill you. There are no old men working at the foundry.

"Perhaps there is better work elsewhere," I ask.

The man spits. His phlegm is dark with soot. "Perhaps," he agrees sourly.

There is an accident later. I do not see it and do not know quite what happened. At the ore gantry, we are far from the work floor, but I can see that a crucible has fallen and spilled molten metal. Several men are burned badly. There are shouts and screams. The injured men are taken away on stretchers. We stand and wait. We are not allowed to move. An overseer comes and waits with us.

"Looks likes there's vacancies on the floor," says one of the men.

"Shut up," says the overseer. "Just sit there and shut up. If I want to hear talking, I'll ask for it."

Eventually, we are told to leave. We are sent out. We cannot use the shower block because the wounded are there.

"Wounded or dead," says one of the men. This time, the overseer says nothing, but he strikes the man hard in the mouth.

We go out back into the city just after high moon. We are not given a full day's pay. Some of the men grumble, but there is no point.

"You're lucky to get half pay," we are told. It is enough for me, but some of the men have families. Half pay means someone will go hungry. Others have habits; a half day's pay to pay for a full night of drink is not enough for some of them.

The city is busy. Again, it is a struggle to get through the crowds. I have to push my way through the streets. The better dressed citizens look at my dirty clothes and face and move out of my way. They do not want to get their clothes dirty. Others try to beat me away with sticks they are carrying. They swish them like swords to clear a path. Sometimes others are not quick enough to get out of their way and get a crack on the back or head from the stick. It is mostly the old, the sick and the slow that get hit. I dodge into the road to avoid one man with his stick. In the middle of the road, horses are pulling carriages and carts. I am careful to avoid being kicked by a horse or hit by a horse whip. I spin around, and I see the crowd gather around a group of soldiers and riders. A kind of hush has come over them. The riders come down the middle of the street and the crowd parts. On a cart is Alaba. She is lying in the back of the cart, and the soldiers are escorting her. She is glowing like the moon. It is her. I see her. They are here. I stop and watch them pass. I see the stupid honest soldier, the one who came after us to pay for a piece of silk. He is walking at the front of the column. He looks well. I had thought he would need to rest till his wounds healed, but he seems to have recovered. The wounds cannot be as bad as I supposed. Utas is marching at the rear of the column. He looks tired. There is a young girl with him, but I don't know who she is. He walks right past me. I look him in the face, but he seems to not notice me. Perhaps he cannot recognize me covered in grime. Perhaps he does not wish to alert the guards to the fact that he has friends here. I do not shout out to him or try to attract his attention. I just stand and watch while Alaba is taken into the city. When they have passed, the crowd starts to move again. I turn and continue to make my way back.

When I get back to the room, Erroi is there. He is sitting by the fire.

"Have you brought anything to eat?" he asks.

"No," I reply, "but I can make you something. I think we have some wine. It is better than the water. Utas and Alaba are here. I saw them arrive. Where is Eskanza?"

"Gone. She has gone to visit her horse, I doubt she will return."

"I thought you said not to go and visit the horse."

"I did, but she did not listen. No doubt the capos have got her."

"We need to help her," I say. "And help Alaba."

Erroi does not reply. Instead, he fishes out the wineskin. It is almost empty, and after he has drunk from it, it is empty.

"We need to get more wine," he says.

"I'll get more," I say, "or you could get some. Anyway, Utas and Alaba have arrived. I saw them being taken to the Great Hall."

"I know," says Erroi. "They have come to meet one of Vatu's councillors. Gutiza, the mayor at Fadu, wrote to him, and he has come to bring the prisoners to Vatu. We must free Alaba tonight. We cannot wait longer. We may not have a better chance."

I am amazed. "Are you mad? Are you suggesting we just walk into the Courts of the Governor, past the guards and locked doors and just carry her out?"

"Yes, that is what I am suggesting. Is the food ready?"

I hand him a plate with some beans and the last of the apples. He eats and clears his plate.

"Thank you," he says, "that was very good."

"It was only beans. What about Eskanza?"

"She will have to wait. She is with the riders. She thinks they will not kill her; perhaps she is right. Come, it is time we started."

We leave the room and walk down the rickety stairs and out into the street. The moon is down and it is dark. The smoke from the furnaces hides the stars. We head out into the mountains of ash at the edge of town.

"Why are we here?" I ask.

"We are looking for something,"

The poorest of the people of Fadu live amongst the ash heaps. They have dug into them and formed little shelters. They dot the sides of the heaps. Sometimes the heaps collapse, especially in heavy rain. Then the people are buried in mud. Many die, but still they keep digging into the spoil heaps. Many of them die anyway. The ash is toxic. It is a poison that you breathe when the wind whips it up and which drips when the rain falls. The poor drink it, breathe it, it is on their skin and clothes and food. First you weaken, then you spasm, then you die. There are lots of dead in the ash heaps, maybe more dead than living.

We walk past the body of a young girl. She cannot have been much more than ten dawns old, much younger than Alaba, but her face seems older, as if her life had the pains of a hundred dawns crammed into it. She is dirty and her hair is matted. Her clothes are rags. She is curled up in a ball. If you do not look closely, you might think she is sleeping, but she is dead. She does not move, or breathe, she does nothing. It is like she has become stone and ash.

"This one," says Erroi. "We must wash her and change her clothes."

I hesitate; I do not want to touch the body. I curse myself as a coward. The girl is gone; this is not her, this is just a shell and emptiness. Do I think I will be harmed if I touch her, or do I think to touch her is disrespectful? I lift her. She is stiff, but very light. I carry her to a dirty pool, and with a rag I wash the smears of ash and dirt from her face and arms.

"All of her," says Erroi, "you must wash all of her, and her hair."

I strip the torn rags from her, which crumple to dust in my hand, and I wash her body. I wash her hair. In the end, she is lying naked and cold and dead. Her eyes are closed. Her clean skin is almost clear against her bones. Erroi hands me a robe to dress her in. It is a simple robe of wool. It is a finer robe than any she wore in life for certain.

"Now dress her hair," he says, and hands me a comb. It is difficult to comb her hair and if I am not gentle, tufts fall away from her scalp.

"Who is she?" I ask. But there is no answer. She is no one. She is a doll dressed and washed. How cruel is life. How cruel I am. Was her own life not cruel enough for her?

"It is no worse than being left in the spoil for vultures and jackals," says Erroi.

I do not think he is right. I feel like a despoiler.

"Why are we doing this?" I ask. But I know the answer.

We wrap the body in silk. I wonder briefly where Erroi got the silk from. Once we have wrapped her... Her? It? The body? Once we have wrapped it... Once we have wrapped the body, we carry her back to the city, the city that killed her. I carry her over my shoulder like a man carrying a bolt of cloth or a rug. We walk through the dark, moonless streets. Erroi walks ahead in the darkness. I carry a small lantern to light my way. I decide to put it out. I have no wish to be seen. Let darkness cover our deeds.

We move out of the mean back streets into the broad avenues of villas and mansions that lead to the Great Hall of Fadu. As the streets get wider, I move closer to the walls of the gardens of the rich. The shadows of vines hangs over me. I stay in the shadows and follow Erroi. Eventually, we come to the Great Hall. There are several guards. They look bored and tired, but they are alert. In the still night, the air is cool around us. We stand in the shadows, looking at them. What now, I wonder, but say nothing. I don't want to alert the sentries.

Erroi walks forward out of the shadows. The guards must see him. They will stop him and ask his business. Perhaps they will take him and lock him up. But they do not. He walks right up to the guards, and they do not say a word. They do not draw their swords or show that they have noticed him in any way. Why do they not stop him? He is standing out in the lamp light. I can see him clearly from where I stand in the shadows. How can they not see him? He is right next to them. There are six guards. I look and see that their eyes are closed. They are standing and have not slumped or fallen down, they are just standing with their eyes closed. Why do they not open their eyes? Erroi motions for me to come forward. I go, but I am afraid. Surely they will see me. How is it possible that they do not see me? I walk forward, and the soldiers neither open their eyes nor move. When I am beside Erroi, I want to ask him how it is done, but I do not want to wake the soldiers, if they are really sleeping, that is.

We walk to the door. It is not locked, or if it is, somehow Erroi has opened it. He pushes it open and holds it for me while I walk through. Then he closes it behind us. We are in the Great Hall. If we are caught here, we will be killed. We will either be killed straight away by guards or taken and brought before the governor and killed. Erroi leads me off into a passage. It seems he knows exactly where he is going. Again, we come to a place where there are guards. Erroi does not pause; instead, he walks right past them. The guards are just standing. I walk past, carrying a corpse wrapped in silk over my shoulder. We come to a small anteroom. There is a door which must be locked, but it opens to Erroi's touch, and we walk through.

"Wait here," he says, and then he is gone. I am alone in the dark with a corpse, in the middle of the Great Hall of Fadu with sleeping guards all around. What else can I do but wait? I put the corpse down and lower myself to the floor. I do not know how long I have to wait. It seems like a very long time, but perhaps it is just moments, perhaps just seconds. It feels like years. I sit in the darkness and think. How can this be real? Surely I am asleep and in bed and will wake. How can this be real? But it is real. I can feel the cool night air against my skin. I can feel the roughness of stone on the skin of my feet. I can feel the stone, cold and hard, pressing against my back. I look and feel the silk wrappings of the corpse, smooth and soft. I can smell the smoke of lanterns and metallic tang of sweating soldiers, and the stale scent of prisoners. It is real.

When Erroi returns, he gestures to me to stand up and bring the corpse.

"Where are we going?" I ask.

"Follow me."

So I lift the frail, cobweb-light body of the dead girl. I do not put her over my back this time; instead, I carry her in my arms as you would carry a baby or a lover. I follow Erroi; there are more guards with eyes closed and more locked doors that open at a touch. We walk in unlit shadow and in pools of lamplight, it is all the same. We are unseen and unnoticed. We go deeper and deeper into the prison. We go past many locked doors. We do not look into the rooms, but I can hear the murmured nightmares of the prisoners. Some scream and cry out. Some babble and weep. Some say nothing, but just breathe out fear.

Eventually, we stop. The door in front of us is heavy and studded with iron. There is a lantern lighting the hall outside the door, but there is no window into the room. Even so, there is light coming from under the door. It is the only cell we have passed with light in it. I listen to see if I can hear the prisoner, but it is silent. Perhaps the room is empty, or perhaps it is an antechamber to more cells. I run my hand against the door. The wood is surprisingly smooth.

"Open it," says Erroi.

"I can't."

"Yes, you can."

He is right, the door opens to my touch and swings open. Inside is a small cell. The walls are rough and cold, just bare stone. There is no fire or lantern. There is no window. The floor is also rough stone. In the middle of the room is a low wooden bed. Lying on the bed is Alaba. She is covered in a single rough blanket, which is pulled up to her neck. She is lying on her back, looking up blankly at the ceiling, and light is shining from her face. The light from her face fills the dark room and casts shadows into the corners. I lay the corpse beside her. I am struck by how similar they are.

I pull the blanket up from Alaba. She is dressed in a simple white silk under-gown.

"Change her."

I hesitate. But there is no time for modesty. I loosen the buttons around the neck of the gown and then pull it up over her head. She is naked and exposed. I look away. The light glows from her flesh. It glows brighter than ever, beautiful, beautiful light; beautiful, beautiful flesh. I swallow and look away. I replace the rough blanket over her nakedness and can breathe again. Now it is time to undress the corpse. Her wrappings are easy to remove, and her flesh does not glow. The wool robe opens down the front and is easier to remove. I put the dead girl's arms into the silk under-dress, and then slip it over her head. After that, I pull the dress down so that it covers her down to her ankles. Now I take the woollen gown and dress Alaba in it. Dressing Alaba is harder, she seems to flop and sway, and I take care to ensure she does not fall and bang her head on the floor. As much as possible, I look away. It is not right to look at the daughter of Utas naked.

"Why do you not help me?" I ask Erroi.

"This is your task," he replies.

Eventually, I am done. Alaba is dressed in the simple woollen robe. I take the wrappings of silk and cover her. I wrap her up and eventually I have wrapped her up enough so that none of the glow from her skin escapes. I lay her gently on the floor, then I lift the silk-clad corpse and lay it in the bed. I take the woollen blanket and cover the body, but leave the face and hair exposed. It does not look like Alaba. I don't think it will fool anyone, but Erroi disagrees.

"No one looks at a corpse," he says, "except those that loved them when they lived. People fear the dead. Even if they look, they will think the changes are changes brought on by death. They look near enough the same."

"It does not glow."

"It does not glow because it is dead. That too will be reason for any change. It will be enough."

"Utas will look," I say. "He will see it is not Alaba."

But Utas will not say she is not Alaba, and if he does, they will think he is lying. How can a sick girl disappear from a locked and guarded room and be replaced by a corpse? But he will not say. He is not a fool, he will look and see and know that we have rescued Alaba, and inside, he will be glad. He will know she is with us.

I lift Alaba and Erroi leads the way. I carry her back the way we came. I want to ask about Utas. Is he well? Is he safe?

The lights are all dead. We walk in total darkness. I can feel Alaba breathing as I carry her. She is still and light, she feels barely more alive than the corpse I carried into the cell. I can see nothing. I can hear my breath and I can hear Alaba breathe, but I can neither hear nor see Erroi. Perhaps he is gone. I touch the side of the wall with my fingertips and use them to guide me forward. Am I going the right way, I wonder? Am I going out of the Great Hall or am I going deeper in? I wish Erroi would say something. I wish he would lead me out. He led me in, he must know the way. But there is no sound other than my breath and the breath of Alaba. If I wish Erroi to lead me, I must ask him. In the dark, I am afraid to speak. Who will hear? Will Erroi hear? Is he even near me? I reach out my hand and turn in a circle. My hand brushes against cloth, ragged, homespun cloth. Erroi is just in front of me. I close my fingers on the cloth and let him guide me through the passages and corridors.

As we go, we do not come to any lighted areas, we hear nothing through closed doors, and we meet no guards, asleep or otherwise. All I have to do is hold on to Erroi and take one step after another, until at last I am in the square before the hall. I look back and see that the lanterns are lit and that the guards are standing sullenly at attention. I look around. There are some windows from which lamplight falls, the skies are clear and I see the stars. I walk slowly back to our lodgings. When we get there, I pass Alaba to Erroi, light the lamp and unlock the door. There is a note pinned to the door. We enter, and I put Alaba on the pallet where Eskanza slept the night before. I pass the note to Erroi.

"I cannot read," I say.

Erroi looks at me. I think he will say something, but then starts to read the note.

"My maid has said she will bring this note to you. You were right, I should not have gone back to see the horse. They were there waiting, and there was too many. I struggled, and it was no use. They have taken me back to my father's house. They will not let me see him. They say he is dead. You must come quickly and save me. It is the large house on the avenue of goldsmiths, the one with six windows at the front. There is flowering jasmine too. I think they will kill me or worse. I hope they will kill me.

"Eskanza."

Chapter Seven
Never Sleep

Never sleep. Dream of light. Touch the light. Always hear. Always feel. Touch the light, the burning light. Voices, small people talking. Always hear voices. Always hear small people talking. See the light. The light runs away. The light escapes. The light burns. Touch the light. Hold the light. The light burns. The light runs away. Hold the light. Lock the light away. Keep the light. Keep it safe. Keep safe from the light. Never sleep. Voices, more voices, small people's voices.

"Great spirit, great dark one, mighty Vatu, keeper of the Sun." Voices, too many voices.

Keep the box closed. Keep the light safe. Keep safe from the light. Never sleep.

Gold. There is gold. Gold falls from small hands. I hear it chink against the stone floor. I hear voices.

"Great spirit, great dark one, mighty Vatu, keeper of the Sun." Voices, too many voices.

Do not sleep, never sleep. Dream of light. Dream of the Sun. The light, touch the light. The Sun, touch the Sun.

"Great master, we are loyal to the Sun." Voices, little voices.

Where is the Sun? Where is the light? In my box, it is safe. I am safe from the light. I keep the light safe. Darkness, I am darkness. I am always.

Time.

It is time.

"Great master, we are loyal to the dark." Voices, little voices.

I must open the box. I must see the light. I must see the Sun.

I must touch the light. I must touch the Sun, the burning light, the burning Sun. Never sleep. Thieves will come. He will come.

Gold, gold falling from little hands, I hear the voice of gold, I hear the voice of the Sun. It is calling me; too many voices.

Time, it is time.

He holds my box.

"Great master, I am loyal to the Sun, I am loyal to the dark."

It is my box. Give it to me. I never sleep. I dream of the Sun. It runs away. It runs from me. It is mine. It is in my box. It is safe; safe from thieves. It cannot run from me. It cannot burn me. Open the box. No! Thieves will come. Open the box. No! It will burn. Open the box. No! The light will run away.

Never sleep. Darkness, I am darkness. The box is mine. I surround it. It is mine. I hold it. Small hands have taken it to the tall tower. Thieves, the box is mine, the Sun is mine. I hold the box, it is mine.

Gold, there is gold. I hear the chink of gold as it falls to the stone floor. Gold, it is my gold. Thieves, they will steal my gold. He will steal my gold. Darkness, I am darkness.

"Vatu, great lord, I stand before you and plead that you may give us dawn."

Open the box. See the light. See the Sun. Touch the light. No! The light burns. No! The light runs away. No! The light is mine.

Gold, there is gold. The gold is mine. See the gold. I hold the gold, I surround the gold. Thieves will steal the gold. Never sleep.

Gold does not run away, gold does not burn. I keep the gold safe. I surround the gold. I hold the gold. The gold is mine.

Voices, I hear voices, so many voices, too many voices. I am darkness. It is all mine. It will not run away.

Time.

It is time.

Open the box. See the light. Dream of light. Dream of the Sun. Touch the light. Touch the Sun. The light is mine. I keep it in a box.

Long ago, long ago, the light came. Now it is mine. Now I never sleep. Long ago, the Sun ran from me. Now it is in a box. I keep it in a box. I keep it safe. I am safe from the light. I must see the light. I must touch the light. The light burns.

"Great spirit, great Vatu, master of darkness, lord of the Sun, we beseech you, open the box of the Sun. Let the dawn break upon the land. Take this gold, it is an offering of our love and loyalty. We are loyal to the Sun. We are loyal to the dark."

Kong is lying face down on the floor. His voice is raised to the heavens. His voice is raised to the darkness before him. His face is down on the floor. All the priests of Vatu are lying face down on the floor, all but one. All their voices are raised to the heavens. All their voices are raised to the darkness before them. They drop gold before the darkness. It is an offering of their loyalty and love. Vatu is forming around the gold. If Kong looks up, he would see the darkness forming, he would see Vatu forming.

"What do you want?" It is the voice of Vatu. He has come.

"Great master, bring us the dawn. This day, bring us the dawn."

They are lying on the floor of the high tower. They are lying before the box of the Sun.

"Great master, open the box."

"Why?"

"Great master, without the dawn, we perish. If we perish, we cannot serve you."

"Darkness needs no servant."

"Great master, have mercy."

"He is gone."

Kong says nothing. It is true.

"Where is he?"

Kong says nothing.

"Where is he?"

"We do not know, master. He fled far from here. Reports say he is captured and is being escorted back. He will return. He will return and face the darkness."

"He will return."

"Yes, master, he will return."

"And?"

"Yes, master, the girl too. She will return. She will return and face the darkness."

"No, she will not face the darkness."

"As you wish, master."

"Where is he? When will he return?"

"Soon, master, a few moon rounds, maybe three, maybe less."

Vatu seems to billow like dark smoke. He swells and flows upwards. He surrounds the tower and the citadel and the City of the Sun. He seems to flow towards where Kong has pointed. Perhaps he will go to Fadu. But he will not, cannot, will not, cannot leave. He cannot leave the box of the Sun. Again he forms into a darkness before Kong. He takes a shape like a man, a great, dark man, but not a man, a shadow, a darkness.

"Great master, we beseech you, open the box of the Sun. Great master, we beseech you, open the box of the Sun."

The dark shadow is still. He stands before the box. He touches the box. The priests press their faces to the floor and close their eyes tight, but even so, they are afraid.

The great darkness touches the box. He longs to open it. He longs for the light, but he is afraid.

"Great master, we beseech you, open the box of the Sun. Great master, we beseech you, open the box of the Sun."

The great darkness touches the box. The priests are afraid, their eyes are shut and their masked faces pressed to the floor.

The box opens just the width of a hair. Light streams from the box; light flees from the box, bright, burning light. The light burns.

The priests press their masked faces to the floor and screw their eyes shut tight, but even so, light floods into their brains. Brilliant, brilliant brightness floods their minds. They see nothing but light, burning, brilliant light. They can feel heat, brilliant, burning heat, light and heat.

They press hard against the floor and back away, crawling slowly. The heavy mirrored plates of their gowns shield the burning, but even so, they can feel their flesh blister and burn. The light burns. They crawl backwards and away from the Sun, the beautiful, burning Sun. They crawl backwards away from the Sun.

Vatu stands before the Sun. He opens the box. Inside, he can see the bright, brilliant, burning Sun. He reaches to touch it with his hand of shadow, but his darkness melts and burns and is gone. He reaches to touch it, but it burns and burns and burns. Touch the light, the beautiful light. But he cannot touch the light. The light burns.

The light burns away darkness. Vatu is darkness. Vatu burns. The light burns Vatu. Again and again, darkness forms. Again and again, darkness burns away. Again and again, Vatu forms. Again and again, Vatu burns away. It is a dance of burning light and darkness.

Vatu cries in anger, rage, agony, desire, joy. The light is his.

He raises his head and bellows a great roar of anger, pain, pleasure and despair.

"Mine!" he cries. "Mine."

And the voice of the dark one, the voice of Vatu, can be heard throughout the dawn.

Below, in the shadow of the great tower, the people rejoice and despair. Below, in the Palace of the Sun, the priests rejoice and despair. In the Valley of the Sun, the people rejoice and despair. Throughout the dawn, the people rejoice and despair.

Light floods the land like a tide. Life bursts. Fields turn green and blossom in an instant. Trees turn green and flower in an instant. Shoots burst from the ground. Buds burst into leaf and flower. Birds fly up from field and forest and cry their great dawn chorus, the sounds of larks and thrushes and warblers. The sounds of sparrows and robins fill the air. All nature rejoices. Fish leap in streams and ponds. Frogs and toads add their voices to the song. Hares leap and course through fields where grasses spring up faster than they can run.

The light caresses them, each and every one, each and every fish and fowl, each and every plant and weed. The light caresses them, each horse and hound and beast, the light caresses them. Each man and woman, each child, the light caresses them.

But there is work to be done, even in the dawn. There is sowing and reaping and gathering. There is weeding and watering and cutting. There is winnowing and threshing. There is cutting and mowing and all the work of the dawn and the day and the dusk.

Each and everything hears the cry of Vatu.

"Mine!"

But the light is not his, it is theirs. It is the labourers' and the workers' and peasants' and the beasts' and the birds' and the trees' and the grasses'. It is a thing of life, not darkness.

They do not spare the whip, the overseers. It lashes out and cuts those who are slow or just too near. There is work to be done, and the work of Pinxo is to whip. He walks behind the labourers and whips. He does not walk fast or slow. He does not whip fast or slow. He feels the heat of the Sun on his back and a trickle of sweat is on his brow. He flicks his whip again, and the labourers plant and move on. His whip cuts the shirt of a girl and shows brown flesh. She does not cry out or flinch. She moves on, planting more corn seed. She is not young, not very young, nor is she pretty. Pinxo flicks the whip again, but this time she has moved out of the way, not gracefully, but easily and lazily. Pinxo can see the patch of bare skin where he has cut the cloth of her blouse. Again the labourers move forward. When they have planted this field, they will have to water it, weed it, and harvest it. In all the fields, there are gangs of workers planting, weeding, watering, harvesting. And in all the fields, there are overseers, shouting, whipping, driving them on. One day is all they have to plant and sow and harvest. Today is the day to plant and sow and harvest.

A small child runs with water for the labourers. He carries a cup and a skin of water. Those at the head can drink. Pinxo calls the boy over; it is time for him to drink. It's warm, the heat of the Sun warms the air; soon, it will be like breathing fire.

He flicks his whip again. This time, he catches the girl unaware, and she gives a start. She does not cry out or even look back. Later she will. Later, when she is hot and tired and the whip is still coming, she will look back and with silent pleas will beg for the whip to be spared. It is always the girls that get whipped the most. It is worse for the pretty ones, but there is no pretty one here, so Pinxo whips this one. She will look back and with her eyes plea for the whip to be spared. And the whip will be spared, for a price. Pinxo hands the cup back to the water boy. He takes time to look at the labourers. They are a mixed bunch of old men, young boys, women and girls, all of them poor. There are no pretty girls. This girl will have to do. Tonight, when the Sun goes down and darkness returns, this girl will do.

A light drizzle falls from the sky. That is good. It makes the air cooler, but it makes the ground soft and muddy. It will be harder to drive the labourers on, and his new boots will get muddy. Pinxo sends forth his whip. Again he misses his target, but Pinxo is not worried; he has all day to whip. The girl has all day to plant and to be whipped. She slips on the wet earth and he sends a sharp lash across her shoulder, once again cutting her shirt. If she is nice, he will buy her a new shirt. A boy helps the girl to her feet. He is small and thin, younger by a few years. He has badly cut dark hair that lies flat and ragged on his scalp. His ears are large and bat shaped. Pinxo send the whip curling towards him. He is aiming for the boy's ears, but misses.

"Move on," he shouts. "Get up and move on."

The girl moves off to get more seed. The seed is being carried in a small cart pushed by two old men. She fills her sack and takes her place back in the line. The other overseer is looking over at Pinxo, grinning. He knows full well what Pinxo is planning.

"What are you up to?" he asks jokingly.

"Mind your own business," replies Pinxo. He would like to whip the other overseer. It is none of his business what Pinxo is up to, as long as the labourers are whipped and the field planted and harvested.

"This is my business; I'm in charge of this field. If you want to single someone out, that's okay. Can't say I've never done the same. But go easy, and make sure the rest of them are working, too. If you've only got eyes and the whip for the girl, then the rest will slack off. There's too much to do. Besides, if you whip her too hard, then she might get sick. Then you won't get what you want either."

"Are you telling me how to do my job?" asks Pinxo sullenly.

"Yes," says the other overseer, "that's what I'm doing, telling you how to do your job. Go easy on the girl. This is your first summer in the field. It's not like in the city."

"I know what I'm doing," scowls Pinxo. The other overseer is trying to take the girl for himself, no doubt, thinks Pinxo. Well, he won't get her. There are plenty other girls in the field, let him choose one for himself.

The other overseer has walked off and left Pinxo to get on with it. It is still raining. Pinxo's hair is now plastered to his skull. Water is running into his eyes, and it is harder to see.

The labourers are also wet and muddy. The girl's blouse is now wet and sticking to her back. Still they keep going. They are nearly at the field edge, only a few more lengths. The field is bounded by a low fence of split timbers. Beyond is a forest. The trees are growing so fast you can hear the timber creak and groan. Just a few more rows to be planted, thinks Pinxo as he sends the whip forward. The rain is good, it is cool and refreshing. He turns for a moment to look back at the planted field. Already at the start of the field, the seeds have sprouted and burst through the wet soil. The shoots of corn are like a thin green beard or like sparse fur. He watches as the shoots swell up and thicken and spread. With early rain, it should be a good harvest, provided it clears later.

Buds burst open everywhere. Bees erupt from holes in the earth and from hollow trees. The hives empty as the army of workers spread out to collect nectar and pollen. The humming of their wings rises to a shout. Each flower is visited again and again and each drop of nectar taken and fought over. The bees are dusted yellow with the pollen released by a thousand flowers. They are weighed down by their treasure of nectar, and still they go back and forth to their hives searching for more. They too are hunted, by birds swooping and grabbing them in flight, by spiders that spin webs like fishing nets cast in the air, by wasps and dragonflies that chase and clasp them in tiny jaws. Bees die by the hundred, by the thousand. An army of ants besieges the hives and warrior bees die defending their homes. Sting and die, sting and die. The warrior bees attack everything within sight. Beasts flee in panic, pursued by warriors. They crawl into fur and into ears and mouths and noses and sting.

In the fields, watchers shout out warnings to the workers, and they fling themselves to the ground while great clouds of black, stinging death pass over. They smear clay over their skin and plug their ears and noses. Still some are stung. For some, a sting is only pain, for some a great pain. But for others, it is death. The victim swells up in reaction to the stings. The skin turns red and blotchy. The tongue swells and blocks the throat, making it harder to breathe. They cannot breathe, they gasp and wheeze. Their chests rise and fall as they try to pull air into their lungs, but it will not come. Their hearts race, they stagger and fall. Death comes quickly, perhaps not quickly enough.

Pinxo counts the corpses. There are three in his work team. He leaves them. There is nothing that can be done for them now, and even if there was, there is no time to do it. The day will not last forever. There is still much work to be done if there is to be food for all this year. Three less mouths to feed is no big deal, especially when they are the mouths of poor peasants. At least, thinks Pinxo, it is not him that is dead, as he brushes wet earth from his clothing. The dead are young. One is the water boy. He signals to the bat eared boy to take his place. If the workers do not get water, then they cannot work as hard. The bat eared boy is too small to do much work anyway. The other two are girls. They are both too young to have been of interest to Pinxo, although some overseers like them that age. Pinxo knows about them. But he tells himself he is not a monster like them. He will not touch a young girl before her time.

He sends a flick of the whip towards his victim. She is caked in earth. The rain will help to wash it off. Already, she has cleaned her face and arms. She has picked up her planting stick and seed bag and has started to plant again. She turns and glares at Pinxo.

He laughs at her and whips her again.

"Don't get too uppity," he says, "there's worse than the whip if you cross me."

The planting goes well and the seeds have germinated quickly and have sent shoots up already. The shoots have come up thick. Not too many seeds have failed. Groups of boys are running up and down the rows, chasing pigeons from the field. The corn has loosened silver tasselled treads that flick back and forth in the wind. The air is powdered with corn pollen. It is thick with it. It settles like a paste on skin and cloth. It too can kill; for some to breathe it is as deadly as a hundred bee stings. But few people die of it, and fewer will die of it while it rains. The rain seems to keep the air clean of these things. It will mostly be the bird chasers that will die of it. They will stop and wheeze and stop breathing. Pinxo has seen boys drowning in air filled with corn pollen. It is a slower death than bee stings. Many do not die, but even so, it is unpleasant to watch. Whipping them does no good. They will either die or they will not.

"Get moving," he shouts, and leads the workers back to the start of the field, where the corn is already being strangled with weeds.

The workers walk back to the field gate. There they swap their planting sticks for hoes. They are given short hoes with narrow, blunt blades to cut through soil. Pinxo stands by the wagon and each worker hands him their planting stick and he gives them a hoe. The girl hands him her stick. He hands her a hoe, but holds it and does not let go. She twists and wants to pull it from him, but knows better.

"What is your name?"

"Luzora."

"That's a pretty name."

"Yes, my mother gave it to me. May I have my hoe, please?"

"What's your rush? Desperate to get back to work?"

"Yes," says Luzora, "there is much work to do. There is not time for talking."

"No," agrees Pinxo, "not now, but later."

"Yes, later," says Luzora, again trying to get the hoe from Pinxo's hand.

Pinxo lets the hoe go. Luzora walks away.

"Later," he calls after her, but Luzora does not look back.

Pinxo calls on the bat-eared boy to bring him some water. The boy is slow, so Pinxo cuffs him across the head.

Hoeing is not as hard work as planting. You take your hoe and push it backwards and forwards through the soil until the earth is bare. Then you step forward and do it again. The workers are lined up and walk up and down the rows they planted earlier. Watering is harder work. You need to carry basins of water up the rows and then water the corn, then walk back and collect more water. Hoeing is much easier. Still, the overseer will whip you if you are slow, or if he thinks you are pretty and is trying to make you give him favours.

Luzora knows why she is whipped more than the others. She is young and fit and a good worker. She works hard. This is not her first day in the field. She knows how to plant and sow. She does her share of the work. The overseer is a pig. He thinks because he whips her, she will beg and ask for favours and offer favours in return. She has seen it happen many times. It has happened to her before, but not every year. She is not pretty enough to attract much attention. Usually, there is someone prettier than her to attract the overseer's attention. Most years, it is fine. Then she can get on with the work of the day in peace. It is bad luck that today she has an admirer and worse luck, that her admirer is a pig. Some overseers will try to buy your favour with extra water or food. Some will give you lighter work and less of the whip. Some will try to talk to you and treat you well. This one is a pig. He whips you harder. He is trying to tear your clothes to see your skin. If he can tear it enough, your skin will burn and blister in the Sun. He is a pig. He thinks only of himself.

Lento comes and offers her some water. Luzora gulps it down quickly and thanks him. She is glad he is the water carrier. It is a good job for him. He is too slow to work in the field and this is better than scaring birds. Her brother is slow. He should have died when he was born, but he is alive, and if he is alive, he will have to work. Water carrier is a good job for someone who is slow. Luzora turns and looks at him. She remembers when he was born. He was small and sickly, and Mother thought he would die. But he did not die. He lived. Luzora remembers her mother telling her not to get too attached to the baby. And she had tried not to. She had tried not to love the small pink creature that cried and fretted, with its lemur-like eyes and ears. She had tried to remember that he would likely die and perhaps he still would. She had tried not to love the slow child who followed her and looked at her with those big eyes and snuggled in beside her crying when the other children had been teasing him.

But it was no good. How can you not love your brother? How can you not love a slow, sickly child who follows you and needs you? How can you not love a brother who loves you? When her mother died, Lento was all she had left, just him and her, two of them alone. Perhaps she should have left him then. Perhaps she should have, but she could not. If she had, he would have perished in days. He would have starved. But so what? So what if she had to share her food? Luzora was hungry anyway. What difference did it make to be a little more hungry? Surely a few mouthfuls of food was worth company and friendship and love. Besides, Lento is slow, but not stupid. Just because he limps and stammers does not make him stupid. They will be fine. They will get on fine. They will be fine, especially after today.

Lento picks himself up from the ground after Pinxo has boxed him down. He has managed not to spill any water. That is good. If he had spilt water, the pig of an overseer would whip him. He would be too slow with his limp to escape from the whip. He takes back the cup from the overseer and goes to bring water to the other workers. He smiles to himself. He spat in the cup before he took it to the overseer. The overseer drank it without noticing. This is Lento's first day in the field. It is hard work. Perhaps the work is too hard for someone with a limp. The factor had laughed when he asked to be taken on, but he had been determined. In the end, the factor had agreed.

"But only half pay," he had said. Luzora had been angry, but Lento did not mind. Half pay was better than none. And anyway, neither of them would be going hungry, not this day. Today would be the day everything changes for them. Lento gathers up the water sack and goes about his work.

Pinxo is pleased with the way the work has gone. The field has been planted and hoed. The ears of corn have swollen and ripened. He is tempted to pull one and strip it and see the golden cobs. Pinxo likes working the corn fields. He worked in the orchards one year. There was really nothing much to do there except gather up fruit as it fell. The workers ran from tree to tree, gathering fruit in baskets and then back. There is more variety of work in the corn fields, and more opportunity.

The corn is high now. It is taller than he is, and it forms dense strips running the length of the field. It is hard to keep an eye on all the workers, but it is easier to trap a worker alone in some quiet corner of the field. Pinxo has his eye out for the proud girl. It is later. Now she will talk, and perhaps more, if he can find her quickly enough. He will need to find her before the harvest starts. He begins to hunt through the stalks, looking for his prey.

In the forest, the trees stretch upwards and upwards. The sunlight pours from the tower and comes flooding in between the massive trunks of the trees. Dark bands of shadow cut across the ground and clouds of violets and bluebells burst open, turning the floor of the woodland into a cushion of purple. The scent of hyacinth rises up, heady and intoxicating. Briers creep out from dark corners and wave spiny, arched stems in the air. Ivy and honeysuckle twist around the boles of trees like corkscrews, spiralling upwards. Birds sing and fly from branch to branch. A column of moths rises up and spins around the wood. Mosses drip from shaded branches. The sound of cicadas fills the air. A light breeze brushes the branches of the towering trees, sending kaleidoscopic patterns of shadows dancing on the forest floor. It is not a quiet place; it is not a still place. Leaves thicken and spread, creating a green filter to block out the burning Sun.

From the edge of the forest, hungry eyes watch the fields ripen. An outcast lies hidden by greenery. He sees the corn, golden and ripe, and from the edge of the shade, he slips into the field. He is hungry. He must eat. He moves, crouching low, through the high stalks of corn. He hides, set low and watching. He pulls a cob from one of the stalks. He strips it bare. The cob is still young and tender. He eats it and then reaches for another, still watching, then another. He can hear footsteps. There is a girl, a young girl. He almost missed her. She is trying to hide. Perhaps she is also a fugitive. He watches as the girl slips between the rows and ducks back on herself. She does not eat nor pluck corn. Then he hears a loud, crashing noise. A thickset man in the robes of an overseer comes through the field. He is not careful about being seen or heard. He pushes his way through the rows and is calling roughly. The fugitive knows he must not be seen. The fugitive knows she must not be seen. He crouches low to the earth. He hopes the overseer will move on. She crawls along the row and hopes the overseer will not notice her. The overseer pushes through the corn and hopes to find the girl.

The outcast is still barely breathing. He dares not move, and yet both girl and overseer are coming closer. It is like a dance. He goes one way and then the other. She goes one way and then the other, but all the time she is going back and back to the edge of the field and to the edge of the forest. Soon, she will have nowhere to go and nowhere to hide. Soon, he will find her, unless he finds the outcast first.

The outcast knows he is in danger. He is in danger from the overseer, and from the girl. He needs to get back to the forest. He has eaten, now he must escape.

"Girl, come here," growls the overseer. He is angry and tired of the chase. He has worked all day and soon, the Sun will go down. Soon, the girl and all the other labourers will go back to the City of the Sun and his chance will be gone.

The watcher thinks; should he run? Should he try to creep back to the forest? Should he stay hidden? If he runs, he will surely be quicker than the overseer. But the overseer might have a bow or spear. If he creeps back, then he will surely be quiet enough to evade the overseer, although who can say? If he hides, then surely the overseer will not find him, not if he finds the girl first. He can feel himself start to tremble like a hare when the overseer gets nearer.

What if the girl finds him? That is possible; she is creeping around and through the rows of corn. What if she creeps into his row? What if she sees him eye to eye? Will she cry out and startle? Will she bring the overseer to them? Will she just be silent in the hope of escape? Again, the watcher trembles and his legs twitch.

He is not afraid, he tells himself. He can run faster than an overseer. Once he is in the forest, then they will not catch him. Once he is in the forest, he will be safe. The girl is getting nearer and the overseer is getting nearer. The outcast trembles again and his heart starts to pump and then he jumps and runs.

There is a shout; well, not quite a shout, but a noise, a commotion or an exclamation. Pinxo turns back to the labourers. What is the trouble, he thinks. There is always some sort of trouble for him to fix. It takes a moment for him to see, but then it is clear, an outcast is running through the field, he is running into the forest. He is running away. Pinxo curses and then shouts.

"Hey! Get back here. Outcasts! Outcasts!"

The other overseers come quickly. The outcast is far ahead. One of the overseers has a bow. He nocks an arrow and takes aim.

"You'll never hit him from here," says Pinxo.

"Yes, I will," says the other overseer calmly.

"Why bother?" says another. "Waste of an arrow. Think you'll be able to find it in this?"

The archer ignores the comments of his friends and lets his arrow fly. It is a good shot or a lucky one, and it hits the runner square in the back. He stumbles and falls to the earth. By the time the overseers reach him, there are already flies buzzing and laying eggs. Worms are wriggling in his skin. The dead man is a poor wretch. He is ill fed and his clothes are worn. He is very dirty. One of the overseers touches him with the toe of his boot.

"Don't," says the chief, "he may be diseased. Good shot, though."

The bowman removes the arrow from the dead man's back. When the runner fell, he twisted and rolled. The arrow is split and is now useless. The bowman grunts and throws it away.

"Waste of an arrow."

"Told you."

"Get the squad in order and back to work."

"There could be others," says Pinxo.

The chief looks at him with amusement.

"So what? What do you want to do? Go traipsing through the forest looking for them? Do you think you would find them? And then what? We got no time for all that. There's enough to do here. Now get back to work."

The chief is right, thinks Pinxo sullenly. Labourers run off to live as outcasts all the time. So what? There's plenty others to do the work, and it just means a few less mouths to feed. Let the outcasts starve or worse. Still, he is angry that the girl has slipped away, back to the other workers. Now he will have to find her again. He will make sure she pays for his trouble.

It is time to harvest. The air is thick with the fragrance of autumn. Fruits ripen and fall. They split and burst. Seed capsules dry and twist, then burst and scatter the seed. Downy heads of thistles and dandelions float through the air. The bald heads of fungi push up through the ground and open up, letting handfuls of spores drop and carry with the wind. Wasps feed on overripe apples; they buzz around like angry drunks. Leaves turn thin and brown and shrivel up, like an old man's fist closing. Again there is rain. This time, it is a heavy, thunderous downpour. The workers cannot stop. They must get the harvest in before it spoils. Corn is plucked and put in baskets, wheat and barley cut and bound in sheaves. The harvest is gathered and bound. Grains are threshed and winnowed. Hay and straw are bound and stacked to dry in barns. The day will not last much longer. Everything must be done, every grain, every ear, everything must be gathered for the long, dark night.

There is no time for Pinxo's pleasure now. But he stands close to the girl. He lets her know she has not escaped. It is time for the workers to leave the field. Huge carts are waiting at the field gate. They have worked hard and they are ushered into the carts with little complaint. The workers are crammed into high cages while the overseers sit up front. Luzora can see Pinxo sitting, looking around at her in the cart. Lento is beside her. She can see Pinxo staring at her. It is not a good feeling. She takes Lento's hand.

"What is it?" he asks, and looks around. He sees Pinxo's baleful, lustful glare. He knows what is wrong.

"Don't worry," he says and puts something into her hand. Luzora looks down and sees the broken head of an arrow, the same arrow that killed the outcast.

When the carts arrive back in the square, the cages are opened and the workers are let out. They clamber into the square, groaning and complaining. As they drop down from the cart, they are handed wooden tokens that they take to a large table. There, the token is changed to money. Tonight, all the workers will have money. They will eat and drink and dance around the fires. Tomorrow, some workers will still have money.

When Luzora descends from the cart, Pinxo goes to hand her a token, but holds it back.

"If you want it, then come and see me later," he says and points to a large barn at the corner of the square.

Luzora flushes with anger, but says nothing. She walks away.

"Tonight," calls Pinxo after her.

Lento runs after her. He has a token, but it is only a half token, a half token to feed two mouths. Luzora is angry and pushes him away.

Kong and the other priests have retired from the presence of the darkness and the Sun. They are in a large room below the tower. They have removed their heavy robes of leather and their padded shielding and their helmets of brass. Now they are lying in cool baths of water. They have calming unguents to rub on burned skin and cold presses to push on eyes that still see flashes of the Sun. In the centre of the room is an hourglass.

They know that soon they must put on their heavy robes and helmets. They must put on their heavy gauntlets, and they must go and plead with the darkness to return. They must plead with Vatu to put away the light and to bring darkness back to the world. There is only so much brightness the world can survive.

It is the last of the Sun. Soon, the box of the Sun will close and darkness will descend again. Soon, shadows will race back and the stars and moon will shine again. Soon, the air will cool and the fierce, burning rays of the Sun will be gone.

Great fires are lit, fires of waste straw and stubble and dried and withered things. Onto the fires, the workers throw manikins of straw and twigs; some are as large as a man, others as small as a finger. They are offerings to the Sun, like the offerings that will be given in the Tower of the Sun. The workers think it will bring them luck.

Luzora walks away from the fires. She is walking to the barn. She knows she must eat and to eat, she must have money; to have money she must have her token, and to get her token she must see the overseer. She pushes open the barn. Inside, it is dark, even with the Sun still out. She pushes the door shut. Light seeps in through cracks; dust dances in the sunlight that shoots across the darkness.

Pinxo is behind her. He does not say anything, and for that at least, she is grateful. He places a hand on her shoulder and leads her forward. She is led like a calf to a stall. The straw is new and clean, at least. He pushes her, not gently, and sends her sprawling onto the floor. He tumbles on top of her instantly. He pins her to the ground with his bulk, and she can feel him fiddling with strings and catches. She does not cry out. If she will live, then she must do this. She screws her eyes tight. Her stomach heaves. Her throat is dry. She will not cry. She will not let tears come to her eyes.

Then suddenly, the overseer gives a sigh and goes limp. His hand falls from her and touches the ground. It seems that he has become heavier still. She tries to look up. Lento is there. He is trying to roll the overseer off from Luzora.

"What have you done?" she asks.

"What needed done," replies Lento. Luzora can see the shaft of the broken arrow sticking out of the overseer's neck.

"Help me," he says. Together, they roll the overseer off. Then they strip the body. He has some money, twenty silvers. The clothes are also worth money, especially the boots. He also has Luzora's wooden token, but he has snapped it in two; now it's worthless. Still, twenty silvers is more money than they could dream of. It would take them a lifetime to earn that.

"What now?" asks Luzora.

"I know what to do," says Lento and together they dress the body in braided straw and twigs. When they are finished, it looks no different from any other corn doll manikin. They carry the doll into the square. No one looks at them twice. They carry the doll to the fire. The fire is burning hot. It is like a furnace. The heat of the fire singes Luzora's hair. The brother and sister heave the doll onto the fire. It is a sacrifice to the Sun. Perhaps it will bring them luck.

Kong has dressed in his robes of leather. He has his helmet and gloves on. He and the other priests escort the girls to the top of the tower. The girls are young and beautiful. They are dressed in gold. The priests lead the girls up to the tower and then bow. Through their robes, they can feel the Sun burning. And though their eyes are shut, they can see the girls dancing naked before the Sun, before the darkness, before Vatu. They can see the girls burning like golden torches as they dance and the gold melts like wax. They can hear the music of the players, joyful and glad, and they can hear the screams of the girls.

Hold the light. Touch the light. The light burns. Thieves will steal the light. Touch the light. Always hear. Always feel. Touch the light, the burning light. Voices; small people talking. Always hear voices. Always see small people talking. See the light. The light runs away. The light escapes. The light burns. Touch the light. Hold the light. The light burns. The light runs away. Hold the light. Lock the light away. Keep the light. Keep it safe. Keep safe from the light. Never sleep.

Burning. Burning. Burning.

Then dark. Never sleep.

Chapter Eight
Gone

"She is gone, she is not here," I say. They think I am talking of her spirit. They think I mean only that she is dead. I look at the body. How could they think this is Alaba? Do they try to mock me? Have they taken my child and replaced her with a corpse? I look again. The body is dressed in Alaba's clothes. It is about the same age and not too dissimilar in colour of hair. Her eyes are closed, so I cannot compare them. Her hands are raised in front of her. They are small, but callused and rough and her fingernails are broken unevenly.

This girl had a rough life; she was not the daughter of a rich man or even a prosperous man. Most likely, she has been abandoned in the streets of Fadu by her mother, who in turn was abandoned by the child's father. I suppose neither the father nor the mother had enough to feed an extra mouth. Maybe they are also dead.

Maybe I am being unkind. Maybe her parents loved her, but died leaving her alone, or maybe she died, and her parents mourn for her as I mourn for Alaba. Either way, she is not Alaba. The body looks flattened and crumpled, like a discarded robe. She is lifeless and so unlike my daughter. Can it be I am too hard on the judgment of my captors? To them, the corpse is not so dissimilar.

There is no glow of light from her countenance, but would Alaba glow if she was dead? I do not know. They must look at her and see only death. If they see any changes in her, they will think that death has wrought those changes. I cover the body again with the sheet, out of respect for the dead girl that lies in front of me; it is the only kindness I can give her now. I hope there was some kindness in her life.

"What will you do?" I ask.

The two nobles look at each other. "What do you mean?" they ask.

"I mean, will you let this child be buried and go to the light?"

Clearly, they had not thought what to do. The Governor of Fadu shrugs. It is not really his concern. We are just passing through his domain. It is the other one, the one from the City of the Sun, who must decide these things. He will have to stand before Vatu or his priests and tell them what he has done. I recognize him now. He is one of the nobles of the outer court. I doubt Vatu even knows his name. I do not. He must have been the friend that Gutiza wrote to. He does not recognize me; for this I am grateful. He opens his mouth to speak and closes it again. He looks like a fish.

"Vatu has commanded that the girl be brought to him," he says at last. "We must take the body to him. He will decide what to do with her."

"It is not her," I say. "He will not want to see her. This is not the girl he seeks."

"He must decide that," says the fish-faced noble. "It is not for me to guess the thoughts of darkness."

No, it is not. He is right. Still, it is cruel to take this body to him. This child should know rest.

"In any case," continues fish face, "you are the man he is looking for."

Yes, I agree. I am the one he seeks. I think of what Vatu will do when I stand before him. The anger of the dark one is terrible. I hope for a quick death. Darkness can be merciful.

The Governor of Fadu is bored. This has nothing to do with him, and he has duties to attend to. He makes apologies to fish face and then leaves. Now there are just two of us, the corpse and some guards. The guards take the body and lift it on the bier and go to carry it away.

"Do you wish to see her again before they leave?" asks fish face. "Once they take her away, they will seal the body in lead so that it does not perish till we arrive. You will not be able to look at her until we reach the City of the Sun."

I am taken aback. I had not expected even this small kindness. A grieving father might wish to linger and look at his dead daughter. That is what they think I am. I do grieve; I grieve for this corpse, and for my daughter and for myself.

"No," I say, "the sight of this child does not comfort me, but I thank you for your kindness. I will remember it."

"Will you," sneers fish face, all his kindness now gone, "and so what? Do you imagine that you will ever be able to repay me? Once you are delivered to Vatu, I will be rewarded. But you?" Fish face shudders and leaves the rest unsaid. He has no need to say anything. I know better than him what Vatu is capable of. I suppose fish face is imagining some terrible torture. Whatever he is imagining, it will not be terrible enough. Perhaps he is right, and perhaps he will be rewarded for returning me to the City of the Sun. Still, the future is always unknown, and he is a fool to discount any help I can give him. Clearly, he does not know who I am.

I am startled from my thoughts as fish face springs forward and strikes me. It is poor manners. "I am your jailer," he says, "and you will address me with respect."

"As you say."

He strikes me again. As is prudent, I let myself fall to my knees.

"Don't talk unless I tell you to. Did I give you permission to speak? And bow in my presence. I am a Chamberlain of the outer court. You are nothing."

I do not speak and bow my head as instructed. Fish face turns on his heel and marches out of the room. I am left alone now with a few guards. When fish face is gone, one of the guards runs over to me and removes his helmet. It is Zintoa.

"I'm sorry," he says and helps me to my feet.

"You have nothing to apologize for," I say. "Thank you for your kindness."

"Let him get up himself," says one of the other guards. "Surely you've seen worse. If not, you'll not last long in this job."

"I owe this man my life," says Zintoa. "He is a good man, he does not deserve to be beaten."

I groan. Zintoa thinks it is from the pain of fish face's blows, but it is not. I am not a good man, and I do indeed deserve to be beaten, beaten and worse.

"Are you in pain?" he asks.

There are tears in my eyes. But they are not tears of pain, they are tears of shame. I have never helped a beaten man to his feet. I have never offered comfort to a prisoner. I am not a good man, and I deserve to beaten, not helped.

When I am on my feet, the guard tells me we can go outside.

"Why?" I ask.

"Have you forgotten what day it is?" he asks.

"Yes, yes I have. What day is it?"

"Sunday," he replies. "Dawn for a whole moon round. Today, even those in the deepest dungeon are taken out to the yard. Not all day, mind, but our job is to guard you and only you. So we can stay out for a good bit. None of us particularly want to go back down to the cells. Not on Sunday. If we can get your promise not to run away, that is."

I laugh out loud; the guard has meant it as a jest, surely. Does he think I could run from an enclosed yard full of soldiers? And if I could, does he think my promise would be worth anything?

"I promise," I say.

The guard nods his head. "Thank you, sir. Zintoa says you're a man of your word."

The door is opened, and Zintoa and the other guards lead me through corridors. We finally stop at a small door. I can see light come in from outside under the door. We stop. One of the guards goes forward and starts to unlock the door. There is much anticipation. It has been a year since we have seen the Sun. Is it really a whole year? Can it really have been so long?

The door is now unlocked, and the guard is opening it. Sunlight streams into my eyes and face. It chases away darkness and shadow. I breathe in the light. My eyes are closed, and yet I see red light pushing through my eyelids. I smile. I have no reason to smile; I have no reason not to. No, that is not true; I can think of many reasons not to smile, but sunlight is a good enough reason to smile. It is like a bath of light, I can feel the light penetrate my flesh and heat my bones. I feel health and energy return to me, and joy. I step out into the blinding white brightness of the day.

I open my eyes and look around. I am surrounded by my guards. They are still wearing their helmets, so I cannot see their eyes, but I can see their mouths and I can see they are smiling.

"Wish I could take this gear off," complains one of the guards. And I realize that I can. I remove my robe and stand naked in the sunlight, except for my underclothes.

"Feels good, doesn't it?" says one of the guards.

"Oh, yes," I agree. If I could, I would stand there forever in the warmth of the Sun. I can see the sunlight flowing from Vatu's distant tower. It is like a captured star. No, it is not like that at all, it is not like anything, there is nothing like the Sun.

I look around and see that I am in an enclosure about twenty yards by twenty yards. The enclosure is bounded by tall buildings on all sides. In the sunlight, the stone looks like pale gold. Windows and doors are cut into the stone. They are not many and they are small. They are like mouse holes, or holes in cheese. About half the enclosure is shaded. But you must not think that the shaded side is dark. Light bounces back into the shadow or curves around the walls of the enclosure so that even the shadows are radiant and bright.

"You should cover up, sir." This is Zintoa. He is worried that I will burn in the sunlight. Can he not see how dark my skin is? I will not burn, at least not at this distance from the Sun. I will stay a bit longer, but then I think of the guards in their heavy armour. The metal of their armour will catch the Sun and turn it to heat. It must be unbearable, as I know too well. It will be better for them if we sit in the shade.

"Come," I say, "let's go sit."

The guards lead me to a low bench in the shaded part of the enclosure. It is good to sit and look and see without lanterns or torches. Even moonlight is just a pale imitation of the Sun. We sit in the shade and look out at the rest of the Sun-flooded yard. It feels so good. I am glad to be alive.

The guards stand or sit around me and Zintoa sits on the bench beside me. I can see he wants to talk, but is afraid that the rest of the guards might overhear him.

"So how did you end up here?" I ask.

"Palaia, that's the man who hit you, he's in charge here, or at least in charge of you and Alaba, he asked Borroka if we would go home. Not likely, says Tito. We caught them and brought them. If there's rewards to be handed out, we'd like our share, if that's square with you. Palaia said yes, there should be enough for everyone and he could do with a few extras, but if we wanted, he could give us a reward now and then we could go back to Riga. Borroka was happy with that. The rest of the boys were happy too. But I thought that you'd be better with at least one friendly face, you and Alaba, that is. Not that the rest of the squad are that bad, but you know. I'm sorry about Alaba."

With that, he is silent. I look at him. He is right, I am glad he is with me. I wonder what he knows. Surely he cannot be fooled. He must know she is alive.

When we came into the courtyard, it was empty. But now from a door, guards usher out more prisoners. They are all men, but some are old and some young. One of the men is huge, almost a giant. I wonder what these men have done to deserve being locked up. They are chained at the ankle and at the wrist and are made to walk in a line. The guards watch them warily, especially the big one.

"So many."

"Yes. In Fadu, there are many bad people. There are always lots of guests at this house. Some of them have been here for many years. But most will be here only until their case is tried by the judges. If they are guilty, they are usually executed. Those not guilty are let go," says the guard.

"Why are some kept so long?"

"They are kept because it is uncertain if they are guilty. The judges do not wish to slay innocent men, nor do they wish to free guilty men."

"How long will they stay?"

The guard shrugs. It is not up to him, nor does he care. "Perhaps forever," he says.

Is that what will happen to me, I wonder, will I just be locked in a cell till I die?

As the line of prisoners approaches, one of my guards shouts, "Keep them away from here, this one is to be kept separate."

The other guards grunt and then lead the prisoners away and around the yard. He leads them around in a circle. The prisoners do not look up. They do not look at the Sun. They shuffle around the yard, raising dust. From time to time, they are encouraged to move faster, sometimes just by words, but also with punches and kicks.

One of the prisoners stumbles and falls. He lies on the ground and the guards beat him till he rises again. He is old. He is dirty and ragged. His eyes look glazed. As they beat him, he cries out softly to himself. I see that his teeth are missing.

I have tears in my eyes. But they are not tears for him, they are tears for me. Is this what Vatu has in store for me? Will I be this old man? Maybe my tears are for him after all.

"Why do they beat him? Can they not see he cannot rise?"

"He cannot rise unless they beat him," says one of my guards, "but do not worry, we will not beat you. Unless Palaia tells us to, then we will have to."

"Could they not help him rise?"

"A guard cannot help a prisoner to rise."

He is right, a guard cannot help a prisoner to rise, a prisoner cannot rise unless he is beaten, and if he cannot rise, he will be beaten until he is dragged away. One day, the prisoner will not rise and will be dragged away and not return.

I am ashamed. I have no sympathy for the prisoner, only for myself. I try to tell myself that he deserves to be beaten. He is a criminal and I...

Anyway, my fate will not be to rot in a provincial prison. Vatu will have other plans for me. I will not grow old. I will be beaten, or worse, but not for long. It is a mercy, a small kindness.

The guards are enjoying the Sun. I am left on the bench alone. Not quite alone, I have Zintoa with me. Now that the other guards have moved out of earshot, he is eager to speak. I try to discourage him, but he speaks nonetheless.

"You saw it?" he asks in a low whisper.

"Saw what?" I ask.

"The body, you saw it?"

"Indeed."

"Then you must know."

"Hush, let's not speak of these things."

"Yes, but you know, don't you? About the body, I mean. We came in this morning, and it was lying there in Alaba's clothes and in her cell. The other guards just thought it was her lying dead, but I could tell because I spent time with her before and had fed her. And, well, yes, I don't know how she did it, but she healed me, took my wounds right away. I don't even have scars. She held my hand and smiled at me. Do you think I would not know after that? If I could tell, then you must have known, too."

"Does anyone else know?"

"No, no one else knows, at least I don't think so. To the rest, she is just the corpse of a prisoner. Why would they even think such a thing? How would it be possible? The cell had guards outside all night."

"I have seen many strange things," I say. "I know that strange things are possible. I have seen them happen."

"Yes," agrees the boy. "Things like girls that glow in the dark and can heal broken ribs with a touch, things like a dark man that can kill a great cat with a single thrust of his blade and walk in and out of dreams."

"Yes, things like that, and stranger things."

"Stranger?" asks Zintoa.

Yes, stranger, things like a fire that never goes out and gives life and death. Things like a shadow that lives. Things like a boy who will not abandon his prisoner, like a stranger met in passing who has rescued my daughter. The world is full of strange things. There is nothing stranger than kindness.

I do not answer for a while and then I say, "You should go back to Riga."

"What, and leave you? No, I could not do that. Besides, I want to go the City of the Sun."

"Yes," I say. "Leave me and go back to Riga. What is the name of your girl? The one you bought the silk for."

"Hosta!" exclaims Zintoa. "She's not my girl. She's my little sister. I don't have a girl, not in Riga anyway." And suddenly Zintoa looks sad.

"Won't your sister want to see you?" I persist. "And your parents."

"She's getting big. In a few years, she'll be looking for a boy of her own. She won't need me. And I'm just a burden to my parents. They don't have much money, and it was hard for them when me and Hosta were little. Now I have my own pay and live in the army barrack, so I'm not such a burden. I try to help a little with money, but they won't take it. I'll see them when I get back from the City of the Sun. Then I'll have so much to tell them. I'm sure they won't believe half of it. I'm not sure I do."

He should leave. He should leave before his innocence is eaten up in the darkness. He should leave and make his own life, a new life far away. He should find a girl in Riga and settle down like his parents. He should not come with me to the Sun, to the darkness.

"Please go," I say and there are tears in my eye. They are tears for him.

"If you want," says Zintoa lightly. "I'll be back later."

He walks off and leaves me alone. All the guards have left me alone. I stand up and stretch. I watch the line of prisoners marching around the quadrangle. They have been marching for about a watch now, and in the full Sun, it must be more of a torture than a blessing. Their bones and muscles will be weak and cramped. Still, the guards keep them marching. Why do they do this, I wonder.

"It is to kill them," says Erroi. "They will march them all day. Some will drop and die from exhaustion and dehydration. It will not kill them all. The Sun is too far away to kill them all, but it will kill some and that will be less work for the guards."

"What do you know of the Sun?"

"I know everything; there are no secrets that can be kept from darkness."

"If there are no secrets, tell me where Alaba is."

But he does not answer, and when I look around, he is gone.

At last, the giant stumbles and falls. I watch as the guards beat him till he gets to his feet. When he gets to his feet, he does not start marching, and the guards continue to strike him with the butts of their spears. The giant cowers and sobs. His voice is wheezy and laboured. It is strangely high-pitched for such a large man. Still the guards beat him. He lifts his arm as if to protect himself. His shock of dark hair has fallen across his face, as his head is bowed to avoid the spear butts. He is crouched and braced against the blows. His ragged clothes offer no protection against either the burning rays of sunlight or the hard strike of the spear shafts. His body is coated in sweat and grime and blood. He sobs are slower now, and he sinks to one knee. I turn away. If they will beat him to death, I have no wish to see. The guards are shouting now. They are striking harder and quicker.

The giant suddenly springs forward. His great bulk lands squarely on one of the guards. He has slipped under the guard's spear and has wrestled it from his grasp. He is back on his feet in an instant. The sobbing, beaten man is gone, and instead, the giant grasps the spear at the end with one hand and whips it around in a circle. The fallen guard rises gingerly; he is injured, but not dead. The giant has bitten the man's shoulder, and there is a lot of blood. Even so, there are many guards and now every spear is pointed at the giant. Although the giant is large and strong, the guards are many and each is armoured and trained to use the spear. The giant is manacled at ankle and wrist and though strong, he has no idea how to use the spear. He waves it wildly in front of him. Still, it will be dangerous to take him down. The other prisoners might join in the fight. If they do, it will make the fight much closer, but they do not. They just stand in a line with their heads down. One of the guards blows a whistle, he gives three shrill blasts. I expect to see more guards issue out into the square, but instead, a row of boarded upper windows open, and I can see archers leaning out and taking aim.

The guards back off. They do not need to risk their lives. An arrow springs from the giant's back and he staggers, but does not fall. Instead, he charges forward, straight at the guards. If he will die, he wishes to die fighting. Two more arrows spring from the lunging giant, and he is lying dead on the ground before he reaches the guards. One of the guards walks forward and prods him with his spear. The giant does not move and so the guards motion to the prisoners to move the body. They will not take the risk of getting close, in case he is still alive. The prisoners lift the body over and drag it by the heels. There is a trail of dirty brown in the dust. Blood is not red, not once it is mixed with dirt and sweat.

My guards have not joined the killing. They are standing in front of me as if they seek to protect me. They have made a shield wall, and they do not stand down until the giant is taken out of the courtyard. When all the other guards and prisoners are gone and we are once again the only people in the courtyard, the guards relax. The officer comes to talk to me.

"Are you all right?" he asks, as if I had been in the skirmish.

"I am fine."

I am not even shaken. I have seen this and worse a thousand times. Erroi is right, there are no secrets from darkness.

"Are you sure?" asks the officer. "It gave us a bit of a fright. I suppose all's well that ends well. You were never in any danger, I assure you."

Is that how things end well, with a death? At least for the guards, it ended well. I suppose that everything ends well for someone, even if it ends badly for someone else.

"Who was he?" I ask, but the officer does not know.

"Nobody," he says, "but I can find out for you if you want. Why? Does it matter who he was, he's dead now."

Yes, I think to myself, he is dead, it does not matter who he was, and I look at the trail of dried blood.

Zintoa comes. He is carrying a flask and I wonder where he got it from.

"It's just water," he says and hands it to me. Perhaps he had gone to get the water when the skirmish happened. For some reason, I am glad. I don't want him to see such things.

The water tastes stale and rusty. I grimace as I drink.

"Yes, I know," says Zintoa apologetically, "it tastes bad. We have to drink it, too. I asked if I could get you some wine or even some lemon to mix with it, but they said no. When I'm off shift, I'll go and buy some lemon and perhaps mint. It will make the water more drinkable. They won't let me give you wine, even if I buy it myself."

I apologize for my bad manners. "The water is fine and gratefully received. You do not need to go to any trouble on my behalf."

"No trouble," says Zintoa. "I'll be buying some for myself anyway. The water really is bad. I think it is because of the mines. They say that minerals leach from the mines into the water. They say the water is not good. We'll only be here a few days anyway, I'm quite sure. We might even be going on our way tomorrow. Fadu is a big place, but I can't believe how dirty it is compared to Riga. Of course, it is closer to the Sun and there are lots more things that can grow here, but even so, I think Riga is much nicer. I'll be glad when we start travelling again. The sooner we get to the City of the Sun, the better."

I say nothing.

"I'm sorry," he continues. "I suppose you're in no hurry to get to the City of the Sun. Still, once you're there, things will go better, I'm sure. Whatever it is that Vatu wishes to see you for can get cleared up and then you can go back to your journey to Kota. Your wagon and goods are still at Riga, I saw the sergeant give you a receipt. I could come with you as far as Riga."

Does he really believe this? Does he really think that I am just a travelling merchant on his way to retire in a distant province? I want to laugh, but that would be unkind.

"I will never leave the City of the Sun," I say.

"Well, if you want to stay, then you can stay," says Zintoa. "I'd like to stay too, but I think I need to go back. My parents and Hosta will be missing me a bit, I'm sure. I'll write to them when we get to the City of the Sun. Maybe if I get a good reward, then they can come and stay there too."

"You misunderstand me; I will never leave the City of the Sun alive."

Zintoa's eyes bulge and he starts. "It can't be as bad as all that," he says. "I know you don't want to talk about it, and none of us know why Vatu wants to see you. Perhaps he has just heard about your daughter and wants see her for himself? After he hears she's dead, he might just let you go. Then you can do what you want. You could stay at the City of the Sun or go back travelling. It will be all right, I'm sure. Vatu is merciful. And we are all loyal to the Sun."

I shake my head. "No." He will protest, but I stop him with a gesture. "You must do something for me."

"Yes, what? I'll do whatever I can."

"I do not know where she has gone. She may be with the dark man or the boy. That is all I know. Will you find her?"

Zintoa looks down. "I saw the boy when we came into Fadu. He was part of the crowd when we came in. He must be here. If she is with him, then I can find her. I could look and find out what they have done and tell you."

"No. You must never tell me where she is. If you find her, do not come back. They will know. Vatu will not be fooled. He will know and then he will try to find out. It will not be good for anyone that has been with me. It will not be good for these guards or for Palaia. It will not be good for you. Go and do not come back. If you find her, stay with her if you can. Do not come back. Do this one kindness for me."

Again Zintoa starts, then he looks towards his companions.

"You cannot save them," I say. "Not without betraying her, not without betraying me. And they will not believe you. Palaia will not believe that a man can walk past guards unnoticed and into locked cells. He will think the guards have betrayed him and will have them put to death, after he has had them tortured. I can save you, but I cannot save them, not this way."

"You should listen to him. He is right, they will kill you. It is better to live than to die," says Erroi as he steps up beside me.

Zintoa is not startled. He looks at Erroi and nods as Erroi fades again from view.

"Where will I find them?" he asks.

"He will show you where to find them, I'm sure. I thank you again for this kindness."

"It is a big thing you ask," says Zintoa. "Not for myself. I will do anything for Alaba, but you ask me to desert my comrades."

"If you leave, they will say, 'Zintoa is a friend of the girl, he must be responsible for her escape.' They will blame you. Vatu will believe them. He will be hunting for you. If you leave, your comrades will escape punishment. If you stay, they will not. It is a hard thing I ask. I ask you to be the scapegoat. You will not be able to go back to Riga and your family. I will understand if you say no. But if you say no, you must go now and tell Palaia that Alaba has escaped or you will die."

"I could not do that, not ever. It does not matter how much I suffer, I can never betray her."

"Then you must do as I say, and you must do it now."

The boy nods and backs away. He turns to say goodbye, but other guards are near.

"Keep him safe," I plead with Erroi.

"No one is safe," he says.

I hold my hand up to the Sun. The sunlight passes through my flesh and turns it into a transparent red glove wrapped around bones. I can see each bone as clearly as if my flesh has been stripped away by worms. I close my eyes, but even in the shade I can see no darkness, only the bright red glow. Even so far from the Sun, its brightness is inescapable.

Eventually, the prisoners return to the yard. Again they are marched in a line. More will die, beaten, tired, and thirsty. I do not wish to see. I have seen enough deaths for a lifetime.

"Please," I ask the officer, "may we go inside?"

He is surprised. Why would anyone wish to go inside on the day of the Sun?

"Don't worry," he says, "we won't make you march around like them."

"Please," I ask again, "may I go inside?"

"Are you burning?" he asks. "One of the others will have salve, for sure. We can get you some. I thought someone with your skin would not burn and we are in the shade. I should have thought to get you salve before. My apologies, I'll get some now."

"No, it is not that. I have lived in the City of the Sun. I will not burn, not at this distance. It is not that."

Before I can say more, a runner arrives.

"Palaia wishes to speak with the prisoner," he says.

The officer grunts in agreement. He calls the rest of the guards and motions me to my feet. Then I am led back into the fortress. There are two guards ahead of me and two behind, with one on either side. I am flattered that they think me so dangerous, and say so to the officer.

"We don't," he replies. "This is for your protection."

As he tells me this, we walk through the fortress. We have climbed stairs and are now in corridors of polished stone floors and walls. There are several ornately carved doorways, decorated with a sunburst motif. These are the upper chambers, and they are very different from those down below. They are lit not by guttering torches that spread as much smoke and flickering shadow as they do light, but by oil lanterns spaced close together. We stop outside a doorway. It is right at the end of the corridor. The guards stop and the officer addresses me again.

"Remember, do not speak unless Palaia tells you to and when you go in, bow as low as you can. Not right down, but on your knees. Don't look at him in the face. I'm telling you this for your own good. I don't particularly want to beat you, but if Palaia says we have to beat you, we will."

The door is opened and I am led through. I do as the officer has instructed. I kneel and bow my head, but I can see we are in a large room with an open balcony facing towards the Sun. Palaia is standing, warming himself in the Sun's rays. He ignores me and then suddenly the Sun stops. Vatu has closed the box of the Sun. Summer is over for another year. Darkness returns and the air cools. Servants step forward and light lanterns. Palaia turns and looks at me.

"Why does Vatu wish to see you?" he asks.

"I do not know, great one," I reply.

"Tell me."

"If I could, I would, great one. I cannot, for I know not. Who can know the darkness?"

Palaia motions and I am beaten. It seems to me that I am beaten for a long time. They stop, and I have many bruises and cuts. I do not rise, but remain on the ground. I do not think anything is broken. I am glad Zintoa has left. It would be hard for him to beat me with the others. But then I wonder if he has betrayed me. Perhaps he has spoken to Palaia and told him that Alaba lives. Is that why am beaten? I raise my head and look around. Zintoa is not present. If he had spoken to Palaia, he would be here to challenge my denials.

Palaia is looking out towards the City of the Sun. In the darkness, he can see nothing, but he is looking and thinking.

"Who can know the darkness?" he repeats. "Perhaps you are correct. Have you nothing to tell me?"

I do not wish to be beaten again, so I say, "Great one, what will you have me say?"

"Tell me why Vatu wishes to speak with a travelling seller of silk."

"Great one, I do not know, it is better I am beaten again, beaten a thousand times than I should lie and deceive you. I know nothing."

"Then tell me, why does your daughter glow? I saw her glowing and the whole city of Fadu saw her riding into town shining."

"Great one, I do not know. Why do stars shine, or the moon? I cannot say. But she shines no longer."

Palaia sighs wearily. It is as if he is too tired to give the signal for the guards to beat me more.

"So you will tell me nothing. Then get up."

I rise to my feet. Our host, the Governor of Fadu, enters. Behind him comes two servants carrying what looks like a mirror draped in cloth.

"Do you know what that is?" asks Palaia.

I know, but I shake my head. "No, great one. It looks like a mirror."

"It is a dark portal, it is a piece of the darkness of Vatu covered and brought here to Fadu. No light has touched it, and it is the same darkness as the darkness in the Tower of the Sun. If a man steps into that darkness, he is stepping into the darkness that is there and when he steps out of it, he is stepping into the Tower of the Sun."

"Great one, how is that possible?" I ask. One of the guards strikes me.

"Leave him," says Palaia. "I do not know. This portal was brought here by our host. It is a great and powerful magic."

Our host turns towards us. He looks excited. "I have never used this," he says. "To use it, the permission of Vatu is required. It was not me that brought it here, but one of my predecessors. Perhaps it has never been used. It is something I have thought of before. But it is something I would be loath to use. Think of it, to step into the darkness and disappear. What if you do not reappear? You could be trapped in the darkness forever. I am faithful to the dark, but that thought chills me.

"Only one can go through the portal," he continues. "I am glad it is not me. Vatu must wish to see you greatly if he has ordered this."

Palaia looks away. He cannot hide his annoyance. I have escaped him. I will walk through this and leave him behind. By the time Palaia arrives at the Tower of the Sun, I could be dead. And when he does return, it will not be to stand before Vatu bringing a much wanted prisoner, but to return to his duties in the outer court. It is unlikely that he will receive any great gift now. Even if he does, it is unlikely to cover the expense he has already incurred. Who am I that Vatu would order such a thing?

The governor motions me to stand before the portal. The lanterns are doused and the window closed. It is complete darkness. I hear the brushing of cloth as the portal is uncloaked.

"Now," says the governor, "step into the darkness and away from the light."

I step forward. Then hands close around me and pull me onwards. I am in the Tower of the Sun. Kong is there.

I am home.

Chapter Nine
Two Places At Once

I cannot leave Alaba.

"You must stay with her," says Erroi.

"What will you do?" I ask.

"It depends," says Erroi.

I look at Alaba. She is very weak. She is not so different from the corpse we left in her place. She is breathing slowly and heavily.

"Is there nothing we can do for her?" I ask.

Erroi shrugs. "Nothing I can do," he says.

I hold her hand. Even though it still glows faintly, it is cold. I rub it and try to warm it. I should light a fire. I should make her eat. Her eyes open and she looks at me. I cannot tell what she is thinking. Her fingers are closed around my hand. Not tightly, but when I go to start the fire, she does not let go; instead, she holds on.

I must save Eskanza. She is rude, ungrateful and foolish. She has put herself and us in danger. If she had stayed here, she would not be in danger. She has put us all in danger. Now the capos can find us. She has put Alaba in danger. But, I cannot just leave her to her fate. She asked for me to save her. I cannot just turn my back.

"You must come," says Erroi.

I look back. I see myself holding Alaba's hand. I turn and go out the door. I follow Erroi down the narrow stairs and out into the street. The moon has not yet risen, but there are many people on the street.

"Why are there so many people out so early?" I ask.

Erroi says, "It is Sunday."

How can I have forgotten? Today is the day of the Sun. It will open soon. For us it is a holiday, a great festival. Many will go and work in the fields. They will earn money and bring home a harvest. Even the poorest can find work today. The Sun is a great blessing. I should go and work in the fields, but I have other things to do.

I have gently eased Alaba's hand from mine and I have piled coals in the hearth. I have lit them and I am standing, watching while they catch. The flames spread and smoke. I will wait until the coals are glowing hot before I will make porridge. I take a pot and mix some meal with water and a pinch of salt. I wish I had some milk, but I do not want to leave Alaba to buy some.

"Where is the avenue of goldsmiths?" I ask Erroi. We are standing in a great crowd of people. The Sun has not yet opened, but there is an air of anticipation. There are stalls selling hot corn on the cob. It smells good and it reminds me that I have not eaten. I should get some for Alaba, but she would not eat it. Fadu is a big city. There are many houses with six windows and flowering jasmine. I curse Eskanza. Why could she not stay in the room?

The porridge is beginning to thicken and I stir it. Then I take it from the coals and let it cool. I do not want it too thick. If it is too thick, Alaba will struggle to eat it. It will thicken more as it cools. Alaba is lying, facing upwards. Her eyes are fixed on the ceiling. I have put her in the pallet bed that Eskanza used and drawn the coverlet up to her chest. She is still dressed in the simple shift that we dressed the dead girl in. I should get new clothes and change her. These clothes could carry some disease or ticks. Alaba is not strong enough to suffer any new illness. I have enough money. Although I should not leave her, I will go and buy clothes and some milk.

"How can we find her?" I ask. Erroi turns towards me. He is holding what looks like a slender thread.

"Here," he says and hands it to me. It is light and insubstantial, a thing of nothing.

"What is this?"

"Follow this."

Erroi hands me a jar, it is full of milk. It will be enough for Alaba and some for me.

"You must stay with her," he says.

"What about the clothes?"

"They do not carry disease," he says. "Hunger is not a disease you catch from old clothing."

"Perhaps I could wash them, at least."

"You must stay with her."

The clothes he hands me are light and insubstantial. They are spun of finest silk and are brightly coloured. I will dress Alaba once she has eaten.

I wind the thread as I follow it. It leads me through the throng of people awaiting the Sun. I have to push through the crowd. I do not remember Fadu ever being as busy in the short time I have been here. It is as if all of Fadu is out on the street, waiting for the Sun to open. Most of the people are facing towards the City of the Sun.

There are people of all sorts. Rich merchants and their wives out in all their finery, laden with enough gold to buy a villa. There are soldiers off duty with girls who might be their lovers or might be prostitutes. There are workers, scrubbed clean and wearing the shabby, cast off clothes of the rich, patched and mended. There are children still in rags and dirty, they have no change of clothes and nowhere to wash except the ditch. There are stall vendors and merchants carrying goods into the city for the festival. There are farm workers being loaded up into wagons to go to the fields. They are lining up and boasting about their strength and skill. The overseers are inspecting them and selecting the best. But there are many overseers and it is likely that even the weakest labourer will find hire. Through all this, my thread runs, and as I follow it, I wind it up into a ball.

I have propped Alaba up. She is sitting up, supported by pillows, such pillows as we have. They are flat and thin.

She is looking straight ahead, her eyes open. I have to open her mouth and spoon the porridge in. She swallows small mouthfuls of thin gruel. Then I wipe her mouth with a cloth and spoon a little more in. She is not eating a great deal, but I am thankful she is eating anything. The fire is burning and the room is warm, very warm, but when I touch her hand, it is still cold. She is so thin. It is as if the light that shines from her is a fire that burns away her flesh, except that her flesh is cold.

> It is always darkest just before the dawn, and coldest. There are a great many lights, they have been lit to welcome the Sun, but it is cold. I can see my breath in the cold morning air, and the breath of the crowd. A few ragged children gather around one of the corn vendors to heat themselves at his fire, but he chases them away. He will not have them get the heat of his fire for free, and he thinks it is bad for business to have beggars clustered around his stall. He chases them away, and they go running off through the crowd to find somewhere else to stand.

She has eaten and will not eat more. She lies still and quiet, looking nowhere. She sinks back to the pallet. "You must stay with her," says Erroi.

> The Sun opens. It is a flood of brightness. People gasp open-mouthed and are momentarily blinded. They blink their eyes. They laugh and stretch out. The light is now reaching up to the sky. The heavens change from inky black to brilliant azure. Clouds of white vapour catch the low light of the Sun and turn pink and yellow. The heart, the eye and the spirit all soar upwards. The brightness of the Sun hurts my eyes, and the warmth of its rays washes over my face and hands. I reach up, stretch up. I am like a sail filled with sunlight.

I reach and pull Alaba back down, but she shrugs me off. How did she get so strong? Now she is glowing brighter than ever, and the sound of her laughter is like the chime of small bells. She is standing up, stretching and turning and shining. She is beautiful. Her radiance fills the room. She steps off the pallet and walks to our small window. The light of the Sun is coming in, streaming in like a river of light and warmth. She steps into the river and twists and turns so that every part of her is touched by sunlight. She looks as if she is swimming, but then I realize that she is dancing. She is dancing in the sunlight. She is glowing brighter than the sunlight. She turns to me and motions for me to join her.

"Come, you must stay with me," she says. She reaches a hand out to me.

In my hand is a ball of thread. Where does it lead? In the sunlight, the thread is like gold, a thin line of gold. I wrap the thread around in a ball, a ball of gold and follow it as it leads me through the crowd of laughing, dancing, singing people. I laugh and sing as I push through.

She is pushing through the crowd of people. She is laughing and dancing. She holds her hand out to me as I follow after her. It is like a golden chain she uses to lead me through the crowd. I laugh and dance as she leads me through the crowd. How did she get so strong, so beautiful?

The crowd parts for her, and I follow. She is leading me through the crowd away from the city. The people gasp and laugh in the sunlight. I push my way through. I can feel the warm of the Sun on my skin. I follow and we have soon left the crowd behind.

> I am standing outside the stable. This is where the thread has led me. I walk in. Eskanza's horse is still here, as is our horse, my horse, or I should say Zintoa's horse. They are both in the same stall. Sunlight is coming into the stall, and the two horses are turning around to look at the Sun. They have food and water. I hold out my hand, and Cavall comes to nuzzle my hand. It is good to see him. Eskanza's horse is also nuzzling against me. They look at me with dark eyes. Cavall shakes his head. He reaches towards me. It is too long since I saw him.
>
> There is a stable boy in the yard barrowing hay. When he sees me, he starts. He loads his barrow and turns to go.
>
> "Wait," I call after him, and he turns and walks towards me.
>
> "Have you seen a girl?"
>
> "I saw a girl with the horse, if that's who you mean. She

came and was grooming the horse. She said she owned it, even though she had not brought her here. The boss seemed not to mind. He told her she couldn't take it away, but she was welcome to groom her if she wanted to. You could see she was really fond of the horse, and the horse seemed to know her. They both seem to know you, too. Most horses are friendly enough if you feed them, but not the mare, she's skittish. I'm surprised she went to you."

"So do you know where she is now?"

"No, sorry, can't help you. She was here yesterday. She might come back later today. She's probably out in the Sun."

"Did anything happen while she was here?"

"Like what?"

"Anything, did she do anything or see anyone?"

"Just the two men, they came in right after her. When she saw them, you could see she was angry. They spoke in whispers, but in loud hissing whispers, if you know what I mean. The horses did not like them, and the mare tried to kick."

"Do you know who they are?"

"No, never seen them before in my life. They were dressed smart. One of the other boys thought they were capos, but their hands were too soft looking, if you know what I mean?"

"No, what do you mean?"

"Well, look at my hands. You can see that they have been used to shovel and work. They are rough and right now they are dirty. A capo's hands are a bit like that. They're not rough like mine, but you can tell that they are working hands. I mean, they're big and strong, hard hands for doing capo work. These men had soft hands, I think they were rich boys. There are a lot of them in Fadu, boys with rich fathers that don't have to work. Some of them dress like capos, but you can tell they are not real capos."

"So what happened next?"

"Nothing really, you could see they were arguing. In the end, they went away together."

"Do you know where?"

"No. The boss might know, he seemed to know them."

"Is he around?"

The boy looks at me like I'm mad. "On a Sunday?"

"Thank you," I say.

I turn to the horses and say goodbye. They are nice horses.

The ball of golden thread is still in my hand. I am following the thread. I am pushing through the crowded streets. Alaba is leading me through the streets. People stop and stare and then move on. It is almost like they cannot see her. It is as if she is made of sunlight, it is as if she is too brilliant and bright to be seen. It is as if she can be glimpsed only for a moment, and then the image of her is burned from your sight. The image of her is burned into my sight, and when I close my eyes, there is a brilliant after-image of a dancing, brilliant beauty. Why can they not see her? The crowd parts for her and I follow. She dances through the crowd and I chase after her. I chase after a thread of gold. There is a thread of gold between me and Alaba.

"Come, you must stay with me," she says. She reaches a hand out to me.

"You must stay with her," says Erroi.

I chase after her. She moves too fast, turning and spinning. It is as if she is being pushed by sunlight. I run to keep up, and she laughs, the tinkling of bells, little bells ringing in sunlight. We are at the edge of the city, and we are turning to the ash and cinder hills. She is glowing brighter than the hot metal in the furnaces. It is like she is a mirror. It is like her skin is a shining mirror, reflecting the Sun. I run after her. I try to catch her. She runs faster, and I hold tight to the golden thread. It is pulling me along after her. I must stay with her.

We are running faster and faster. She is still dancing and turning and twisting in the sunlight. It is hard for me to keep up. Her hair spins around her as she dances. Her hair is like flame, flickering and flaring in all directions. We are running through the mountains of ash and cinder. There is no else here. There is just us. We are running and dancing. She is so beautiful. We get to the foot of a great mountain of ash. It is the tallest of all the piles of ash; it is taller than the tallest building in Fadu. It is taller than any hill or mountain. We start to climb the heap of ash. She dances and skips up the mountain and her feet barely touch the dirt. I climb, and my feet sink into the ash like sand. Each step I take brings piles of ash sliding down, but still I race to keep up. I must stay with her.

I breathe heavily as I climb after her. The thread of gold tugs and twists in my hand. How did she get so strong? I cannot keep up with her, I cannot stay with her.

"You must stay with her," says Erroi.

"Then help me," I say, and she puts out a golden, glowing hand. I grab it and she tugs me up like I am nothing, like I am air or sunlight. She pulls me and dances, and I go spinning around her as she pulls me along and upwards. It is like I am a sail filled with sunlight. It is like I am pushed by sunlight up the mountain. My feet barely touch the dirt. Instead of sinking into the ash, I skip over it. I race after Alaba and I laugh. Now the thread of gold is like a ribbon that twists and turns and dances as we race up the mountain. It is like a live thing, a thing of light. When we get to the top of the mountain, Alaba stops. She leaps into the air and twists. It seems like she will fly, but she does not.

Now that she is at the top of the mountain, there is no shadow. The Sun is far away, but we can see it clearly as it shines below us. Alaba dances and turns in the sunlight, and as she does, she glows brighter still. Her clothes are fire, they catch fire and burn. Her clothes are transformed into gossamer flames that billow like clouds. The thread of gold spins like a ball as she turns and dances. The thread twists and weaves in golden patterns. I hold tight as I watch, awestruck. She spins and spins until she is like a shining golden ball.

I hold the ball of gold in my hand and wind the thread around it. I follow the thread as it winds through the busy streets. It leads me to a street, and I take it that this is the avenue of the goldsmiths. The crowd here has thinned out. Many of the houses have large windows that are facing towards the Sun. They are open and there are people standing in the sunlight. The houses are all large and built with stout stone. They stand on one side of the avenue only, with the other side open to let the sunlight stream unhindered into the houses. Each house is protected from the street by a low wall. The walls are tall enough to protect the houses, but low enough that they will not cast shade on the houses. The thread leads to a house. It is not the largest house on the avenue, but still very big. There is a fountain in the garden and there is flowering jasmine. The smell of jasmine hangs heavy in the air, sickly and sweet. If this is the house of Eskanza's father, he must be very rich. She must be very rich. This is why she is so disdainful. She must have slept every night in a feather bed and dined on fine porcelain plates with cutlery of silver. She will have had a cook and eaten meat every day. No wonder she showed no gratitude for the meagre fare we could provide.

I should go. Surely she will be happy here. This is where she belongs. She has run away and now has returned to where she belongs. I stand outside in the sunlight. I can hear laughter and the sound of drinking coming from the open windows of the house. I turn to leave.

"You must stay with her." It seems to me that I can hear Erroi telling me to go on. Why? We saved her life once before when she rode off wounded and fell. Even then, she would not trust us or show any gratitude. Why would she want our help now? And help for what, to take her away from her family? I look at the people in the window. They are wearing summer clothes and are bedecked in gold. They are laughing and drinking, and I can hear music starting. They will feast and party and when the Sun goes, they will burn fires till moonrise.

It does not look like a home where the owner has just died. I look through the window. If I can see her, I will know she is fine, and I can go. I just need to be sure. I don't owe her anything, but I still want to make sure she's all right. No doubt her letter was just some hysterical girlish nonsense. Now she'll be with her family, enjoying the Sun. That is what I should be doing. I should be with Alaba. I should not be wasting my time on that ungrateful girl.

I look up at the open windows, where the family is standing around, enjoying the Sun. There are many girls who look a bit like Eskanza, but I do not see her. Perhaps she is sitting in the shade towards the back of one of the rooms. If I could see her, I would know she is fine and could go. Alaba is waiting for me. I should be with her. I go to the gate, but there are servants there in livery. They are watching me. I walk past. I am the only person in the street. Why am I here? Is there is nothing I can do? What could I do? I cannot get past the servants and walk into the locked and guarded house, and then what?

I walk up to the servants.

"Is there a girl called Eskanza living here?"

The two servants look at each other.

"What business is it of yours who lives here?"

It is none of my business. I should leave. I turn to go, but there is a shout from the doorway. A servant comes over.

"Stop," he says. "You there, stop now."

The two other servants are as surprised as I am. I stop, although part of me wants to run. Perhaps Eskanza has seen me from one of the upper rooms and sent her servant to speak with me. I wait to hear what the servant will say.

"Bring him in," the servant says to the two gatekeepers. The gate is opened and two sets of large hands are set upon me. I think to resist, but then, why should I when they are taking me where I wish to go? After I have seen Eskanza, then I can go. I'm sure she is fine. The two gatekeepers lead me around the back of the house. I am taken in through a door and then led up a staircase. They are steep, spiral stairs such as a maid might use to move through the house without disturbing the family of the house. They lead me into a small room.

"Wait here," they say and then leave. The door is locked behind me. I go and sit on a small stool. The room has no windows and I cannot see the Sun. It is lit by a single lantern hanging from the ceiling. There are shelves and it looks as if it is used mainly as a store room. In a short time, I can hear the door being unlocked. It is pushed open and the two gatekeepers enter. I am expecting them to be accompanied by Eskanza, but instead, a man comes in behind them. He is a young man. He carries himself with the air of confidence that comes with money. He is finely dressed, and he is wearing gold chains around his neck and wrists. He is carrying a glass of wine in one hand.

"It is you," he says. "I thought so. How did you find us?"

"How did I find what?" I ask. "What are you talking about?"

"No need to be coy. I remember you. I suppose you've come here to spy us out. You'd have done better to wait till after the summer. You were fairly obvious standing out there in the Sun."

"I have no idea what you are talking about."

"Really. No matter, I remember you clear enough. So what do you want?"

"What do I want? I just want to see Eskanza."

"Is that all? Well, she's not here. Don't know where she is. No one has seen her for months. There, what do you say to that?"

"I've seen her, I've seen her just a day ago."

"Really, where is she now, then? We all want to see her. We all miss her. We all long for her to come back. What are you saying? I hope you've not kidnapped her. I warn you now, if you have, then you better hand her over, or else we'll hand you over to the guards. Tell me where she is and I'll go easy on you."

"I don't know where she is. She was with us and then she left. I had thought she had come here."

The man laughs. It is not a pleasant sound. It is high pitched and false sounding. I remember him now. He looks different without riding gear on.

"She is not here."

"I think she is."

"You do? What makes you think that?"

"A ball of thread. No, not just that, a letter and a stable boy."

"What is this, a riddle? She is not here. We don't know where she is."

"She is here."

I stop and listen. I can hear him not denying it. I can hear him not bringing other family members to argue with me, or calling for the guard. I can hear him not saying too much in front of the gatekeepers.

"You knew me," I say. "It took me a while to recognize you, but I do now. Where are you keeping her? In a room like this, locked up? You have kidnapped her. Why?"

The man's face flushes with anger. He gets up from his seat. He is angry and worried. What do the gatekeepers know, and what will they tell?

"Is her father dead?" I ask.

"Yes," hisses the man. "He is dead and has been dead for over a month."

It is a lie, I can hear it in his voice.

He walks to the door.

"Keep him locked up here," he says as he leaves.

The gatekeepers will do as he says. I do not try to escape. They are bigger than me and stronger. They take the lantern from the room and lock it behind them. I am in darkness.

"Well done," says Erroi, "now we know she is here."

"Yes, she is near," I say as I watch Alaba dance in the sunlight, "but she is in darkness."

"Then we must bring her out of darkness."

I sit on the stool with my eyes closed to keep the darkness out. With my eyes closed, I can see golden ribbons spinning and twisting.

Eventually, the door opens again. The man has returned, and this time he is alone. He places the lantern between us and sits, looking directly at me.

"Where is the dark man?" he asks.

"You mean Erroi? I don't know. Why?"

"You have come here as his spy. Now we know he is coming, we will be ready."

"What makes you think he is coming? Have you seen him? I know you're one of the riders who were chasing Eskanza. I didn't recognize you at first, but now I do. I take it you took her at the stables. So you have her here somewhere. Why can't I see her?"

"No one can see her. She is dead. She is not here. No one has seen her for months."

"Have you got her hidden in a room somewhere? I'll find out in the end."

"No one will find out. Not you or anyone."

"Really, you're that worried about someone finding out, are you? That's why you've locked me up here and sent the gatekeepers away? So that no one finds out. Why, what will happen if they do? If her father is dead, then what can anyone do? You're afraid. That's why you and your friend were after her. That's why you never just paid some capos to kill her. It would have been easier, but the risk of being found out would have been greater."

"Be quiet. She is dead, I say."

"No, not dead. If you wanted her dead, you would have used a bow when you were chasing her, although you did almost kill her. We found her and if we hadn't, she would have died. You should thank us for that."

"I don't know what you're talking about."

"Yes, you do. You already said you recognized me. You were there. You asked me about Erroi. You remember him all right."

"I should kill you now and shut you up."

"What, and have a corpse in your house that you need to get rid of? I don't think that would be very smart."

"I'll say you came to rob us. The gatekeepers brought you up here and we fought when I wanted to question you, just a pity that you were killed."

"Yes, and then there will be a big search of the house. Maybe I had an accomplice or maybe I'm part of a gang. There could be others in the house. They will want to search everywhere. Where will you hide Eskanza then?"

"I could kill her too and blame it on you."

"Don't be ridiculous. No one has seen her in weeks, then she turns up here, dead and locked up in a room. I don't know who you're afraid of, but I doubt they will be stupid enough to believe that."

"You don't know what you're talking about."

"If you say so. Still, I think I'm pretty close. I can guess whose house this belongs to and who you're afraid of."

"Shut up, shut up. You know nothing."

The lantern starts to flicker. Even though there are no windows in the room, it seems as if there is a wind blowing.

"How are you doing that?"

"I'm not doing anything."

The man, I call him a man, but now I see he is still a boy. It is only the arrogance of wealth that has made him seem older. The boy gets up and leaves. Again, he takes the lantern with him and leaves me alone in the dark.

"You should not have frightened him so," I say to Erroi.

"It was you who made him afraid."

"No, he was already afraid."

"Should I kill him?"

"Is killing always the answer?"

In the dark, I cannot see Erroi's face, but when I close

my eyes, I can see him looking at me as if he expects me to answer.

Eventually, he replies, "Usually. Often, at least, it is one answer, but it is an answer that raises more questions."

I close my eyes again and watch Alaba dancing in the sunlight. She is spinning golden ribbons around her head.

"Should we go now?" I ask.

Before I can answer, the door is opened again. The two riders are here. It is still dark. There is no lantern. There is the click of the lock opening and a patch of light expands and contracts while the door opens and closes. Then the door is locked again.

"You should not be here in the dark," I say. "I cannot guarantee your safety."

"Our safety? You should think more on your own safety."

"You cannot kill me, Erroi will not allow it. I will not allow it. Have you really learned nothing?" I can hear the creak of footsteps and the swish of cloth as they try to creep towards me. "You are very noisy for assassins; I can hear where you are you quite distinctly."

"Yes, and we can hear you. We have knives and you are unarmed."

"Right, so what will you do with my body?"

"There is a trap door in the ceiling above, we will pull it up there. It leads to an unused loft space. We will leave your body there. It will only need to be there for a short time."

"Really? You are not worried I will come back to haunt you or that I will drip blood through the ceiling? I'm not saying I will, but you should think about these things. Besides, with it being summer, my body will start to rot very quickly. The smell will be noticeable in a couple of hours. The whole house will smell of death. Perhaps it does already."

Erroi is standing behind them. His hand is reaching for his sword. I shake my head.

"The same is true if they were to die. No doubt the room would smell of death very quickly."

"You think you could kill us," says one of the boys incredulously.

"Certain of it, especially in the dark. You don't even know where I am. For all you know, I could be right behind you."

"We can hear your voice."

"All right, then where am I?"

"He's over there in the corner furthest from the door. No doubt he's trying to keep as far away from us as possible."

"No, he's in the middle of the room, between us."

"You see, you have no idea where I am. You'd have been better to have come with a lantern than try this in the dark."

"He's right, put the lantern on."

"Don't be stupid, he's trying to trick us. He's in the far corner, like I said."

"Or I could be behind you, or by the door. I could be anywhere."

"You can't be anywhere, you have to be in this room. And if you are in this room, we will find you."

"Very well, try and find me."

One of the boys does turn around to check that I am not behind him, but the other charges in the far corner. He trips over the stool I was sitting on and spins into the shelves. The other boy lunges forward.

"Got him."

"That's me, you idiot."

I am relieved that neither of them are injured, not seriously injured. The bolder of the two has bashed his shins and bumped his head, but they are trivial injuries.

"Right, let's keep hold of each other, that way we won't mistake him for one of us again."

"How do you know it's not me you're holding right now?"

"I can feel my brother's clothes. You were not wearing silk."

"Good," I admit. "Unless I have put on one of the silk gowns on the shelves. Perhaps I put one on so I could pass as a house slave."

"This is not the silk of a house slave's robe."

"If you wish," I reply.

Again, they begin to inch around the room. They make two circuits of the room without any success.

"This is hopeless," says the bolder of the two boys. "Put the lantern on."

They take the lantern and lift the shutter. Light spills out.

Now it is possible for them to see me. I have taken my seat on the stool in the middle of the room again. The boys look around. In the shadows, they can see Erroi standing.

"How did he get here?" one of them blurts.

The other says nothing, but makes a scramble for the door. He is trying to unlock it, but he is shaking too much to get the key in the lock. Again, I shake my head. Erroi shrugs. It is nothing to him.

"How did he get here?" the boy asks again.

"I don't know," I reply truthfully. "He seems to just go where he likes."

The other boy has dropped his key. I spring forward and kick it under the door.

"That is the only key we have," he hisses at me. "Now we are all stuck. If you kill us, you will not escape."

"That's not quite true," I remind them. "I could go through the trapdoor into the loft and escape that way, but I have no intention of killing you, or letting him kill you, either."

When I say this last bit, I look at Erroi severely, but I doubt he had any intention of killing them anyway.

"So what will you do?" they ask.

"Nothing," I reply. "Or at any rate, nothing to you."

I pick up the ball of golden thread. It is time to follow it. I go to the door, and it opens at my touch. I push the door closed behind me. I can hear the boys scrabbling at the door, but it is locked. It will do them no harm to sit in a locked room for a few hours. The thread leads on through the house. I walk through the house, following the thread. I walk past all of the party-goers and servants. Some of them look at me as if they will say something, but then they are distracted and go back to what they were doing previously, eating or drinking or talking to a friend or serving guests.

The thread leads to a room at the back of the house. It is locked, but that means nothing. I enter and close the door behind me. The room is very grand. It has a window that faces away from the Sun, so the window is quite small. Only moonlight will come in through that window. Lying face down on a large bed of black lacquer and brass is Eskanza. Although she is finely dressed in silk the colour of moonlight through clouds, she is dishevelled, and her eyes are red and puffy. Her lip is also swollen and slightly bruised.

When I enter, she turns around and looks at me.

"So," she says, "you have come at last. Where is the dark man? I have work for him."

"He does not work for you," I reply, "or anyone else."

"My cousins, did you see them? Are they dead?"

"I saw them, they are fine."

"I want them dead."

"Then you must kill them. If you want them dead enough, then you should do it yourself, otherwise don't ask. I think they are stupid boys, but to kill them would be wrong. I will not do it."

"Where is the dark man? He will do it."

"No, he won't. Besides, is this the first thing you want, death? You're no better than them if you do. They have not killed you, and they could have."

"That is because they are afraid. I am not afraid."

I let it pass. There are other things to talk about.

"What of your father?"

"He is here. I am certain."

"Do you wish to see him?"

"Yes, yes, take me to my father."

"Come, then."

I push the door and again it opens at a touch. Eskanza straightens her dress.

"Wait," she says and rushes over to a black lacquered cabinet. She brushes and combs her hair and puts rouge on her cheeks and lips.

"Now I am ready, take me to him."

I follow her as she leads me to the main chamber. She pushes the doors open and enters with a flourish. The room hushes as she walks in. There is an old man lying on a couch. He is grey haired and breathing heavily. She rushes towards him and he looks up. When he sees her, he smiles.

"Where have you been?" he asks.

"I came here as quick as I could when I heard you were ill. It is good I am not too late."

"Yes, very good, but even so, I will not last long."

"Nonsense."

"No, not nonsense, I'm old now, and old people die. I

don't know how long I have. I will die soon, not today, but not many moon rises. I'm sure of it."

She holds his hand.

"Have you reconsidered?" he asks.

Eskanza stiffens. "No."

"You should be wed. It will keep you safe."

"Safe? I'll never be safe. Not as long as people plot to take what should be mine. I am your heir. It should pass to me. And if I marry, it will be someone of my own choosing, you cannot make me marry Fribolo."

"He is your cousin. Marrying him will keep the money in the family. It will keep it together. They will look after it for you."

"He is a fool. He has tried to kidnap me and force me to marry. He would not let me come to you."

The old man nodded. "So, there is a bit more about him than you thought. That is good. But you escaped."

"You knew about this?"

"Of course I knew. Why do you think they did not just kill you? Don't you think they will just kill you when I am gone? I can protect you, Eskanza, I have protected you. But I will be gone soon. My brother and his children will look at you and say, 'If she dies, who will inherit?' You know the answer to that."

"Then kill them now. Kill all of them. That was always your weakness, you are too soft."

The old man chuckles. "Yes, I have always been too soft. I should have whipped you and had you married long ago. Too soft, like you say."

"I will not marry Fribolo."

"Then what will you do? I'll be gone soon, do you think they will listen to you? You are fierce, but you are a woman. If you do not marry Fribolo, I will leave it to him anyway, to save your life. They will not have a woman set at the head of things. It cannot be done."

"Father, I am your daughter."

"Yes, my disobedient daughter, my only child. If I had a son to inherit, then you could have married as you wished, but not now. I do not know how you escaped from your room. One of the servants let you go, no doubt. They will be punished. Now take her back to her room, until the wedding."

The old man gestures and two thickset servants take Eskanza by the arms. She does not resist. Her head is bowed and there are tears in her eyes.

"Who are you?" says the old man as I step forward.

"Do you want to go?" I ask Eskanza. She cannot reply, she is choking back tears, but she nods her head.

Alaba is dancing and glowing. Her clothes have turned to fire. Now she is naked and golden. I reach out a hand to touch Alaba, to take her away. My hand touches her glowing breast. The fire burns. The Sun shines in through the window brighter than ever. Then it is dark. No one can see. The Sun has gone, Vatu has closed the box of the Sun.

I take Eskanza's hand and lead her through the darkness. I am blind.

Alaba's brightness has burned away my vision. In the darkness, I travel, holding a ball of thread. I follow the thread through the darkness.

The people are shouting: "Where is Eskanza?"
I am shouting: "I am blind."

Alaba takes my hand and leads me through the darkness. I am holding onto a thread that I cannot see.

Eskanza is holding my hand. We leave her house. She is crying because she will never come here again. I am crying because I am blind.

"Don't cry," says Alaba as we climb the stairs and Erroi opens the door for us.

We are all here.

Chapter Ten
Home

I step into the darkness and through the darkness. In the darkness, rough hands seize me and pull me forward. I let them pull me forward out of the darkness, the comforting darkness. In the light, I see I am surrounded by the priests of Vatu. Kong is here. They have brought me here. He has brought me here. I stand and wait.

"Well, will you say nothing?"

I shake my head. I will say nothing. I will reveal nothing. I will tell nothing. They cannot make me speak. I am struck in the mouth.

"You will speak," says Kong. "You know they all speak. Speak now and make it easy for yourself."

I look at Kong. He is not afraid to meet my eye. Why should he be? Once more, I am struck from behind. They would like to torture me. I can see it in their eyes, bloodlust. I am ashamed of them.

"What happened to the girl?"

I do not speak to them. Why should I, they cannot make me. I have nothing to say to them. They are less than nothing. I can see they wish to kill me, but they cannot, not yet. Kong smashes his helmeted forehead into my face. I stagger backwards, and I can taste blood. There is blood coming from my mouth and nose. I am dazed. I stagger and hands reach out and hold me upright.

"You're a fool."

I cannot disagree.

"Did you think you could save her?"

Yes, that is what I thought. Perhaps I have saved her. The thought is a comfort.

"She is dead. You have robbed Vatu of what is his."

Have I? Was she really his? Was I really his?

Kong is shaking and his speech rises and falls like an actor's. He is talking quickly, and spittle sprays from his mouth. Is it anger that makes him shake? Is he really so angry? Anger is weakness; I had thought him stronger. I can see he wants to kill me, to torture me till I scream. He could make me scream in agony, I am sure he could. I am sure that he will. He has a dark imagination. He was always good at making people scream.

I look around the rest of the circling priests. They are wearing their robes and masks. But I do not need to see their faces to know they are all here. I can tell each of them by the way they carry themselves, by their height and bulk. I recognize the colour and length of their beards. All twelve priests are here. All of them will seek revenge. Kong is wearing the jet amulet of the chief priest. He leads them now. He always wished to lead. I look around. I have no friends here. I never had friends here. I am cuffed across the face by a heavy leather gauntlet. It is Kong; he is angry and afraid.

"Why?"

It is a single word I have heard so many times. Why? I am not sure why, other than that I had to, there could be no other way. Why?

I wonder how long they will keep me before I am offered to the darkness. They will not kill me. They will not give a corpse to Vatu. His anger would be great. Still, there are many other things they can do. I am kicked from behind. My legs are kicked out from under me. I fall to the floor and a priest grabs each of my limbs. I am held and lifted, then carried onto a low bench. They have decided what they will do.

Manacles are attached to my hands and feet. The chains are tightened so that I am spread eagle and rigid. A clamp is placed around my head and in my mouth. I will not be able to move my head.

"Still nothing to say?"

I am surprised to realize I have nothing to say. What can I say that they do not know, other than what I will not tell?

"I would kill you," says Kong, "I would kill you now."

Yes, but you cannot. Now I realize it is not anger that is making Kong shake, it is humiliation. How long he must have pleaded with Vatu to let him kill me. I find the thought amusing, and then I am ashamed at my unkindness. I realize how much Kong must hate me, always hated me. Even now, he cannot kill me, after all I have done. Vatu will not allow it. I am his and he will have me. Poor Kong, I pity him. A life filled with hate is no life.

Kong gestures, and four priests carry a large, flat stone and place it on my breast. It is heavy, but not excessively so. It is not heavy enough to break bones, but is heavy enough to make breathing difficult. They will not put on more weight. To do so would make me die quicker. They cannot let me die. Still, it is painful. I wonder how long I will lie here.

Kong is bending down and his face is pushed towards mine. "Tell me, what did you think you could do? Did you think you could hide from the darkness? You must have known you would be caught. You must have known she would die anyway. Why? What did you hope to achieve? You have achieved nothing; nothing except your own death and hers."

I focus on breathing. Each breath is an effort. To raise the stone takes all my strength. Each breath is a torment. To inhale, I must push the stone upwards so that air may enter, and each time I exhale, the weight of the stone pushes down. If I do not brace myself and exhale slowly, the weight of the stone falls like a hammer on my chest. I try to slow my breathing. I try to make each breath last as long as it can. I hold each breath until my lungs are bursting. My lungs are like fire. My brain is dizzy from lack of air. A face mask is brought. It is made of brass and covers my mouth. It has a tube of brass that is thrust into my mouth and throat. There is a tube running from the mask to a bellows. Kong signals and one of the priests, is it Zauria, pushes down on the bellows. Air is forced into my lungs. They fill like balloons and push the stone upwards. I feel as if my lungs will burst. Then, the bellows are emptied and air rushes out of my lungs. My chest falls and with it, the stone comes pressing down. I judder under the impact. Again and again Kong signals. In and out go the bellows, up and down goes the weight on my chest. I must congratulate Kong, his imagination is dark indeed.

I hear a voice crying out in pain, and then I realize the voice I am hearing is mine. It sounds far away and weak. My voice is muffled by the face mask. Kong motions for the bellows to stop and then he pulls the mask from my mouth.

"Not so silent now. No one stays silent for long. You think that if you stay silent, then it will be better. You are wrong, you know you are wrong. This is not a game, or competition. I do not need to make you speak. What could you tell us that we do not know? That you are a betrayer? That you are a thief? We know that, we do not need to hear it from you. What do you think we wish to hear about, your journeys and people you met? Why should we care? We have you. That is what we want. There is only one thing I want to hear, and that is the sound of you sobbing in agony. Now I have heard it. It sounds sweet."

If I could, I would turn and look at him, but my head is held firm in the clamps.

"I could make your lungs explode," he says. "I could blow them up until they burst, or I could empty them completely. I could kill you and make you scream. But you've already been screaming. I could have taken your tongue and voice box out first, but then you would not have been able to scream. Would you have liked that? Would you have liked to suffer in noble silence? I thought you might have. I did consider doing it. But I didn't have the time. Besides, I'd have needed to let the surgery heal up before putting you on the ventilator, or else you'd have likely bled out and drowned in your blood. So, sorry not to let you stay silent, I know how much that would have meant to you. Besides, I wanted to hear you scream. Thank you for letting me have my little pleasure."

I am breathing heavily. I doubt I could have spoken even if I wanted to. I roll my eyes around, and I can see Kong out of the corner of my eyes. He is bending towards me. His mouth is near to my ear. His face is covered by his mask, and I cannot see his eyes. But I have seen his eyes before, and I know they are the eyes of a madman. Everyone is mad in the Tower of the Sun.

He is still speaking to me, but I have stopped listening. I do not care what he has to say. I never did. I am wondering when he will start to torture me again. Then I realize, this is torture, it's all torture. I close my eyes and wonder if I could sleep. I have seen prisoners faint and often thought it must be pleasant relief for them. I close my eyes and try to let my mind go blank. But when I close my eyes, there is still pain. When I close my eyes, there is nothing but pain. There is no relief.

He is still talking. Perhaps I should be listening, but I cannot concentrate. The stone has been lifted from my chest and I am able to breathe easier. Now water is dripped onto my chest. It is cool and welcome, it is a mercy for which I am grateful, and then the water is dripped into my face. I open my mouth and let it enter. It is warm and mixed with blood and dirt.

Then the water is dripped onto my head just above my eyes. It runs into my eyes and fills them like twin pools, then the water runs down each side of my head like tears. Each drop of water strikes my head, like a tapping finger. It is not hard, but still I feel a jarring go through almost to my brain. It is like a drill going into my brain. I cannot move my head and each drop falls in exactly the same place. One after another they fall, and I try to keep count. Why? Why count them? There will be many, many drops falling. Each drop is tapping. Each drop is drilling. It is going into my brain. I keep my eyes shut, but at each drop, they open involuntarily. I keep my eyes open and with each drop, they screw closed involuntarily.

I do not scream. I am not in pain, but there is a drill going into my head. It is getting deeper and deeper.

"Still silent? How brave." Kong is mocking me.

I do not know how long water drips on my head. Eventually the water stops. What now?

"Did you like that?" asks Kong. "They say it is like having a hole drilled in your skull. It drives most people mad if you leave them long enough. I would like to drive you mad. I would like to see you gibbering and witless. Sadly, Vatu will not allow it. He wants to see you whole. I did plead with him. I begged and begged, but no, he would not allow it. Not dead, not mad, not maimed. He wants you whole. I begged and begged, for your sake of course. You know that you'd be better to die under my hand than have to face him. He's very angry with you. He's been angry with all of us, but mostly angry with you."

The clamps are taken from my head. Now I can turn and look at Kong. He is standing, facing away, pacing back and forth. Why am I still silent? Do I say nothing just to rile Kong? Once, I thought of him as my friend. Even now, I do not hate him. He is doing what he must. He is doing what he is driven to do. He is driven by madness.

He turns and looks at me. "Why will you not speak to me?"

Because I have nothing to say.

He stands over me and brushes a gauntleted hand over my face. It is surprisingly gentle. "I did not want this," he says. "We did not need this. All you needed to do was tell us why. We would have listened. We will still listen. We would have understood. We could have been friends. We were once. This is all so wasteful. Soon you will have to go. Vatu will call for you and we must obey. Then you will be gone, and this time wasted. You will have taught us nothing."

He would not have understood. I do not understand. It is like I am a puppet that must do what the puppet master commands. Even now, even as I lie in chains and blood and agony, I know I could do nothing else except what I did. Could you understand that, Kong? Can you understand that you and I are nothing but scraps of paper, blown by the wind? We are playthings for some creator, evil or benign. That is why I cannot speak, because the puppet master will not put words in my mouth. I pray for kindness, for my agony to end. But I receive no testament. Instead, I am filled with bleak despair. I have done my best. I have given all. Will this sacrifice be enough?

One of the other priests comes forward and loosens my chains. One by one, he takes the shackles from my wrists and ankles. It is Gezuri. I can tell because he is small and slender, his beard is thin and fair. He helps me to rise. I am seated on the torture block. He lifts a cup to my mouth. The water is foul. It is warm and gritty with dirt. Still, I am grateful. I drink deeply, and the water washes away the blood from my mouth and throat. I can feel the water give me new strength, and with strength comes hope. Hope for what? I have no hope. I will be offered to the darkness and perish. I can hope only for death. What does death hold for me? Can I have hope in death? It is absurd. I can hope only for the peace of not existing. And yet, as strength comes, hope comes unbidden.

Gezuri removes the cup from my lips. I would drink more, but I am denied. Gezuri will not let me have more water, more strength, more hope. The puppet master will not allow it. He is cruel. He gives and takes away.

"Feeling better?" asks Kong.

Better? Better than what? Better than being tortured till my lungs burned or till I almost went mad? Yes, I am better than that.

Kong comes and stands above me. He is looking down. I cannot see his eyes, as they are hidden by shadow. He brings a torch close to my face. The brightness hurts my eyes. I can feel the heat singe my hair. Does he think the heat of a torch will harm me? I have stood next to the Sun and have not burned. I have walked through fire and darkness.

"There is so much to say," says Kong.

There is nothing to say.

"When you escaped, it was us who met the wrath of Vatu. It was us who had to tremble and quake as he raged. It was our lives he played with and thought to take in his anger. It was us who paid for your crime, not you. Even now, we have done nothing compared to what he did to us, what you did to us. We stood naked in the dark, and the dark consumed us. The dark stripped us to the bone, and then brought us back."

I understand, it is no wonder they are mad. There is only madness in the Tower of the Sun, there was only ever madness here.

"This torture is a mercy. It was a mercy we pleaded for. 'Let us take him,' we pleaded, 'Let us kill him.' But he would not allow it. He would not grant that mercy. He will have you. And this will be like a sweet memory. We tried, we pleaded. But all we are allowed is to delay your time with him. He will have you."

I realize that I am being stripped naked. I am too weak to resist. My merchant's robes are being removed. I have worn them now for many days. They are worn and ragged and dirty. They are stuck to my flesh with dried blood and sweat. The hands that strip me are not gentle. When I am naked, I am led to a bath. Again I am taken by my hands and feet. Gloved hands hold my head. I am lifted into the bath. Will they drown me? But I am lifted into water, cool, clean water. The dirt and grime of my body is washed away. I am so tired. I think I could sleep. Water, soothing water, blessed gift of the heavens. I am lifted from the water a new man. I am clean.

Gauntleted hands grasp my arms and shoulders. Naked, I am led away from this place. I am led through familiar tunnels. Why? Do they think I have forgotten the way? Do they think I will try to run? I suppose I cannot blame them. I ran once.

I let them lead me. I follow the pressure of their grasp. I do not try to escape. I am wise enough to know that escape is impossible. The tunnel turns and twists, but does not branch or divide. There is only one road to follow now.

Voices in my head say kill them, kill them all and run away. Escape. But I cannot. There are too many, they are too strong, I am too weak. Besides, this is right, this is just.

The door in front of us is low and narrow. Only one person can pass at a time, and to do so, they will have to bend almost double. I am released. Now, it is the priests who will not speak; they are more afraid even than I am. Kong is beside me, and I can taste his fear. He always was a coward. But that is not fair, he is right to be afraid.

They stand in a crowd behind me. I cannot retreat. The only way forward is to open the door and enter with my head bowed. I turn towards them. In the dark, I know they are there only because of the sound of their breathing and the rustle of their robes. I can feel the heat of their bodies behind me. They will not open the door. They will not force me through. I am pushed towards the door. No one speaks, and I do not know who it is that pushes me, perhaps no one. I turn and reach out, and my fingers brush against the heavy, bronze door. I feel for the locking bolt. Why does the darkness need a lock? It is a thought that has just occurred to me. Still, my fingers find the mechanism. I turn it, and the sound of bronze jarring on bronze fills the silence. Then I push the door. It swings forward. This time, there is no sound, the noise is swallowed by the dark. Now there are no other priests. There is nothing but me and the waiting darkness. I lean forward. I duck my head. I take a step and then another. I pass through the doorway to where Vatu is waiting.

The door closes, not by my hand or by any other. I stand naked in the dark. There are no secrets from the dark. I step forward into the great arched and vaulted blackness. Although I cannot see, I can feel the darkness reaching up high. What is darkness? I breathe in darkness. I am surrounded in darkness. I am filled with darkness. I reach out, and I am swimming in darkness. I am drowning in darkness. I am suspended in darkness and space. Darkness washes me, as cool and soothing as water, as endless and restless as water. My eyes open and close, but I cannot tell if my eyes are open or closed, there is no difference. I step forward, but there is no forward, only darkness.

Vatu is here. He is all around me. He surrounds me. He fills me. The sound of my bare feet slapping on stone make a dull thump that echoes and then dies away. He is here. I wait. I can feel darkness swirling around me. I can feel it moving over me. It fills my mouth and my lungs. I reach to touch the darkness, but it moves away like water. This place is darkness, this place is Vatu.

I wait; for what? I do not speak. There is nothing to say. I walk forward again. I will not be afraid. I will not hide from the darkness. I will face Vatu. Let him do what he will. I have stood in this hall many times. I heard the great vault echo to the song of the priests, to my song. I have seen darkness and shadow fill this space like a flood. I have seen the figures on these walls and on the ceiling; darkness on darkness, a thousand shades of darkness. I have stood with the dark lenses over my eyes and seen it all. I have no lenses, I am naked and yet I see. What is darkness? How can you see in darkness? I look up and imagine the great barrel vaulted ceiling above. I see the carved scenes of black figures, black bones, black stars, black earth, black air, women, men, and children. All in darkness, dead, dying, decaying. The whole world is here. The whole world is in darkness. What is light? It is merely the surface of things. The depths belong to darkness.

I see Vatu, darker than the dark. He is everywhere, and he is all around me. He gathers himself up like a dark cloud. He is the eater of light. He gathers himself together, he is before me. He lies before me like my own shadow, a shadow of darkness in darkness. His vastness stretches out before me. He is my shadow. Vatu gathers himself. From every corner, darkness comes. Shadows come and gather before me. He is standing before me in the great chamber of darkness. He forms a solid shadow in the shape of a man. He forms a solid shadow in the shape of me. He is my shadow, come to torment me.

His black eyes look into mine. I cannot look away. They are not eyes, they are emptiness. There are no secrets from the dark, you cannot hide from darkness. He reaches out a hand towards me. It is the hand of darkness. I will not flinch. Let him do to me what he will.

His hand rests upon my shoulder. Dark lips move and the voice of darkness echoes through the chamber of darkness. "Welcome, friend," he says. "Welcome home, friend."

Tears form in my eyes, and a sob escapes my mouth. I fall to my knees and cry out. It is the cruellest thing he could do. His hand reaches down to me and he raises me to my feet.

"Do not cry, friend," he says. "I am sorry for your loss. But now you are home, things will be better." Then, the darkness withdraws.

I am blind again. I can hear my voice sobbing. It echoes around the chamber like a choir of mourners. Again I fall to the floor. I am home where I belong, in darkness.

How long do I kneel, sobbing? I cannot say. Eventually, I stand. I have no more tears. I turn back to the door. It opens as I approach, and I bow my head to leave the chamber. Behind me, the door closes. I stand and in the darkness, the twelve priests bow. Kong has shuffled forward on his knees. He is holding out something. He is handing me the jet amulet. I lift it and place it around my neck.

"Lappura," I say, "fetch me my robes," and the youngest of the priests runs to bring them to me.

In the dark and silence, we wait. The remaining priests are kneeling before me. None of them would have expected this. That I would return, that I would be restored. None of them could have thought that I would live, or that I would be forgiven. Do they fear me now? Each of them has laid hands on my flesh. Each of them has tormented me. Now I stand before them, waiting to be dressed in the robes of the chief priest. How Kong must hate me now. So short a time the amulet of darkness hung around his neck. Now it is mine again. It was always mine. I cannot escape who I am. I am no longer Utas.

"Has the body arrived?" I ask.

"Yes, lord," says Kong. "It arrived when you came. It came through the same portal."

I did not know that. The coffin must have been in the same room and then passed through behind me. When I was taken, there must have been others there to move the coffin. Or had the coffin been moved before I arrived?

"Has she been brought to Vatu?"

"No, lord, it was you he wished to see."

"Where is the body now?"

"It is in the upper chapel. It is to be burned with great honour, as befits the daughter of the high priest."

They knew this, but still tortured me. Vatu allowed them to torture me. Now he knows there is a wedge between them and me. They fear me now and will forever fear me. It is not good to be feared. It is far better to be loved. Was I ever loved? Yes, once, at least.

Lappura has returned. I stretch forth my arms. In the darkness, the same hands that tortured me clothe me. Their gauntleted hands are gentle now. A priest is shaking as he holds forth a boot for me. Although I cannot see, I look towards him. He is shaking. Even in the dark, I know who he is. I know each of them by their touch or by the sound of their breathing. It is Irruzura.

"Do not be afraid," I say. But after I have said these words, he shakes more. I place my foot into the boot and allow him to draw back. Now that I am dressed in my robes, they have all drawn back. They think I will punish them. They are waiting to hear me command their punishment. They have dared to torture the high priest. They must be expecting death.

Is this my punishment? Vatu would allow their death. He would allow their torture. I could do as much and more to each of them as they have done to me. I could make their ends terrible. My imagination is darker even than Kong's. In my mind, I see tortures of unthinkable pain and duration, unthinkable to the sane. The desire for revenge wells up within me. Can it be denied that they deserve to suffer for what they have done to me, and to others? I have but to reach out my hand, or utter a word. Here, the shadows will obey my commands. Here, I have power absolute. Kong, he is the chief of them. He is the one who sought to take my place. He sought to take my life, and only the command of Vatu prevented it. Even so, he is the chief of them. But…

I am ashamed. I have walked from darkness and into light. Will I return so quickly? Will I give myself to darkness? Vatu has been merciful in his way, or cruel. Can I be less merciful, or less cruel?

"Light," I say. It is a command.

The shadows withdraw. There is light. I can see the twelve priests kneeling before me. Kong has removed his mask. His head is bowed, and his neck is bare. Does he hope to tempt me into giving him a quick death? Irruzura is still shaking.

Lappura is looking towards me. "I was always loyal," he says.

Greba turns towards him. Even with his mask covering his face, I can see his contempt. He would strike Lappura if he could.

They are all here, all the servants of the dark. If I slay them, they will spring up again, them or others just like them. There will always be servants of the dark. I could kill them all. It would be just.

I am ashamed. There is so much darkness within me. Even now, I would stretch forth my hand and smite them. Now it is me who is shaking. I am just like them. I am darkness. But I will not.

"Stand." I mean to be kind, but my voice is rough. They stand instantly. "Let us go to the body," I say.

They part and let me take the lead, as is fitting. It is I who should lead them in the darkness. We follow the twisting tunnel upwards. Then we enter the tower. The upper chapel is on the highest floor, and is reached by a broad stair that turns and spirals. I start to climb and realize I am out of breath. Zauria rushes forward to assist me. I push him away and continue to climb the stairs. Zauria seeks to placate me, but I give no heed. When we reach the top, we pause outside the upper chapel. I catch my breath.

What is going through my mind: hate, revenge, fear. There is a body in the chapel. It should be the body of one precious to me, one for whom I gave up everything. Now she is dead. Now she is lying in a coffin in the dark chapel. Now I must make them think she is dead. Now I must make them think she is lying in the dark chapel. I motion for the door to be opened, and two priests rush forward and push them open. I am more afraid to enter than I was to face Vatu.

The coffin is lying by the altar. Sweet woods have been piled around her. Spices have been placed around the coffin. The lead casing has been opened, but the grave cloth still covers her body and face. I step forward. I can hardly bear to touch her.

"I am sorry for your loss." It is Vatu. He is here, in the darkness. He coalesces before us. I do not know what to say. "It is my loss, too," says Vatu.

I want to turn, I want to strike him, but you cannot strike shadows. His loss, he has lost nothing. He has nothing.

"Burn her," I say.

The priests rush forward, but Vatu motions them to stop. "So soon? Should we not grieve together? Come, let us gaze upon her one more time. Lift the sheet from her face, and let me see her loveliness again."

What can I do? I cannot refuse. I am the servant of Vatu. I am the shadow of the shadow. I step forward and put my hand on the grave cloth.

"Is it too hard?" asks Vatu. "Should I have one of the twelve draw the cloth from her? I do not wish to cause you grief. But it is right to grieve."

No, I will not have one of the twelve touch her. If the body were truly my daughter, I would not let them touch her. I will not let them touch this unknown child. I shake my head. The priests have begun the low, steady song of the dead. I lift the grave cloth.

"Look," says Vatu, "is she not lovely? Even in death, she is beautiful. How beautiful she is, how dear to us."

Is he mocking me? I cannot tell. I start to sing the sorrowful song of death. To my surprise, tears well up in my eyes. Here is a child taken before her time. Here is a child dead. Is that not reason enough for tears? Should I only weep for myself and for my own lost child? Again I look at the dead girl's face. My voice mingles with the voices of the priests. The sound is low and heavy and sad.

How can he not know?

I motion for the flames, and this time Vatu does not halt the priests as they come and light the pyre with their lanterns. Flames lick the wood, like the tongues of harlots. They twist and twine though the timbers, burrowing inwards. Pale smoke lifts from the pyre slower than a snowflake falls, slower than a shadow crossing the moon. There is no heat, not yet. There is a quiet crackle. Inside the timber pile, the fire builds and grows. The red, glowing flames cast shadows across the chapel. Vatu flickers in between them.

She is beautiful. Not as beautiful as Alaba, but what of it? She is beautiful. Her eyes are closed. I hope she is at peace, I hope the darkness has been merciful to her. I hope her short life brought some measure of joy. I hope she found kindness and was kind to others. Life is so cruel. Death should not be crueller. She is beautiful.

How can he not know?

I am crying and tears are in my eyes. Perhaps it is the smoke. My voice still sings the words of sorrow.

"Go, return to darkness. He will have you and hold you. Go, return to darkness. He is waiting and will make you welcome. Go, return to darkness, peace is his gift for you and for all others."

Now the flames are caressing the coffin. The black paint starts to blister and peel away from the coffin sides. The heat of the fire is strong, and the flames roar as they consume the timber. Dark smoke now rises in columns and forms a curtain around the coffin. There is so much smoke, I can no longer see the face of the dead girl. Flame has climbed the sides of the coffin and dances higher and higher.

"Go, return to ash. Let fire consume your form. Go, let fire take you from here to where you will be next."

Still I am singing. Still I am crying. The smoke is heavy now and the scent of burning fruit wood and spice is gone. Now the smoke smells of death, of flesh. Vatu is flitting between the flames. He is hovering amidst the smoke.

How can he not know?

The coffin is like a boat of fire. Flakes of soot dance upwards. The heat of the fire is strong enough to make me step back. The smoke starts to choke and smart. I can no longer sing. I bow my head and listen to the priests singing. Now Vatu is behind me. Now he is beside me.

"I am sorry for your loss," he says.

We stand before the fire and watch as the child is consumed. The flames are too bright and the smoke too thick for us to witness her burning, but we know she is burned. She is consumed, she is ash. She has gone to the darkness. Vatu is beside me. He is wrapping me in darkness.

"Soon," he says. "Soon you will be with her. She will wait for you, in the darkness."

Is he mocking me? Is he comforting me?

How can he not know?

How long do we stand? I do not count it in hours, but until the flames are gone and the smoke fades, until the embers have died and the ashes are cold. How long is that? Vatu waits with me. When the fire is dead, truly dead, she is dead also. There is nothing. There is ash and there is nothing. She is dead.

How can he not know?

Kong approaches me. What does he want? I turn towards him and he averts his eyes.

"Speak."

"There is much to do, Lord. I have reports, will you see them?"

There is always much to do. There is always much to decide.

"Later."

"As you wish. There are prisoners to be dealt with."

He is right. Now I am chief priest, I must be chief priest. I could just tell him to deal with them; perhaps he is hoping for that. Kong always enjoyed judging and punishing. I must show them that I am chief priest. I will take on my duties. I will not let Kong think he can supplant me.

The prisoners are kept at the lowest level of the Tower of the Sun. It is one of the smaller cells that they are held in. They are brought there by the officers of the outer court. Often the cells are crowded with more people than they can hold. We do not have to see prisoners until we so wish. Then we open the inner door of the cell and bring the prisoners through the tower to the place of justice. They are brought through the tower from the lowest place to the highest. Justice is the highest virtue of the darkness. That is why it is on the highest level of the tower that we carry it out. Also, it makes it easier to carry out executions. Most prisoners are cast to their deaths from the tower. Some have other deaths granted to them. Some are not granted death.

"Where are the prisoners?" I ask.

"They are in the cell," Kong tells me. "Do you wish them to be brought to the place of justice?"

"Yes, it is my wish."

"Very good, Lord, we shall bring them to you."

All twelve of the priests withdraw and head off to the cells. I am alone. I glance again at the ashes that lie upon the fire-blackened altar, then I turn and make the short climb to the place of justice.

When I climb to the top of the tower, I see that the moon is full. It is standing high in the sky. Stretching before me is the City of the Sun. It is ablaze with torchlight. Farther away, I can see other cities lighting up the darkness. I could jump from the tower, it is not too late to escape this fate.

Vatu is beside me. It is too late to escape my fate.

I sit on the seat of justice. It is hard and uncomfortable, made of black volcanic rock. It is unyielding. Kong arrives with the prisoners. There are only two prisoners, a girl of about twenty and a boy somewhat younger. They both look poor. The girl is not pretty, or not especially pretty. The boy is lame. Is this so urgent? Could they not sit in the cell for a while? There have been times when the cell has had twenty and thirty bodies all crammed in, waiting. Sometimes the prisoners fight and often will kill each other. It does not matter if they do. It is punishment and that is just. The killers are also punished.

Prisoners in the Tower of the Sun have no accusers. We have not sent for reports on their misdeeds. We are the darkness and there are no secrets from the dark. Truth is always found, and the guilty always revealed. Punishment is always given. It is just.

"What are your names?" I ask. Although it does not really matter, we always ask. Some refuse to answer; their refusal does not help them.

The girl looks at me. She is still defiant. "Luzora, my name is Luzora. This is my brother, Lento."

"And why are you here, Luzora?" I ask.

"For justice, they say."

"Who? Who says for justice?"

"Guards, they take us and put us in the cell below. 'In there, justice will find you,' they say."

Justice has found you, Luzora.

"And why did they take you to the cell?"

"I don't know. They came to where we were eating, we had bought food from a street stall. 'Come with us,' they said, and then we are here."

"Is that all? They did not search you or beat you?"

"Yes, they took our money, they are thieves. Justice should find them."

"It will, but tell me, was it much money?"

"Some shillings, maybe ten shillings."

"As much as that," I say.

"Yes, maybe more."

"That is a lot of money for a poor girl to have, is it not? You cannot have ten shillings in your pocket very often."

"No, a man gave them to me."

"A man gave you ten shillings?" No man would give her ten shillings. She is not worth more than half a shilling. "Where can we find this man?"

"I do not know."

"His name, then? Can you give me his name?"

Luzora shakes her head.

"Can you describe him?"

Luzora is looking down. "He did not give us all the money. We found some. It was in a barn. There was money and some clothes. We took the money and sold his clothes. We got a lot of money for his clothes, especially his boots."

"This man was in the barn?"

"Yes, no, there was no man. Not when we were there. A man left some money and clothes in a barn, and we found them."

"So you killed this man and took his money and clothes. That is why we cannot find him. That is how you came by the money. Did you kill him in the barn?"

Luzora looks at me in shock. Did she really think she could lie to me?

"Yes, you killed him in the barn. Did you promise him something to make him follow you into the barn?"

The boy blurts out, "It was not like that. He forced himself on her. He was a pig. He took her work token and would not give it to her unless she went to the barn. Then I killed him. He deserved it."

"So," I say, "justice found him. Now it has found you."

"No," says Luzora, "he is lying. He was not even there. I killed the pig. Me, and then I took his money and clothes. I am glad I did it even now."

It is nice she wishes to protect the boy, but it will do her or the boy no good.

"So where is the body? Is it still in the barn?"

"We took it and put it on the fire of the Sun. We sacrificed it to Vatu."

"Vatu is grateful for your sacrifice."

I see how it is. They are not lying. They are poor, and the man they killed oppressed them. I feel sorry for them. Now they must die. It is justice. It is always justice. I motion for them to be cast from the tower, but Vatu stops me.

"No," Vatu commands. "They gave the body to the Sun; it is fitting to give them to the Sun."

It is justice, always justice. He seeks to try me. I will not fail him. "As you command."

I rise and descend to the chamber of the Sun. The prisoners follow, escorted by Kong. Vatu stands beside the box of the Sun. The boy and girl stand in the place of exposure. Vatu will open the box and then the light will consume them. It is a painful death, blistering and burning in the Sun, but it is a quick one. I stand behind the screens of black glass with Kong. The prisoners are restrained with chains of iron. If they are not restrained when they start burning, they will run around and can cause the fires to spread.

The girl is looking down, sobbing. She should not. She should cherish her last minutes. The boy, Lento, is that his name, he is looking at me. Why is he looking at me? He is smiling. Vatu is billowing behind the box of the Sun. Still Erroi is smiling at me. His smile dancing on the face of the boy. Why is he smiling? The girl tries to sink to her knees and cover herself with her arms, but the chains will not allow it. The boy, Lento, is still standing, unafraid and smiling. Why is Erroi unafraid?

Lento is holding my hand. "It is all right," he says.

I feel peace. My eyes close. It is all right.

The box opens and they are gone. The children have escaped, they are gone. I open my eyes. The box is open. Kong is lying prone on the floor. Vatu is a still pool of inkiness. They are gone. The boy and girl are gone. The box is open, I can see it by torchlight, but there is no light, no heat coming from the box. There is only peace and stillness.

I awaken Kong. He starts when I touch him, and he thinks I will kill him and shrinks back. But I point and he sees. The box is open, but the Sun is gone. We rush to the box. Vatu is a pool of still calm; we are ripples that cause the pool to waken. Slowly, the shadow rises up, sleep falls away from him. Then he sees. Then we all see. The box of the Sun is empty. Vatu reaches in and draws from inside the box a single black feather.

"He has come, the thief has come."

Chapter Eleven
Blind

"Is everyone here?" I ask.

"Who is everyone?"

"Erroi, Eskanza, Alaba, are you here?"

"I'm here."

"Who are you? I can't see. Is Erroi here?"

"What is wrong with you?"

"I can't see. I can't see."

"Are you blind?"

"No, not exactly, I can see shapes and things, colours floating, but it is all fuzzy. I can't see my hands." I hold my hands out in front of me. I can see nothing. No, not nothing, I can see circles and blobs flashing.

"Can you see anything?"

"No, yes, shapes, outlines, I can feel things. I can feel the wall." My fingers brush against the wall. I must be near the door. If I turn to the left, I can follow the wall to one of the cots.

"Why don't you sit down or lie down?"

"I'm not sick, I just can't see."

"Let me help you. What are you trying to do?"

Soft hands take hold of me and try to guide me.

"I was going to make food. We should have some lentils. And onions, I can make something."

"No, you can't. You can't cook over a fire if you're blind. You could set yourself on fire. No one is hungry anyway, unless you're hungry. If you are, then I think I saw some apples. You could have one of them. Do you want me to get you one?"

"No, I'm fine. I think. It's just…"

"It's just you're in shock or something, I think. It must be difficult. You should stay still. Perhaps you will be able to see in a while."

"Yes, you're right. I'll be fine in a bit. I just need to wait." I let soft hands guide me to the cot and I sit down.

"Why don't you sit down, too?"

Who is that? Who is she talking to?

"Why would I sit down?"

"You don't look right either."

"What do you mean?"

"You know what I mean."

"No, I don't, sorry."

"You don't know that you're glowing like a fire?"

"Oh, that. Yes, I've been glowing like this for a long time now, it's nothing."

"So you say, but it's not normal."

"Yes, but it's not sore or anything. It's not a sickness. I'm not ill, or at least not now."

"Still, it's not normal. People don't glow. People will stare. What is it?"

"I don't really know. It fades. When it fades, then I get sick. Well, not really sick, it is more like I get really tired. It's like all the energy has flowed out of me. Were you with the boy when he went blind?"

"Yes, I was."

"How did it happen?"

"I'm not sure. We were in my father's house and it went dark. He can't see now."

"Can you see?"

"Yes, of course."

"Is Erroi here?" I ask.

"Who is Erroi?"

"I think he means the dark man."

"Him?"

"Yes."

"Is he here, or not?"

"Kind of."

"Kind of?"

"Kind of."

"Kind of."

"What do you mean kind of?"

"Right, he's here, definitely."

"Where?"

"I'm here."

"What has happened to me?"

"You've gone blind. That's what you said."

"I don't remember."

"Is it sore? Do you want to put something on your eyes? Is the light hurting them?"

"No," I reply.

"Are you sure?"

"Here." A wet cloth is pushed into my hands. "Put it over your eyes." I'm not sure why, but I do as I am told. The cloth feels cool against my eyes, but I still cannot see.

"Is Erroi here?"

"Why? What does it matter?"

They are right, it does not matter. He will come and go as he pleases.

"Who are you?"

I do not know who is speaking or who they are speaking to. I assume they are speaking to me.

"My name is Mukito. I am a friend of Utas. He saved my life. I am here with Erroi, we have come to save Utas and Alaba. We have saved Alaba. We rescued her last night."

"Who is Alaba?"

"I'm Alaba. I'm the daughter of Utas."

"I see, but how did you save her last night?"

"I'm not really sure," I reply. "We got her out of the keep. You were in a deep dungeon."

"How could you have got her out of the keep? That's ridiculous. No one could get in or out of the keep. Never mind walk into a dungeon and carry the prisoner out."

"I know it sounds crazy, but it's true. I'm not really sure how we did it. I could not have done it without Erroi. Is he here?"

"I think I was in a dungeon. I'm not sure. I was very tired and nearly asleep. Someone came in my dreams. It must have been you, I suppose. I don't remember very much about it."

"There were two of us."

"Was there? I don't remember."

"I still don't believe it."

"Why not? We just walked out of your father's house and no one stopped us. That was Erroi. He can do things like that."

"I remember him helping fight with my cousins. We fought our way out. I had fainted, no doubt. You brought me here, while I was sleeping."

"No, I took your hand and we walked into the darkness. We followed a thread."

"I don't think so. No doubt, you went blind when you hit your head in the fight. Erroi has brought us here, and now I have woken up and you are blind."

"We need to stay here until he comes."

"Who?"

"The dark man, Erroi. He will know what to do."

"Who is Erroi?"

"I wish I knew. He's just some traveller. But he's strange. He can do things."

"He's just a man."

"I don't remember him."

"He was there when we came for you."

"I don't remember. I remember you from today. You were holding my hand. I tried to get away, but you would not let me go."

"Erroi told me to stay with you. You will need our help."

"Why does she need your help? Who is she? Why does she glow like that?"

"I don't know," I admit. "She's glowed for as long as I've known her, which is not very long. But the first time I saw her, she glowed, and she's been glowing more or less every time I've seen her since."

"It's the Sun, it makes me glow."

"Why does it do that?"

"I don't know. It just does. It just happened one time, and since then, it happens every time the Sun is out. It's not a problem, as long as the Sun is shining. What about my father, did you see him?"

"No, never. I think Erroi might have seen him when we went and got you out of the dungeon, but I never saw him. If he was here, you could ask him."

"Who is her father?"

"Utas, he's a merchant I met on the road. He was travelling with Erroi, and we tried to hold them up, me and Kilhanga. They killed Kilhanga, but they let me live."

"You're a bandit? I knew you were no good."

"Not really. Kilhanga was a bandit. Yes, I suppose I was, too."

"My father is not a merchant."

"Well, he certainly seemed like one. He had a wagon full of silk that he was selling."

"Did he? How strange."

"I'm feeling a bit better; I think I could make something to eat." I stand up and follow the wall, my fingers brushing against the plaster. I can feel the edge of the hearth.

I can hear someone lighting a fire. I reach to where the pot ought to be, and it is in my hand. I reach to where the oats should be and put them in the pan, then water.

We are interrupted by knocking at the door. I raise my head. I would say that I look up, but I cannot see, I cannot look at anything.

"Are you expecting anyone?"

"No."

The knocking comes again.

"I can..."

"No, you can't. Not glowing like that, you can't."

"You need to stay out of sight, too; it could be from your father."

"I can..."

"My father does not know about here, or at least I don't think so. If he did, then he would have come for me earlier."

I get up and walk forward. I can hear my footsteps on the floor. They are like the beat of a hollow drum. As I walk farther from the wall, the sound is louder; as I go nearer the wall, the sound softens again. I think I am next to the door. I am next to the door, I can feel air slipping into the room through the gap beneath the door. I reach forward and open it.

"Who is it?" I ask.

"Me, don't you remember?" It is a man's voice.

"Sorry, no. Who are you?"

"May I come in?"

"I'm not sure why should I let you in."

"Well, because it's me. Don't you remember me?"

"No, I don't. Maybe. It's dark. I can't see you properly. Who are you?"

"Is he from my father?"

"No, I don't think so. If he was, he'd be more aggressive, I'm sure."

"Yes, I'd recognize him, he's not from my father. Besides, I don't think he knows about this place."

"I think I recognize him."

"You? How can you know him?"

"I don't know him, I just think I recognize him. I've seen him before, I'm sure."

"Yes, you have, lots of times. So have you. I can't remember your name, but you were with Utas, and the dark man. You tied a bandage around me when the cat ripped my chest open."

"Zintoa? Is that you? Why didn't you just say it was you?"

"I thought you'd recognize me."

"He can't see. He's gone blind."

"Really? How did that happen? I'm sorry to hear that. Here, let me help you."

"I don't need any help. I'm fine. I'm sure it will pass. I just looked too long at the Sun."

"Can I come in?"

"Yes, of course, sorry. Come in, I am about to make porridge." I step aside and let him enter and then I reach to where the door handle should be and close the door behind me.

"Why are you here?"

"Erroi sent me. Well, not exactly. I was with Utas, I thought I should stay with him, but it turns out I can't, and he didn't want me to anyway. He told me to leave and go back to Riga. I wasn't going to, but they took him and pushed him into this pool of shadow or something. It takes you to the Tower of the Sun. So he's gone. I could not stay with him. No one else got to go through the shadow gate. I never even got to see it. Apparently it's very strong magic that Vatu keeps for special things. Your father must be very important."

"Is he well?"

"He was when last I saw him. He was out in the sunshine. He seemed to enjoy it. I don't know what's happened to him now. After he left, Palaia dismissed me. Said he had no need for me. So I left and then when I was out in the street, I saw Erroi. I've only seen him a few times since he killed the cat, but I recognized him straight away."

"Yes, he's not someone that you are likely to forget."

"No, he's not, is he? I saw him across the street. Of course, the Sun was still up, so it was easier to see, but even so. I had to hurry across, the streets were still busy. I was going to shout at him, but thought I better not, so I followed him and when he went down an alley, he turned. I think he meant for me to see him and to follow him."

"So what did he say?"

"'Wise choice.' That's all he said. I'm not sure what he meant by that."

"Anything else?"

"No, that was it, and then it was like... Well, it's hard to explain. I'm not sure you'd believe me."

How can he say that as we sit talking beside a girl that glows like the moon?

"I remember you now."

"What?"

"Yes, you were one of the guards."

"Yes, that's right. I was one of the guards that came from Riga, that's where we caught your father."

"Was it? I'm not sure I remember that bit."

"You don't seem to remember much; I think you must be soft in the head."

"She's been sick," I say. "I think she almost died."

"And this sickness has left her brain scrambled."

"No, I don't think so. She seems just like a normal person."

"A normal person does not forget everything."

"Who are you, by the way? I know Mukito and Alaba, but I've never met you. My name is Zintoa, pleased to meet you."

"No doubt you are pleased to meet me. But don't get your hopes up, soldier."

"Ignore her. Her name is Eskanza, she seems to think every man is desperate to take advantage of her."

"No, I would never do that. Ask Alaba or Mukito, they'll tell you."

"Sure, ask a blind bandit and girl who can't remember anything. So you're here and Erroi sent you. So what?"

"If Erroi sent him, then he's welcome here. No doubt he's come to help."

"Sorry, but who is Erroi?"

"He's a friend of your father's."

"He's a bandit."

"I'm not really sure who he is. But we wouldn't be here without him."

"Where is he now? Why is he not here?"

"I thought you said he was here?" I ask.

"He was here, for a while, then he just seemed to disappear. He was here and then I couldn't see him. Maybe he's still here. Why, what's the big deal? He must have slipped out. He'll be back when he wants. It's not like he was ever here that much anyway."

"It's just, I don't know. Maybe I've just come to depend on him. He always seems to know what to do. I mean, we've got Alaba, but not her father. He's at the Tower of the Sun. What do we do now? Should we go and try and save him? That was the idea. At least, I think it was. I'm not sure what we do now. I was going to say we can't just walk into the Tower of the Sun uninvited, but we walked into the citadel here. Maybe we should be heading out after him."

"You're crazy, blind boy. Do you think a blind bandit and a glowing girl can just walk into the Tower of the Sun and say, 'please sir, can we have our friend back?' The soldier says Vatu went to a lot of trouble to get this man, he's not going to say 'here, have him back.' I'd forget about your father and get on with your life. That's what I'm going to do."

"I suppose you're right. I mean, I know it will be hard. I don't know what we'll do."

"Why do we need to do anything?"

"Well, let's make something to eat. I'm definitely hungry now."

"Let me make it. You're blind, and I'm a good cook, or a reasonable one, at least. What have you got? I can see oats and onions. Have you got any vinegar?"

I try to protest, but Zintoa is adamant. "Go and sit down, I can do this, easy."

I sit and close my eyes. It makes no difference, I can still see golden brightness swirling in front of me. I suppose it is better that Zintoa cooks, but I would have liked to do something other than just sit. I can hear someone come and sit beside me. It is Eskanza, I can tell by the guarded way she moves. She is sitting about a foot away. She thinks I don't know she is there. I think she wants to speak to me.

"Are you all right?" I ask. It must have been a big shock to realize that it was her own father who tried to kidnap her and force her to marry her cousin. I do not remember my father. My stepfather... I never thought of him as that. I thought I hated him. Eskanza is different. Perhaps it is always different for daughters, or maybe not. In the end, he hurt her more than Kilhanga ever hurt me. I never expected any different, but Eskanza did.

"What do you mean?" Eskanza's voice bristles with

indignation.

"I never meant any offence," I say, trying to keep the peace. "I just thought that you're only just up out of your sickbed, and then held at your father's house. It must be draining."

"What, you think I'm going to lie down beside you? Don't get your hopes up, blind boy."

There is no point in arguing.

"Who are they?" she asks. I realize she has never met any of them before.

"I don't really know them very well. When I met Alaba, she was very weak. She could hardly eat. She was travelling with her father. He kept her wrapped up in the back of his wagon. Even then, she glowed. Not like now, now she shines like the moon, then she glowed soft as starlight. That's really all I know. When the soldiers took her, I knew I wanted to help. Erroi wanted to help too. I couldn't do much without him.

"Zintoa was one of the soldiers that caught her. Really, he was the only soldier that caught her. He's... how can I put it?"

"Stupid?"

"No, not stupid, or at least not slow, he's just a bit trusting. To be honest, I don't really know him either. I only met him twice, once at the check point coming out of Riga, and then when he came to our camp. He seemed nice enough; in fact, if I'm honest, he seemed very nice."

"Nice, trusting? Like I said, stupid."

"All right, stupid if you like. But that's all I know about him. He seems to know more about us, or about Alaba and Erroi, at any rate."

"So you trust him."

I have to think. Do I trust him? What does trust mean? "I don't think we have any choice," I say eventually. "If Erroi really has sent him here, then there's not much we can do about it."

"And you think he has? You think he is not just making this up?"

"Yes, I do. How else would he know where to come? He could have found us, I suppose, but then why not just come with a squadron of soldiers and take us all into custody?"

"I suppose."

"It would be easier if Erroi was here. Then he could tell us why he sent him."

"Maybe he sent him to cook. You're not a great cook, and now you're blind, it will be difficult."

"I doubt Erroi is concerned about my cooking."

It seems as if Zintoa has been doing well with the cooking. I can smell the gruel. It's not really porridge, more like a thin stew of oats and onions and smells good.

"It's ready," he calls.

Eskanza goes and fetches two bowls. I could have gotten my own, but I am grateful and tell her so. She merely snorts in reply. The stew is good, as good as it smells. After we have eaten, Zintoa starts talking again.

"I should tell you what Erroi said. He says we can't stay here. 'They will come.' He said, 'Tell them they will come.'"

"Who are they?"

"I'm not sure. He seemed to think that you would know who he meant."

"It does not really matter who they are. We don't want to meet them, and the only way to avoid meeting them is to get moving. We need to pack up and go. Did he say where to go?"

"No, he never said."

"Well, we can worry about that later. For now, I guess we just have to get moving."

"Aren't you forgetting something?"

"Am I? What am I forgetting?"

"Her, we can't go around with her like that. We may as well just light a beacon in the dark saying here we are. In fact, that's exactly what it's like. It's like a shining beacon. You've forgotten because you're blind, but I can see it plainly."

"No, I've not forgotten. Utas was able to travel round with Alaba because he had her wrapped up. We could do that."

"No, we couldn't. He took her round in the back of a wagon. We can't just go round with her walking about wrapped up. People will wonder what's going on."

"I could wear a habit like a nun."

"That would not work. It would not cover your face. Besides, we don't have a habit, and why would a nun be walking round with two desperadoes?"

"I'm not a desperado."

"We could leave her here; we could get away and leave her here."

"Why would we do that? We've just gone to all that trouble to save her. Why would we leave her here? No, I've a better idea. Is the fire out? There should be plenty of soot and ash."

I think of when I worked at the foundry and my body was

black with soot. I think of the body of the girl I collected in the ash pits. It was thick with grime, so thick that you could not see her skin until I washed her. It seems as if Alaba is truly going to take her place. She will wear not only her rags, but her filth too.

"That's a brilliant idea. I can rub soot and ash over my body and then no one will be able to see the glow. And it won't be odd. I'll just look like a pauper."

"It could work, and it would not be so strange, people would think you were with these two and that you sleep with them for money."

I cannot see Alaba blush. Does her blushing show above her glowing skin? But I can hear the hurt and embarrassment in her voice.

"Yes, like you say, it won't seem odd. And you can dress like a pauper, too. Then it will be like two gallants that have picked up a pair of girls."

Eskanza snorts, but says nothing.

"Unless I pretend that I'm with you instead of with them. You look like the kind of girl that prefers that sort of thing."

"Enough," I intervene. "I think it's probably better if we all dress like paupers. To be honest, I'm dressed like one already. And now that I'm blind, I'll definitely pass for one. It's really you two that will bring attention. I'm not sure either of you would ever pass for paupers, but we can try, unless anyone has a better idea?"

"I think it will work," says Zintoa, and I am grateful for his support.

"Very well, but if we are to get dressed, then you will need to wait outside, I'm not going to get changed in front of you. She might not mind, but I have standards."

"The boy is blind, he can't see anyway. He does not need to go."

"I'll go," says Zintoa, and starts to leave.

"I'll come, too," I say. I hope the girls will not kill each other in our absence.

Zintoa tries to lead me out.

"I can manage," I say and open the door. Zintoa follows and closes the door behind me.

"I should have brought a light," he says, and then remembers that I can't see. "I'm sorry, I didn't think."

"No need to be sorry."

"I should thank you, by the way."

"Thank me? What for?"

"For tending my wounds. I know I might have died if you hadn't."

"I thought you would have died anyway. You were pretty cut up."

"Well, yes, I was."

There is silence for a while, and then the door opens.

"In you come."

"You look..."

"Hideous, just say it, we know."

"Where did the clothes come from?"

"I had some that were left here when I went to the stables."

"They're a bit big for me."

"What are you saying, you think I'm fat or something?"

"No, it's not that. I'm sorry. It's just..."

"She's teasing you, just ignore her."

"No, I'm not."

"Yes, you are."

"Anyway, if we have to dress as beggars, then so do you."

"I think I'm already dressed like a beggar."

"Yes, you are, but he's not. He looks like a soldier."

"Perhaps I could pretend you're my prisoners."

"I doubt you could pretend anything, you're too stupid to pull anything like that off. Besides, one guard for three prisoners? No one will believe that."

"I've got my work clothes, you could wear them."

"All right, but the girls need to leave while I get changed."

"Modest, are we? It's nothing I've never seen before."

"Really, is that why you..."

"All right, I'm leaving, we're leaving. Come on, Alaba, let's leave the boys to it."

I can hear them leave and then Zintoa asks me where the clothes are. I point to where they should be and wait. It does not take him long to change. I turn and face the wall, even though I cannot see. When he is dressed, I call the girls back into the room.

"Well, you look like a beggar."

"Yes, but these clothes are bit small."

"Beggars can't be choosers. Besides, do you think workers can just buy new clothes every time they grow?"

"I think they look fine."

"How would you know? I'll bet you've never seen a beggar."

"I have. Well, not beggars, but labourers. There are lots of labourers in the City of the Sun. We need them for the harvest during summer. You look like one of them."

"Good, I think."

"Great, so we can pass as ordinary. What now?"

"Now we leave. We can't stay here. We should have left by now."

"To go where?"

"We should go back to Riga. That way, we can get as far as possible from here. We need to take Alaba to safety. We need to get her away."

"They know we have come from Riga. It will be the first place they look. Besides, what is for us there? We could not stay. Utas had left it and gone further on."

"Alaba, do you know where your father was headed?"

"Speak up, have you forgotten he's blind? He can't see you shaking your head."

"No. I don't know where he was headed. I don't think he ever told me, but if he did, I don't remember. I think Mukito is right, we can't go back to Riga. What would the point be?"

"We should go to try and save your father."

"Don't be stupid, even I know no one comes back from the Tower of the Sun. If the darkness has him, what do you think you can do? You can't even see."

"Do you know any place we can go, Alaba?"

"Not really. I was brought up in the Tower of the Sun. This is all very strange to me. I don't know anywhere else."

"Did Erroi say where we should go?"

"Not exactly, he just said be sure to leave."

"That does not sound like him."

"No, his exact words were, let me see. 'Do not wait, go quickly, we have only a little time till he comes. Go quickly.'"

"That does sound like him, but it does not help us."

"Little time till who comes?"

"Vatu."

When the word is said, we fall silent. Vatu is coming. We must flee.

"Come," says Eskanza. "We must hurry."

She leads off and the others follow. I do not know where she is taking us. It does not matter, in the end the darkness will find us. All we can do is run.

"We should take the horses," I say. "There is no point in

trying to hide, we need to be quick."

"You are wrong. If we go for the horses, they would follow us. They would find us. It is better this way. The horses will be fine. No horse can ride fast enough. It would be pointless."

We do not go to the gates. Instead, we walk through the mountains of ash. They do not make a wall, just a barren land around the city. Sometimes patrols check the ash piles, but mostly not. If people want to come to Fadu, the city is happy for them to come. The city is always hungry for more people.

The ash rises in puffs as we walk. I can hear it like a grey whisper. We walk quietly, watching for patrols, but we do not meet any. Our journey is uneventful and dull, but for all the dullness, our hearts are racing. I can hear Zintoa swallowing and Eskanza shaking. Only Alaba seems undisturbed. We are walking, marching as quickly as we can. We do not run, we will have far to go, and we do not want to be spent too soon. Eventually, we are walking downhill. The ash ponds beneath our feet, and we almost slide down. If anyone is following us, they will have no difficulty following our trail. It cannot be helped. We step forward and onto solid ground. We should not stop. We do not have time to stop, we must keep going, but we stop.

"Why have we stopped?"

Erroi is standing in front of me, or at least I think he is.

"Why are you wearing a rag round your eyes?"

"Because I'm blind. I think I have burned my eyes out. I looked at the brightness too long. Since then, I can see only shapes and flashes. It's not too bad. It's like you said, I just need to listen. Mostly things are where they should be when I reach for them."

"You looked too long at the Sun. That was stupid."

"Yes, I suppose it was. I've never been so close to the Sun before."

"That can't be how you went blind. You were with me at my father's house and then everything went dark. I can see, so why can't you? I never went blind. You weren't staring into the Sun. How did you go blind?"

"He was with me. I don't know how to describe it. It's like I was sleeping and then all of a sudden, I woke."

"The Sun woke you. When it shone into the room and touched your skin, you woke."

"Did it? I still don't really remember. But I remember you. We were dancing, dancing and running. I was running really fast. I felt like I could run for ever. I ran and ran. I ran from the house and from the city and ran. It was like I was running away from everything. But you stayed with me. I felt like I was going to run to the end of the world, or maybe fly there. But I couldn't, not while you were with me. Not with us tied together."

"What nonsense."

"Yes, it must sound like that, but it was real. I know I never dreamed it, even though it was like a dream. I remember dancing and fire. Then you reached out towards me. It felt strange, and it was like a fire going right through me. It was like; I don't know if I can describe it. I don't remember it all."

"It was like the air around you was on fire," I say. "It was as if the Sun shone from your skin."

"Is that when you went blind? Did I do it? I'm sorry, I did not mean to."

"It wasn't your fault." It was mine, my own fault.

"I can help you." It is Erroi. I remember how he helped the boy with the injured leg in Riga. There is always a price for Erroi's help. I take the rag from my eyes.

"What will you do?"

I can feel his hands at the side of my head. His thumbs are over my eyes.

"Which eye will you give me?" he asks.

"Wait, you're going to push out his eye? How do you think that will help him? He's only been blind for less than a day. His eyesight could come back."

"It is the price," says Erroi. "There is always a price. If he will pay it, then he will see."

"I know he can do it," I say. "I have seen him heal people before. I'm not sure why there is a price. I had thought it would be a finger or something. Can't you give two eyes for a finger?"

"No. That is not the price."

"Wait, I've seen healing done too, and it didn't involve any eyes being gouged out. Remember when I was cut up by that cat? Well, I was cut up bad. You patched me up as best you could, Mukito, but it was still bad. I think Utas hoped I would die on the way back. I probably should have. I certainly felt like I was going to, but I didn't. I was healed. Here, let me show you. I should have a scar, lots of scars, but I don't have any."

I can hear him lifting his shirt, but I can't see anything.

"I know you can't see, but here, put your hand on the skin.

You can see it's smooth, no scars. And it happened almost straight away."

"So you're saying you can heal me?"

"No, not me. I never did it, I was just sitting, lying really in the cart. I felt like I was getting weaker and weaker. I did not want to die, but it would be all right if I had died. Then Utas and Alaba could have just carried on. In some ways, I'm the reason they were caught."

"So who did heal you?"

"You did. Don't you remember? You reached out and touched me, and it was like a glow; no, more than a glow, like a brilliance. It only lasted a few seconds, but afterwards, I could sit up and then I could feel my skin. I don't know, it was like just being whole again. I took my bandage off, and I was healed, like I am now."

"I did that? Did I really? Do you think I can heal Mukito, and give him back his eyesight? I want to. It's my fault he's blind."

"There will still be a price," says Erroi. "Only it will be you that is paying it."

"Really, I don't mind. What price would it be? It's only fair. It's my fault. What do I do?"

"Don't you know?"

"No. I don't remember what I did. I don't remember anything, or at least not much. I don't remember, or I kind of remember. What did I do? I think I just touched you or something."

"Why don't you try that? Why don't you touch him, just put your hands on his face."

"All right, I'll try it. I'm not sure it will work."

I can feel her fingers on my face. They are warm and soft. They stroke my forehead, they are soothing and gentle.

"Nothing is happening. This is a waste of time. Put his rag back over his eyes, and let's get moving."

"No, wait, I'm sure something is happening. Can you feel anything?"

"Kind of, I think."

But nothing is happening, nothing.

"Why is nothing happening?"

"Wait," says Zintoa.

We wait. I can feel warmth flowing from her fingers and then into my eyes. I can see. I look around and can see for miles, even in the darkness.

"Your eyes are shining like torches," says Zintoa.

"The Sun will never burn your eyes again," says Alaba.

I turn towards her and her face is before me. Even through the ash, it is glowing. I can see her features. Her eyes are closed. I reach forward... but she slumps. I catch her and hold her.

"What has happened?" I ask.

"There is always a price," says Erroi.

"Yes, you said that. What has happened?"

"She is weaker now," Erroi says.

I lay her on the ground.

"Will she be all right?" I ask.

"I'm fine, it's just... Well, it's hard to explain. But anyway, I'm fine now. Here, help me up." Alaba's weak voice.

Zintoa and Eskanza help her. I can see she is weak. Once is she is on her feet, it is time to go. Zintoa and I will help her if she needs it.

"Where are you going?" asks Erroi.

I do not know. I had hoped he would know where to go. "Where should we go? This is all so pointless," I say.

"Not pointless, futile. It is different," he replies.

"Then where should we go, what can we do to make it not futile?" I ask.

"He will come here, we must leave," Erroi tells us.

"And go where? Can we not save Utas?"

"He does not need saving, at least not in the way you think," says Erroi.

Zintoa and the girls are standing, and Alaba is catching her breath as the others hold her upright.

"So you have no plan," says Eskanza.

"It is not me that needs to have a plan. It is you who must decide," replies Erroi.

"What are you talking about? I should leave you, if you are being hunted. They are not hunting me. At least, only my father is hunting me. I do not need to run from Vatu. I have done nothing." Eskanza cannot hide the fear in her voice.

I understand that she is afraid. I understand that she thinks the things she says are true. She is wrong. If she is taken, they will know that we helped her, and that we were with her.

"I should leave now. I could leave, I could find somewhere. I do not need to run." Even she does not believe this now. "Gods, how did I come to this? Betrayed by my father and now wanted."

I am angry. None of us wanted this, none of us asked to be hunted by the great spirit of darkness. We know what this means. Alaba has done nothing, but she will suffer more than any of us. Eskanza may even be allowed to live. Before I can speak, Alaba shuffles over to her. I can hear the whisper of her rags rubbing against her skin as she puts an arm of comfort around her.

"It's all right to be afraid, we're all afraid, or at least I am. I've been afraid for a long time, so long I've forgotten what it's like at the beginning. I can't say it gets better, because it doesn't, but you get stronger. I know what it's like to be too afraid to walk, or speak, or eat, but eventually, you find you can."

"How do you bear it? How can you stand to know you will die?"

"I don't know. I don't know what to tell you."

"Talk, talk, talk. I told you we cannot stay here. We must go now," interrupts Erroi.

"We go to Riga." It is my voice that says it. "Let's get going." At least one of us has a home to go to.

"Riga. Now you have decided, let us go."

We head out, skirting around the city to the road.

"Not that way," says Erroi. He motions to us to turn back the way we came. We turn and see no mountains of clinker in the moonlight, instead we can see the moon shine on low, mean walls of brick.

"How?" asks Eskanza. "It's not possible."

"And yet it is," I say. She is right, though, these things should not be possible.

"Follow me," says Erroi and leads us to the gates. They are still closed. The moon is not yet high enough.

"Is this Riga?" says Eskanza. "It looks like a dump."

The guards are coming to unlock the gate. "Hurry up," says Erroi, "hurry up. We've been travelling all moon down."

"Not my problem," grumbles the guard. "You'll just have to hold your horses."

"We don't have horses," says Zintoa.

"Ha ha, very funny. Is that you, Zinty? Thought you'd not be back for a while. Who are your friends?"

"We're not his friends," interrupts Erroi. "We are here on business, and Zintoa is our guide. Here, I have letters from your mistress."

"Not from my mistress. I got one wife and no mistress, much

safer that way," says the guard. Nonetheless, Erroi hands over the papers, and then the guard opens the gate. The guard hands back the papers. "I can't leave here and take you to her, so you'll need to go by yourself."

We walk into the town. Erroi passes me a wallet of coins. "Get ready," he says, "We will need to leave soon."

I head off towards an inn, but Zintoa stops me. "This is my home," he says. "Come, we can stop by my parents'. Hopefully they'll have breakfast ready. I don't know about you, but I'm starving."

"Just like a man to think of his stomach," Eskanza teases him.

"Well, when you're a soldier, you never know where your next meal is coming from, you've got to be on the lookout all the time. Besides, I've not seen my parents for weeks, or Hosta."

"You have a girlfriend." I think there was a hint of disappointment in her voice.

"No, that's my little sister. She's about your age, you'll like her."

"Will I?" she asks.

"Sure, why not?"

I had not thought about Eskanza and how old she is. She had always seemed older than me, but Zintoa is right, she cannot be more than sixteen years old. She carries herself like a grown woman, but she is younger than me. She cannot be older than Alaba, she could be younger.

Zintoa leads us through the alleyways, then stops at a door. He bangs against the rough wood and pushes it open without waiting for a reply.

"Who is that?" says a voice. It sounds like a young girl.

"It's me. Why, who else were you expecting? You've not got a boyfriend since I left, have you?"

The girl squeals with pleasure and rushes towards Zintoa. She throws her arms around him and hugs him.

"When did you get back?"

"Just this morning, of course. I came straight here."

An elderly couple come through from the next room. They are clear-eyed and healthy. It is from his parents that Zintoa has inherited his good looks. They too rush towards him.

"Have you eaten?" his mother asks. "Who are your friends?"

"No, I'm starving," says Zintoa. "Have you started breakfast?"

"Yes, we have some sausage; if you like, we can put more on for all of you."

"Go on, Dad. They won't say it, but I'm sure they're as hungry as me."

"So tell me," asks the girl. "Did you get to the City of the Sun?"

"No, the nearest I got was a place called Fadu. It's much nearer the Sun than here. They have big mines and furnaces. They smelt metal. There was big heaps of slag around the place."

"Sounds horrid."

"Well, yes, it could be, but there was lots of money there. All the houses were tall with maybe three stories, and the palace was probably as big as the whole of Riga. People there had lots of money and dressed very fancy."

"We dress fancy here too," says the girl.

"Indeed we do," laughs Zintoa.

"So what happened to the prisoners?" asks the old man.

"Better not ask," says Zintoa. "He's on his way to the Tower of the Sun."

"Why, what did he do?"

"I'm not really sure. This sausage is good. Our sausages are better, that's for sure. And our water, the water there was terrible. They say the mine spoil gets into the water and taints it. It tastes awful."

"I'd have thought you drank only wine in the big city," said Hosta. "So how do you know Zinty?" the girl asks Eskanza.

"I met him in Fadu. I don't really know him very well. We were travelling the same way, me and my sister," says Eskanza, pointing to Alaba. "It was safer to travel with other people, so we stayed together."

"Will you be staying in Riga?"

"No," says Zintoa. "They have to travel on, and so do I."

"But you're just back, can't you stay a couple of days, at least?"

"I wish I could, but it's important work. No one else can do it except me," says Zintoa with a grin.

"I don't believe that for a moment."

"It's true, ask Mukito."

"Mukito, is that your name?"

"Yes, we will have to leave. I'm not sure how long we can stay."

"Long enough to eat, at least."

"Hopefully," I agree as the old woman hands me some sausage. The sausage is good. I had not realized I was so hungry. I look around. Eskanza is eating, but Alaba is not.

"You must eat," I tell her. "We can't have you fainting on the journey."

"They're coming with you? I thought you said it was important," says Hosta.

"It is; you just have to trust me."

"Are you in trouble?"

"No."

There is a knock at the door. The old woman pushes forwards and opens the door and Erroi enters.

"It is time," he says. "We need to go."

Chapter Twelve
Hunting, Running

Darkness, I am suspended in darkness. Darkness seeps into my being, into my brain.

"You brought him here. You betrayed me."

Are they words I hear? It is like black letters etched in my brain. It is my own voice speaking, it is my own mind forming the words, not words, thoughts. I am thinking darkness. I am speaking darkness.

Yes, I betrayed you. I have always betrayed you. I have always despised you. Darkness, you cheat life. You cheat me. I will always betray you.

You have always betrayed me.

"Where has he gone?"

I do not know. I cannot know. I relax. Torture me if you will, I can do nothing to help you. I cannot tell what I do not know. He has gone. He has taken her, and he has taken the light. He has set the Sun free.

"Where is she?"

He knows. He always knew. How could he not know? But I cannot tell. She could be anywhere. She should be gone. I pray she is far gone. May the gods be kind and send her far from here. Vatu, your darkness shall not touch her. You will not see her. You will not find her. It is a kindness to know she is safe.

"Where did you try and take her?"

Nowhere, I just tried to escape. I just tried to keep her safe. I just tried to keep her as far away from you as I could. I just ran and kept running until I was caught. She will be running. Erroi will be running with her, I hope. May the gods grant that she is running, running fast.

"She cannot escape, he cannot escape. I will find them."

The darkness seeps into my brain. It is as if I am back in that cell in Fadu. Erroi is there. He sees it all. The darkness sees everything. There are no secrets from the dark.

"So, we will start looking there." Darkness wraps itself around me. It is like a cloak, like a skin. *"Come."*

I feel my body move. We walk up to the top of the tower, wrapped together like lovers. From the top of the tower, we can see nothing. I can see nothing. The darkness cannot see, but it can know, it knows everything. Before us stretches the dark lands. Above us stretches the sky. The moon has not risen, but stars are scattered across the sky. Points of light, points of pain. I can see nothing.

Vatu raises my arms and blackness forms like wings. I leap from the tower, we leap from the tower. I hope to plummet to my death, to land on the hard rock and burst and bleed. Let me fall, Vatu, let me die.

I do not die, I do not fall. Instead, my arms beat and wings of darkness carry me across the land. I can see nothing, but the darkness sees everything.

"Do you wish to see?"

No, I have no wish to see. I know where we are going. We soar across the sky like a black cloud, like a shadow across the starlight. We spread darkness down below. We blot out the stars. We soar across the sky, and my wings raise me higher and higher. Cool air rushes past us. My blood is chilled.

Vatu opens my eyes. I look down. Even by starlight, I can see the fires and lanterns of the people below. It is as if the stars are mirrored in a still pool. Perhaps the stars are only fires in the sky. The lights are patterned and gathered into towns and cities. I can see single lanterns crossing the dark lands between them. Unwillingly, I gasp. It is beautiful. I have never seen anything like this. I have never done anything like this. No one has done this, to fly like a bird, like a bat. Vatu stills my wings and stretches them out. Effortlessly, we float over the land.

Where are we going?

"Fadu. We will be there soon."

I pray again that she is running, but how can anyone outrun the wings of darkness? I can see the furnaces of Fadu burning before us, and we tilt and lose both height and speed. We spiral down and down until we land.

I am in the same room that I was taken to and pushed through the portal of shadow. The room is not empty. Palaia is here. He is sleeping. He is not alone. The darkness gathers and shrinks around me. I am now only man sized, only man shaped.

The room starts to shake, plaster falls from the walls and ceiling, a lantern tips. One of Palaia's sleeping companions wakes and screams. She covers herself with a sheet. Vatu brings shadows around her and crushes her in an instant. Her broken body slumps to the floor, and her blood and ichor stain the ground. It is chaos. There are shouts for guards, and handmaids running to and fro.

Darkness solidifies in the room. Darkness crystallizes. Darkness stills everyone, trapping them in black amber, freezing them in black ice.

"You have failed me."

Palaia cannot speak.

"You have let her escape. You must tell me everything."

Palaia cannot speak, yet I can hear his thoughts. Is it because Vatu is in my mind and his? I hear him.

"Please, Master," he says without words. "What do you mean? I came for the prisoners as soon as I could. I could see it was them. I saw her glowing with my own eyes. It was her, I swear it."

I can see with Palaia's eyes. No, not his eyes. I do not see blackness. Instead, I see myself being dragged before him and Alaba. It is not his eyes that see these things, it is his mind, it is his memories, they are being ripped from him.

"Yes, it was her. You had her and then you let her go. You sent me a corpse."

"Master, it was not our fault. She died in the night, alone. There was nothing I could do. Nothing, I cannot bring her back from the dead. I knew you would kill her anyway. I knew she would perish at your command. I could not bring her back. There was nothing I could do." Palaia continues to beg for his life, for forgiveness, to plead. Does he not know the darkness has no forgiveness, heeds no plea, grants no request? Are they all fools in the outer court?

I can no longer hear Palaia's thoughts. Instead, I can see darkness, a cell. It is my cell. I am sitting in a cell not far from where I now stand. I am sitting, waiting through the night. I am praying that the gods may be kind. I can see only darkness, but Erroi is there. He tells me he will save her, he tells me to come. I tell him no, that I must stay, or Vatu will come after her. The fullness of my betrayal is made plain. My thoughts are sifted through a black sieve, but they fall through like ash, leaving nothing. Vatu does not find what he seeks. I cannot tell what I do not know. Surely now he will slay me. Now I will have my release. May the gods be kinder in the next life.

But I do not die. Instead, the darkness returns to me. Light fills the room. It seems so bright now, but it is only the absence of darkness that makes it seem so. Palaia falls to the floor. I can hear him sobbing. I can hear him gagging and choking, I see that darkness is in his mouth and in his lungs. Suffocation is an easy death. I had thought Vatu would be harsher.

"We have not the time for more, unless you wish it."

What is he saying?

"Will you spare him?"

He is toying with me.

"I will let him live if you wish it."

Really, I can save him, just by a word? I can save him. Do I wish it? I have no reason to be merciful, to be kind.

"There is no need for him to die," I say. Vatu has given my lips leave to speak.

"That is not what I ask."

Hate is a hard thing to find within you. It is just, but it is not kind. I hate Palaia. I hate him for his arrogance, and for the blows I received at his command and from his hand. I hate him for his weakness and pettiness. I hate him for his greed and for his fear. Is hate reason enough to kill? Is hate reason enough for unkindness? Hate is not reason, it is unreason. I could spare him. I could let him live while my daughter will die, I will die. I could let him live and he will return to the outer court to bully and steal and plot. Live, what a word. What is it to live? Now this is my gift. I can let him live. Is death a gift? I could give him death.

"Let him live." It is decided. I have slain many, but never at my wish. I have slain those that Vatu and the law demanded, not all of them, all but one, all but two.

Palaia stops choking and is able to breathe. He stands up and holds his hand to his throat. When he sees me, he is amazed, but he sees only me. He is blind.

"You," he says. "How are you doing this? Why are you doing this? Seize him!"

I had not thought him such a fool. Does he think I will be overpowered by his prostitutes? Even without the darkness in me, they would be no threat. Vatu moves me to speak.

"Bow! Do you not recognize your master? He has spared your

life."

Darkness drags Palaia to his knees.

"I am not your enemy," I say. "No one is your enemy. Vatu is here. He is looking for what you have lost and for what I have stolen from him."

"I have stolen nothing."

"I never said you did. He wishes to find my daughter. She is with a dark man. I know him as Erroi. There may be others with him." Vatu searches my mind.

"There may be a boy with him, he is small and fair. His name is Mukito. He is of no importance. And a soldier, a tall, good-looking man. His name is Zintoa, he is foolish. He was with them before they were taken to my tower."

"I know Zintoa, he was here. He travelled with the prisoner from Riga. He asked to join my company. As far as I know, he is here."

"He is not here, I would know him. The prisoner told him to run. The soldier is a fool, but he has had good advice. Where is he now?"

Palaia looks bewildered. "Let me call the guards, maybe they will know."

There is no need to call them. They are banging on the door. I look towards it.

"Open." The door obeys my command, and the soldiers rush into the room.

"Stop."

The soldiers obey my command and stop.

"Zintoa," says Palaia hoarsely. "Where is Zintoa?"

"You mean the lad from Riga? Gone. He changed his mind about coming with us. Said he had a girl back home that he wanted to see. Said he was missing her, that she had written a letter, took his pay and left."

I turn black-filled eyes towards the sergeant.

"He left this for you, you were gone before I could give it to you," the sergeant continues, and fumbles in his belt. He hands me a small bag. How does the sergeant have the courage to approach me? I am impressed. The bag is filled with herbs to sweeten foul water. Even now, filled with darkness, I smile. Small kindnesses are kindnesses none the less.

Vatu rakes through their minds, but Zintoa has said only that he will travel to Riga and that he will see a girl. I guess the girl he speaks of is his sister or perhaps that is where Alaba is. Vatu knows this, too. I cannot hide it from him. I can hide nothing from him.

"We can search for him," says Palaia. "We will find him. We will catch him before he gets to Riga. He has only been gone a day, he will not have gone far."

I silence him. We are not gentle. But the sound of a fool is distracting. Vatu has eaten his tongue. Now Palaia is making mute noises as we leave the room. The guards try to follow us, but we melt into shadow and are gone.

Are they still in the city? Only if they are fools. Erroi is not a fool. They will be gone. I pray that they are gone.

"I will find them. They will not escape."

I cannot doubt it. How can anyone escape from the dark? We are in Fadu now, in the square. I, we, he is standing in a darkened square lined by windowless buildings. I look around. Where to begin?

"We begin here."

I can feel darkness seeping out across the city. It creeps through doorways, it enters cracks, and it speaks with shadows. Darkness spreads out, seeking what belongs to it.

"She does not belong to you."

"Nor to you either, but I will make her mine, just as you sought to make her yours."

"She is my daughter."

"Is she?"

I will not answer. I will not let darkness sow doubt. But then, if she is not my daughter, would I do anything different? I hope not. I hope I would do everything the same.

"You would not."

The darkness has returned. It has found nothing.

"They are not here," our voices sound.

"I will find them."

"Perhaps she is dead. She was ill when I left her."

"If she were dead, she would be here, they would be here."

"Perhaps it is not as you think. Perhaps she is dead and they are gone. Perhaps the soldier has gone to Riga. It is possible."

"You saw the boy, Mukito, here. He would be here if she were dead."

"How would the soldier know where to find them? He has gone to Riga, like I told him. The boy is nothing, he was here before I arrived, why should he stay?" My mouth is stilled by darkness.

"We shall find out. We will find them all. We will find her. They are not here. We will find them."

Again, dark wings are spread and I leap into the night sky. The moon will rise soon. When the light of the moon shines, we will see them. They cannot escape. Where, what way to go? There are twelve points to a compass, which way will they go?

"You would go to Riga?"

I nod, I am still unable to speak.

"You think that it is the most obvious way to go and therefore the least likely. You try to trick me still."

Vatu lets the dark bindings fall from my mouth. "I am not with them. They will be led by one wiser than me."

"Wiser or more foolish, it makes no difference. The boy will go to the City of the Sun. He thinks he can save you from me. He has come this far to save you, he will not stop now. Is that wise, you think?"

"The boy is not alone, it will not be his decision."

"You think the dark man is with them, Erroi. You think he will lead them. You think he is wise. He will not go to the City of the Sun. He came as a thief and fled like a thief. He will not try to best me again. He will not escape again."

How did he get there? How did he escape? How can he keep the Sun hidden? Sometimes even the box of Vatu was barely sufficient to keep the Sun hidden. How can this man keep the Sun secret?

"It is no matter. He will not escape. I will find him."

The moon is rising over the horizon. Moonlight is casting long shadows across the dark land. It shines directly into my face. It brings gentle warmth to the cold air around me.

"Are you cold?" Vatu wraps me in dark folds, but they have no warmth. I am cold. I am cold and tired. Vatu lets me close my eyes for a moment.

"Flesh is so weak. How do you bear it?"

"Because I must. I have no other choice."

"Really? You could escape whenever you like. Not now, of course, but before. It takes nothing to die. You should know, you have slain thousands. You think that to take these lives is wrong, but you have been merciful. In the end, you have given them all peace. I often wonder why you do not all die. Do you wish me to be merciful? Do you wish to die?"

"Would you be so merciful? Or would I be reborn once more?"

"I might. It might be enough just to let you go. I could let you plummet from here. You would not survive."

He is correct, I could not survive. I look around and see the moonlight through clouds. I feel cool air on my face, I feel pain and worry, I feel hope. Why do I not wish to die? It is a mystery, a divine mystery. If I died, what then, would the next world be free of pain and worry? Is it not right that I worry? Is this not the thing that saves me, to care for others? It is the thing that relieves my pain. I cannot go into the next life ignorant of the fate of those I love. I cannot desert them. I will not desert them.

"You can do nothing for them. You should die."

"I can pray for them."

Vatu's laughter fills the air like the monstrous song of a dark, demonic bird. I see below me, flocks of birds rise from the forests and fields and take flight. They too think it is the song of a great predator. They are not wrong.

"You are mocking me."

"No," I reply.

"Very well then, live. You will regret it."

Vatu stretches my wings. We soar and swoop through the air. The blood in my veins rushes to my head and to my hands and feet. The skin of my face is pushed back into a bizarre grimace. I want to close my eyes, but Vatu will not permit it. It is terrifying, and I scream in fear, yet there is also pleasure. It is good to live, even now.

"Look, torches, moving. That is the road to Riga, or at least it is in the direction of Riga. It could be them."

"It could be, but so many?"

"They could have met up with others and be travelling with them."

"What others would be travelling when the moon is just rising?"

"All the more reason to look, to be sure."

"Very well," I agree, and swoop and circle downward towards the little trickle of light crawling across the dark landscape, like a caterpillar. I let the shadows billow out in a great black parachute and drift downwards. I flow down like a black river, like a black rain. I land in front of the travellers, and draw Vatu back inside me.

The lead rider startles and draws his horse to a halt. He is speechless, and I cannot blame him. He dismounts and bows. I recognize him.

Of course you do, it is the soldier who brought you to Fadu.

Then we have found them.

No, not him, the other ones. This must be them returning home. You knew this and brought us here to waste time.

My prayers have been answered then.

You took a risk. It might have been them, and then I would have found them.

Life is risk. Is that why it is so short? We do not have time for this.

"It's you." The soldier has recognized me. What was his name? Borroka. I see the girl is here too. She has not murdered him, not yet. Why is he afraid?

We come from the sky in clouds of darkness and you can ask that?

No, it is something else, he is remembering the wagon he stole from me. He is thinking I am angry because he confiscated my wagon when he arrested me. Why is he worried about that? Does he think these things are important to me now?

"How may we help you?"

"I am looking for your friend."

"My friend," he says, startled. He thinks I mean Juana. He thinks I will take his whore from him. Juana comes forward.

"Not her, Zintoa."

He is relieved, and when I look at her, so is the whore.

"He's not here."

"I am looking for him."

"He stayed with Palaia. He stayed with you. I think he wanted to help you. We all did. We wanted to help you and the girl, but we couldn't."

I will let it pass, this admission of disloyalty. It is of no importance, not now.

"He has left them. He says he is returning to Riga. He says there is a girl there he wishes to see."

Juana bristles at this. Even now, she would wish that he was hers, or at least could be hers. Can she not see the boy had no interest in her? He had eyes only for one, and she was unobtainable. I frown to think he is with her now. A father always has concern for his daughter. They are not alone. They may not be together. She will be with Mukito, and Erroi.

"He had no girl. I'm not saying there couldn't be one, but Zinty was a bit slow that way. I don't think he even figured that she'd taken a liking to him." Borroka indicates the whore. "Anyway, if he were headed for Riga, he'd be behind us."

"Unless he is travelling with the dark man," Juana says. "The man who killed Gutiza."

She is right. They could be at Riga already. They could be anywhere.

"We should go there."

"Why? They could be anywhere."

They could be anywhere. They could be at Riga.

It does not matter, we will find them.

"Come," I say, and I let the darkness stretch out and take them. We are wrapped in a column of darkness, and silently torpedo through the air. We are pushed back hard by the speed of travel. The air is thin, and we cannot speak. Juana vomits, and her spew trails out behind her. It is bare moments till the pillar of darkness stops, and we are thrown down. We are standing before the Lord Mayor's house. Once again, I am struck by how mean it is, low and with few windows. It is barely different from the other mean homes of the town. I recover my breath, and Vatu shouts with my mouth. Guards come. They look uncertain and confused. They are pointing spears at us.

"Best put them away, lads," says Borroka as he gets to his feet. "They won't do you much good, and anyway, you know me. I'm not trouble, at least except to myself."

"What's happening, Sarge, what's going on? How come you got here out of nothing?"

"Just a little visit, lads, from him."

"Who is he?"

"Good question. I knew him as Utas, but I'm not sure that's his real name."

"Are you a fool?" snaps Juana. "Can't you see who this is? It's him, or at least it's him as well. Vatu, great spirit of darkness, keeper of the Sun. Utas is gone. Vatu has eaten him. Eaten his insides, there's nothing left of him. I knew him too, as good as you or better. Utas is dead. This is just a glove for the darkness."

A tear forms at my eye. It is true. I am dead, or at least trapped. My mind is caught in black pitch. I can struggle, but I am drowning, I am weaker. I am as good as dead.

I told you I would be merciful.

Is this mercy?

"Utas is not dead, not until I say so. He will die. All who are unfaithful will die."

"We all die, faithful or otherwise."

Vatu turns inwards towards me and hisses in my brain. *Be silent, I did not give you leave to speak.*

"If I am not dead, I will speak. I will struggle until I can struggle no more."

"As you wish."

I turn to the soldiers. They are standing wide-mouthed and their spears are slack in their hands. "Take me to the Lord Mayor, no, the

Lady Mayor." I remember that Gutiza is dead. "Bring them," I say, indicating Borroka and Juana.

The guards lead the way. They open the door and lead me up into a large, but bare chamber. It is poorly lit, but there is a large fire at one end. It is pleasantly warm.

A woman enters from a doorway and sits on a large chair by the fire. I motion to the guard, and he pulls her to her feet. He tries to be neither too rough nor too gentle.

"I did not give you leave to sit," I tell her. "I have questions for you."

"Who are you?"

I allow the darkness to enter my eyes. It is answer enough. She falls to her knees. She is not as foolish as I thought. I remember her husband. He was a fool. I see now why they were so ill matched. She should have killed him years ago.

"We seek travellers who may be here. One is a dark man; he is sometimes called Erroi."

She makes no attempt to lie or to protect herself. "He was here and now has gone. He came a few weeks ago. He is a hunter, he says. I bought a great cat skin from him, and the teeth. It was clear he was more than a hunter. I asked him to slay my husband. I had tired of him. He was a fool, and he humiliated me by sleeping with whores. Yesterday, the hunter returned. My husband is dead. I paid him. I would have had him stay longer, but he refused. I do not know where he has gone. My guards tell me he left with four other travellers, one boy and two girls. The other is a soldier that worked for me. He is called Zintoa. I assume he has deserted his commission. They tell me the boy was here before. The first time the dark man came, he was with him. The girls are not known to me."

Her answer pleases me. "Rise."

She rises to her feet, but keeps her head bowed and her eyes averted.

"The guard has family here?"

"Yes. Do you wish them brought for questioning?"

"No, they will know nothing. Erroi will have made certain of that."

"Great spirit, had I known they were traitors, I would have had them slain. Riga does not harbour traitors."

"You were not to know. Besides, I doubt you would have been able to slay them, they are more than they seem." See, I can be merciful. "Your husband is dead?"

"Yes, great spirit, at least so I am informed. I have no reason to doubt it."

"He's dead, all right," says Borroka. "I saw him die."

"Was it painful?" asks the Lady Mayor with greedy eyes.

"It was quick, but yes, it was painful."

"The dark man slew him. He thinks I poisoned him, but I never. I would have, though, he was a pig."

"Who are you?"

Juana shrinks back. She should not have brought attention to herself. Now her enemy sees her.

"Who are you?" the Lady Mayor says again.

"Nothing, no one, his," says Juana, and points to Borroka.

"Great spirit," says the Lady Mayor, "grant that I may replace my fallen husband as Lord Mayor."

Why do they squabble over petty things? Does she really covet this cold, drafty hall at the edge of the dark lands?

"It is normal for the sergeant to take responsibility until a new Lord Mayor is appointed. It should be my husband that is acting Lord Mayor," interjects Juana.

I see now. If the Lady Mayor is appointed, she will have Juana killed. If Borroka is appointed, Juana will have her rival killed.

"Are you married? Either way, she is still a whore," says the Lady Mayor to Borroka. "I am now a widow. It might be a convenient union."

Now Borroka is caught. He must decide. He can throw his lot in with the lady, but if he does not and she is made Mayor, he too will perish. He would have been killed anyway. The lady could not risk him being resentful at the death of his lover. Be wise, Borroka, remember the fate of her last husband. If he was beneath her, how much further do you think a common soldier would be? Do you really think she will be kinder to you?

This is amusing, I decide not to stop them. Borroka hesitates. He knows he is caught. Perhaps he is thinking the Lady Mayor is a better option than Gutiza's castoff whore.

Juana does not hesitate. She knows her life is hanging by a thread. She is quick. She must have had the knife hidden in her robe. She pushes it into the Lady Mayor's throat. Blood spills down and stains her gown. It is a surprisingly fine gown for such a mean town. It is quite beautifully embroidered with coloured silks. She must have lived in the outer court at one time. No wonder she hated Gutiza, if his stupidity brought her here.

The Lady Mayor slumps to the ground. She puts a hand to her

throat. It is useless, the life blood flows from her. She dies quickly, and in some pain. Borroka and the guards have taken hold of Juana. Now they are looking to me to decide what should happen. Will I let the murderer go unpunished? Did I wish to confirm the Lady Mayor in power?

"What have you done?" hisses Borroka. "You murdered her."

"It was not murder," says Juana. "She would have killed me if she could, and you too, husband. Even if you had left me for her, she would not have let you live."

She is right. I cannot argue with her logic. Even if I had let Borroka take charge, she would simply have killed him and taken over. She would have had many ways to kill a simple soldier if she has lived in the outer court.

"Great one, what will you have done with her?"

As if I am interested in their petty squabbles. Let them do as they will. I have other things to do. Let them deal with trivial things themselves. I turn and leave.

"They have escaped."

"For a while. They were here a day ago. We are close."

"They could be anywhere."

"They could be, but they are not. They are near."

I walk through the narrow streets of the town. When I get to the gate, a soldier shouts at me to halt. I walk on, and he comes running after me. I turn and let the darkness flow out of me. He stops, and I continue on my way undisturbed.

The moon is now high, it's a full three quarters out. It is waning and tomorrow will be brighter and warmer.

"Where now?" I ask. But I do not reply, the darkness urges me on. It leads me on.

I walk on. *I will find them.*

"We must keep going."

The moon is now high. Moonlight streams across the moor. We have walked for hours.

"We should have brought horses, my feet are sore," complains Eskanza.

I say nothing, but part of me agrees. My feet are also sore.

"Mukito and Alaba cannot ride fast enough. It would be a waste of time buying horses and getting them ready. Besides, we can travel ways that you cannot take a horse."

I open my mouth to protest, but before I can speak, Zintoa interrupts. "You'd be hard put to get five horses for sale in Riga. The army have horses, and some of the merchants, but not all of them, and of course, even if they have them, they might not sell them."

Eskanza laughs. "I was not thinking of buying them," she says.

"In that case, I'm glad we didn't take them. I know things are different now, but I've never stolen anything in my life and I don't want to start now."

"I doubt the dark man and the boy would need your help. Mukito is a bandit."

"No, I'm not, and neither is Erroi."

"Really? Then what are you?"

Again, Zintoa interrupts before I can answer. "Friends, they are my friends and Alaba's friends. I thought they were your friends too. They saved your life, maybe twice. I've never seen either of them steal anything."

Eskanza frowns.

"We need to keep going," says Zintoa.

"Why? He will catch us eventually."

"You don't need to stay with us if you don't want to. You could go back to your old life, or head back to Riga and start a new one," I tell Eskanza.

"Yes, you could go back and stay with my parents. They'll take you in until this is all over."

Again, she frowns. "No, if I go back, they will take me. If I go to your parents, they will take them, too. They may have taken them already. If they take me, I will be tortured. Of course, I will tell them everything I know before they start, but it will make no difference, they will still torture me. They will torture all of us and then kill us. If we are lucky, we will be pushed from the Tower of the Sun. If we are unlucky, we will be exposed and burned by the Sun."

"You're cheerful."

"Yes, actually, I am. I am here walking in the wilderness right at the edge of the Sun's reach with two bandits, a sick, glowing girl and a soldier. What could be better?"

"We must keep going," says Erroi.

I look ahead. I can see nothing but low scrub stretching out ahead of us. "Where are we going?"

"To the mountains."

I can see the mountains rising up ahead. They are like blunt, black teeth. They are far away. It will take days to get there. Do we have days before the shadow finds us?

"We will never make it." I had not thought to say the words out loud, but they come out anyway.

"Yes, we will." To my surprise, it is Eskanza who speaks. No one answers. Instead, we push forwards with renewed vigour. We will make it, and even if we are taken, we will have done something.

Erroi has led us off the track. We are wading through thick brush. It comes up to our knees and sometimes to our waists. The brush is thick and wiry. It tangles around us as we push through. Sometimes it whips back and catches us. All of us have scratches on our legs where needle-like leaves have caught our flesh.

"We should have stayed on the road, walking through this slows us down too much."

"If we stayed on the road, we'd be going the wrong way."

"Really? There's a right way and a wrong way? I thought we were just heading out toward the mountains. There isn't any kind of a track, not even a sheep track. I don't suppose there are even sheep out here, but there could be deer or wild goats. You'd think they'd make tracks through this stuff."

"We are going the right way."

"How do you know? It all looks the same."

"That's because you are only looking at the surface."

Now Alaba speaks. "I see. Yes, you're right, I see it now."

"What? What is he talking about?"

"I'm not sure you can see it, but I can."

"See what?"

"Water, I can see water."

"Where?"

"Under the ground. No, not under it, in it, it's flowing and we're following the flow."

"Are we? Why?"

"I don't know."

I look and I can see it too, silvery flows. It is like waves of hidden silver leading onwards.

"We must keep going," says Erroi.

We push forwards. I can see the water moving slowly beneath our feet. I can feel the ground getting moister and moister. It is a good job we did not bring horses, we would not be able to bring horses here. Soon, the ground is wet at the surface. Water seeps into our shoes. Farther on, we start to sink into the muddy ground as we walk. The scrub is more open, which makes it a bit easier to walk, or it would if the ground were not so boggy.

"It is a good job I am dressed as a peasant anyway," says Eskanza. "My clothes will be covered in mud."

"Once the mud is dry, it will just brush off," says Zintoa. "Remind me and I'll show you."

Erroi holds up a hand and we stop. He beckons us forward and there before us is a chasm. It reaches down hundreds of feet, but it is only a few yards wide. At the bottom, we can hear water, a raging river, but even by moonlight, it is difficult to see.

"So what now? We are stuck."

"No, we are not stuck. We go down to the bottom, and we will follow the river. It will lead us to the mountains."

"It looks very deep. Are you sure we can get down? What if we go down and can't get any further? We could be trapped."

"We will not get trapped, I have been this way before."

"So how do we get down? We don't have a rope."

"This way," says Erroi, and he walks along the edge. As he walks, the chasm gets narrower. Soon, it is only a few feet wide, and then the gully narrows to less than a foot.

"Here," he says and steps out over the gully. He places one foot on one side of the gully and the other on the other side. He wedges himself between the canyon walls and starts to climb down.

"Can you make it?" Zintoa asks the girls. "If you like, I think I could carry you down on my back."

"It's all right," says Alaba. "I think I will be fine. I'll go next, if that's all right. I think I'd rather get going than wait here and have the chance to think about it. If Erroi has been here before, then it will be fine, or at least I hope so."

"Let me help you anyway. Here, take my hand, at least until you are into the canyon, then you'll need your hands to keep yourself steady."

Alaba lowers herself into the canyon after Erroi.

"It's not too bad," she says, "as long as you don't look down."

"Me next," says Eskanza. "I hope you're going to hold my hand."

"Yes, of course. Here, take it." Zintoa offers Eskanza his

hand, but she just scowls and starts to climb down without holding Zintoa's proffered hand.

"I don't need any help. I'm not afraid."

"Sorry, of course not. That's not what I meant."

There is no answer.

"Your turn."

"All right," I reply. I stand over the crevice and start to climb down. I brace my legs against the wall and then my hands. I lower my legs and brace them again, then my hands, over and over. My legs start to tremble. It is not difficult to stop looking down. There is not much to see anyway in the darkness. It is like climbing into a cave. The walls are of soft stone which is banded and ridged. They make it easier to climb. There are small ledges where you can rest. In the cracks of the wall, there are short grasses, ferns and herbs, which Erroi says not to hold on to, as you could pull them out and slip. Sometimes there are shrubs which look stronger, but I still don't trust them to bear my weight.

I look up and see that Zintoa has not started to come down. "What's the matter?" I ask.

Zintoa's head appears at the top of the gully. I can see it outlined by moonlight.

"Are you coming?"

"What's it like?"

"A bit tight, but not too bad. Alaba is right, as long as you don't look down, you'll be fine."

Zintoa does not move.

"It's fine," I say again, but still he does not move. "You have to trust me. You have to trust Erroi. You've come this far, what now, are you going to just leave Alaba?"

"No, I won't," says Zintoa, and begins to lower himself down.

"What's keeping you?" calls a voice from below. I think it is Eskanza, but it's hard to be sure. The voice echoes off the walls and mixes with soft roar or the river below.

I continue to climb down. "See, it's not too bad," I say to Zintoa. He does not answer, but I can hear him breathing heavily.

Eventually, we reach a wide ledge about ten feet above the water. We stop here and wait for Zintoa. It is only a few moments before he descends beside us.

"What now?" I ask. I can see that the walls of the canyon have opened out so that there is no way we can climb down further. Perhaps we can follow the ledge to an easier place to climb down.

"We jump," says Erroi, and steps forward and lands in the pool below with a soft splash. Eskanza leaps into the pool and then I jump. As I jump, I can see Alaba and Zintoa following me. Alaba is holding Zintoa's hand.

When we land in the pool, we sink deep into the river. Suddenly, there is light everywhere. It is as if the river is glowing, or as if we are in a river of milk rather than water. I wonder where the light is coming from, and then I see Alaba. The water has washed the ash and dirt from her skin. It is her light that has turned the river into the Milky Way. It is like swimming between the stars.

When we break the water, we swim to a rocky beach. I am wet and tired, but exhilarated. Erroi's hair hangs dark and wet over his face. Zintoa is helping Eskanza out of the water. Alaba is sitting by the water's edge, a figure of brilliant white.

"He will find us now," says Eskanza, pointing to Alaba.

"It does not matter," says Erroi. "Come and help."

He pulls back a tarpaulin to reveal a boat. Our boat is a magical boat, it is lighter than air. It is soft and yielding like flesh, but smooth and shiny. We push it out into the pool and climb in. It is broad and flat with plenty of room, but when we move, the boat bends and flexes with our weight.

"Tie yourself on to the boat," Erroi instructs us, and we wrap cords around our wrists. Then we paddle the boat to edge of the pool. The current starts to get stronger and starts to pull the boat along. Now we do not need to paddle. We are moving very fast. The river bed is full of boulders. The water breaks up into falls and rapids. We have to paddle to keep from being thrown hard against the boulders, but even with our best efforts, the boat glances against the rocks, and when it does, it seems to almost bounce from the rock. If we have not braced ourselves, we sprawl backwards. It is good that we have cords binding us.

The boat is moving fast, very fast, faster than a horse can gallop, perhaps as fast as a bird can fly. Water splashes over us, and we are soaked. We try to shout to each other over the noise of the river, but it is difficult. Gestures are better. Mostly, we point to boulders or rapids, and Erroi indicates which way to paddle. As we travel, we can see the canyon narrow and close over us. It seems we will not go over the mountain, but under it. It is good that Alaba is glowing, otherwise we would have to travel in the dark, and we would not be able to see. It would be too wet to use a lantern, it would get washed out, or worse, tip over and set fire to the boat.

Now we are travelling through caves, and, by the light of Alaba's face, we can see great pillars of stone coming down from the roof. The rocks are twisted into strange shapes; some of them look a bit like faces. We are still travelling fast, but not as fast; the river is broad and smooth and the current much gentler. We do not need to paddle, which is good. I think we are all too tired to paddle. Eskanza is leaning against the side of the boat. I think she is sleeping.

"You should sleep too," Erroi says.

"I can't; not yet, although I'm as tired as I can ever remember."

"Alaba is sleeping."

I look around and see that she too is asleep, although she is lying curled up in the bow rather than leaning against the side. Zintoa is sitting next to her as if he is guarding her. Guarding her from what, I wonder. He also looks tired. He might be asleep too.

"I can't sleep, I have too many questions."

"And you think I will answer them."

"No, I know you better than that, but I wonder where we are, and where we are going."

Light reflects from the rippling water and dances over the high ceiling of the cave.

"You know where you are."

"Oh, and where is that?"

"In a boat."

"Will he find us here?"

"Yes, he would, eventually. But this is not where we are going."

He motions to the shore, and in the brightly lit cavern where the water shines clear and crystal, we paddle to the shore. We pull the boat out of the water. I go to tie it up, but there is nothing to tie it to. I start to carry rocks to place in the bottom of the boat to stop it from floating away. Zintoa and Eskanza help.

"Leave it," Erroi says. "We must be going."

"Going where?"

"There."

Erroi points, and for the first time I notice a low cave. Was it even there before Erroi pointed to it? He enters the cave and we follow him through the opening and there is a staircase, a winding stair of sorts. It is not a spiral staircase like the one in my tenement in Fadu, nor a broad, grand staircase like the ones in the great citadel. It twists and turns seemingly at random. The steps are uneven in height and length, and the ceiling is a dark crack reaching upwards. The steps are not worn, at least not by human feet, nor do they look as if they were cut by human hands. It is as if the mountain has made a staircase for...

For what?

"Where are we?"

"Never mind that now. Keep going, we must keep going."

Alaba has moved ahead of us, but there is still enough light to see.

"Do you know where we are?" Eskanza whispers, and I shake my head in reply. At least I hope I don't know where we are. I hope I am wrong.

"Keep going," says Erroi impatiently. "Keep up."

The stairs are steep and narrow. In some places, I have to push sideways to get through. At others, I have to crawl on my knees as the ceiling narrows and lowers. It is a difficult climb. Eskanza is struggling, and I help her. Zintoa is behind us. He is keeping guard again. Erroi is ahead, pulling Alaba impatiently.

"She's going as fast as she can. Be patient, we're all going as fast as we can. We can't go faster."

"You must, we must be quick. We cannot let him find us here."

"What difference will it make," mutters Eskanza. "He will find us anyway, even here, wherever here is."

Erroi glares at her. It is a stare full of anger, but he says nothing and does nothing except pull at Alaba.

"Keep going, you must keep going."

But he says this only to Alaba, and I hear unspoken the words he does not say; those others do not matter to me, only you, you must keep going. I push on; I will not abandon her to him. I will not leave her alone with Erroi, not here.

"You can do it," I tell Eskanza. "You can do it."

"Is it much further?"

"Yes, much further," says Erroi. "We must keep going."

Zintoa is just behind us. I would let him past me, but the stairs are too narrow. Erroi pulls Alaba around a twist in the stair and we are in darkness. They are gone.

"Let me catch my breath, we'll catch up."

In the dark, we rest. I do not know how long, I think it is only minutes. We start climbing again. Now we are climbing in the dark. It is harder than before, and we need to feel along the floor with our hands and feet.

"Wait," I say, "let me guide you."

Erroi can see in darkness, so I think to myself, why not me? It's just a question of seeing what is really there. When I was blind, things were always in the place they should be. Now it is steps and walls that are where they should be. I step forward. Yes, everything is where it should be.

"Hold on," I say, and lead them forward. We start to make progress and climb. It is a long climb, and we do not catch up with Alaba. They must be able to climb quicker with light, but even so, I would have thought we might have caught up enough to see the light of Alaba's face.

When we eventually reach the top, we are tired. My knees are shaking and weak. Before us is a door, or it feels like a door. It is locked. It is a real door, not one conjured out of the mountain, like the steps.

"It is locked," I say.

"Can't you open it, like you opened the doors at my father's house?" asks Eskanza.

"How did it get locked?" says Zintoa. "If they came through it, then they must have opened it. Perhaps we have gone past them on the stair."

"We couldn't have," says Eskanza. "There was nowhere for them to have passed."

I'm not sure Eskanza is right. Erroi could find a place to hide, I'm certain, but I still think this is where they have gone. I close my eyes, and I can see a golden thread leading under the door.

"Perhaps I can break it down," says Zintoa, and he hammers on the door with his fist. To my surprise, it splinters and falls to pieces before his blow.

"So strong," says Eskanza mockingly. I am not sure if she mocking me or Zintoa. Perhaps both. Probably both.

"Come on," I say, and we push forward through the door.

We are standing in a room cut as a perfect square, or so it looks. I say cut, but the walls are of dressed stone, polished stone. There are two giant slabs of stone on either side of the room; they are set upright like walls and are a little over the height of a man. No, they are not stone, they are black glass. In the centre of the room is a square box. It is hard to say how big it is. Sometimes you look at it and it seems massive, other times it looks small enough to fit in your pocket. It is made of back stone, and the lid is closed. I notice that the floor is paved in gold. Not all of it, just here and there, like puddles. Alaba is sitting on a stone shaped like an executioner's block; perhaps it is an executioner's block. She is sitting with her head bowed and her arms are drawn around her. Erroi is standing behind her; his hands are on her shoulders.

"Do you know where this is?" asks Eskanza, but she knows where this is.

Has Erroi betrayed us?

Chapter Thirteen
Darkness and Light

I have found them. I know where they are; they are where I want them to be. I must go. There is no need to hunt them, they have returned to me. They are in the Tower of the Sun, Vatu's tower, my tower. I must go. I must find them. They must tell me where the Sun has gone. They must give it to me. The Sun is mine. The thief must give it to me. It is mine.

I spread wings of darkness out and wrap myself around Utas. He must come, too. He must also pay. He betrayed me, and for what; for a few days more of life for the girl? How pointless. It will be mine, it will be mine forever. It will always be mine.

I reach up with black claws and drag myself into the sky. I reach forward and claw my way back to the dark tower. I will find them, I will make them pay, all of them. They will give me back what is mine. It is mine, it will be mine forever.

I alight upon the tower. They are below me. Did they think they could hide from me here? It is absurd. Did they think they could hide anywhere? It is absurd. It is mine and they cannot take it from me. They will give it back.

Utas walks down the stairs. It is only a short walk. Now I will be reunited with my daughter and friends.

Are you not glad?

I am not glad, not at all glad.

It does not matter. You will be together soon and perhaps in the next life also. You did not think I would let you go?

Now we are standing outside the hall of the Sun. They are mine. The door opens at my command, and I enter.

"Utas," a cry comes from a boy. He has a name, and the soldier, he also calls to me. He runs towards me. He thinks I have come to save him or to save Alaba. I hope I have. I have not.

Black ropes bind the advancing soldier. No, not ropes. I do not wish to harm him. Instead, I wrap him in black wool, and black tissue. I put my soldier away. I take him and put him in a black box safe from harm. There is a girl. I do not know her. She is pounding on the box and calling his name.

"Zintoa!"

Yes, that is the soldier's name, I remember. Who is the girl? It does not matter. I take her and wrap her and box her up. Now all the toys are put away. It is time for business. It is time to finish this.

I leave Utas. I let him fall to the floor like an empty skin and step forward. He is nothing now.

I am lying on the floor, I feel empty and worn. I turn to watch. I see Vatu growing in front of me. He is a vast shadow, an evil smoke. I see Alaba, may the gods protect her. I will for her to live with every fibre of my being, I will for her to survive. I see Erroi. He has brought her here. Why has he brought her here? Why?

I have seen Vatu enter. He is more terrible than I supposed. He has discarded Utas and tossed him aside. How did he know we were here? Why did Erroi lead us here?

"Why are you here? Where is it? Give it to me. Give her to me."

Each of Vatu's words, his demands echoes through the chamber.

Alaba is sitting with her head bowed. Erroi has moved and now stands in front of her. He stands between her and Vatu, as if he will protect her. How can he protect her, who can stand before Vatu? I will run to her. I will save her.

Vatu reaches out to Alaba. He is like a dark cloud. Dark coils reach forward to surround her. Erroi stands. He draws his sword and black slices through black. Vatu surrounds him. Darkness struggles with darkness. Back and forth they go. I can see only darkness and yet it is a swirling, churning darkness full of strife.

He has forgotten me. I am nothing to him. I am less than nothing. I move forward. I inch forward. I will go to Alaba. I will die with her. I will save her.

The darkness is like a wind, like a tide. It flows and turns back, fighting with itself. I can see nothing, but I can feel it.

I will not let her die alone. I will move forward.

"Thief, thief, the thief must die. Give it back to me. Give her to me."

Erroi dances in the darkness, his blade slicing darkness into shards. But the darkness is not broken, it simply reforms and returns. He cannot win. He cannot stand against Vatu.

I break into a run. I think that Vatu would stop me, but he ignores me. I am nothing to him, nothing. I am standing beside Alaba.

"We must go," I say. "We must run."

"No." It is all she says.

Vatu is fighting with Erroi. They are like two clouds of ink swirling in water. How can he stand against the darkness? No one can stand against the darkness. I cannot stand. I am empty. I look at the boy beside Alaba. He is trying to get her to rise, but she will not. Run, Alaba, can you not see that is your only hope? Can you not hear your father? Obey your father, run with the boy. It is your only hope.

"Why," I ask, "why will you not run?"

Why will she not run? The boy does not run. He stays with her. He is brave, and foolish. They will both perish. The darkness will take them both.

Alaba takes my hand and shakes her head. "Do you not see?"

"No."

What are they doing? Why are they not running? They must escape. May the gods grant that they escape. Alaba is standing up. She has been sitting on the box of the Sun as if it were a stool. Will they run now? She is talking to the boy. I cannot hear what she is saying. The boy is shaking his head.

"No."

Vatu reaches out towards her.

"Thief, give it me."

"She is no thief."

"It is mine."

"No."

Vatu is screaming.

"Give it to me!"

He is a towering pillar of darkness. He has stopped struggling with Erroi. He is shouting at Alaba. I cannot hear what he is saying.

Erroi is still standing. He is still holding his sword. I can see his face. He is beaded with sweat and is breathing heavily. He has a strange expression on his face. Is it a smile? Why is he smiling? He is looking straight at me and smiling.

We stand on either side of the box. It's what she says must be done. I don't know why, I do not wish to die, but if it is her wish, then how can I argue? At least this way we will not die in the darkness, and we will not die alone.

"No!"

They are going to open the box, they are going to free the Sun. They are going to burn all of us. I have my robes, but my head and eyes are uncovered. I will burn to death. It is only just, that after all the darkness I have lived, that I should burn. Vatu will not burn, he will survive. The boy will perish too. Can he not see that he should run? He should take Alaba and run.

"No!"

I will not leave her. Even if I die, I will not leave her. I promised Utas that I would save her, and I can't save her. But I won't leave her. I won't just run away. Where would I go anyway? If I run, where would I go?

"No!" Vatu shouts, but cannot reach over to Alaba. Each time he does, Erroi slices him with his dark sword. He cannot reach.

I cannot reach them, I cannot stop them. They will open the box.

We open the box. I have my eyes closed. I am waiting to die. But we do not die. The box is empty.

"No!"

The box is empty. Erroi has stolen it.

The box is not empty. There is a black feather in the box. I reach in and bring it out. I turn it over in my hand. Why is there a feather here? Where is the Sun?

"Look again."

"You stole it. Where is it?"

Erroi cannot have stolen the Sun. He could not take it, it would consume him.

"Look again."

I look and see.

"Come."

Together, we reach in. There is a layer of darkness, it is thin as ice. It is black ice, melting away.

"No!"

But they do not listen to my cry. They do not listen to Vatu's cry. They break the darkness, they crack the darkness and the Sun hatches.

I am blown back from the box by streams of light, by torrents of light. Rods of light push me and pin me down. I am thrown back. I feel my skin blister and my eyes melt. Like before, I am blind, blind to everything except the brilliant, golden, white light of the Sun. No, not to everything, I am not blind to everything. The Sun melts the darkness. It has pushed me to the corner of the room. Vatu has turned to motes of dark dust turning in the light. Utas is lying on the ground. He is shielding his eyes, and his hair has started to smoulder.

I am burning, I am dying. It is just. Erroi comes towards me. He falls over me, shielding me. It is like cool night falling after a day of fire. I am saved for a while at least. It is not a kindness. Can he not save Alaba?

I can see Alaba. She is not burning, she is glowing. She is reaching into the box. She is holding the Sun in both her hands.

"No!" screams Vatu, but she does not hear, or if she does, she does not listen.

"No!" I cry, but she does not stop. She clasps the Sun to her. It seems to enter into her flesh. It seems as if they have become one. It is as if the Sun has become a new beating heart in her bosom. She is glowing brighter than ever.

"We do not need this now," she says. She waves her hand, and the four walls and all of Vatu's dark imaginings are gone. We are standing in a forest clearing.

We are standing in the clearing next to the abandoned cottage. The ghosts come and hold my hands. "It is over now."

"Yes," says Erroi, "It is over."

"No!" shouts Utas, and runs towards his daughter, but she is rising up and up, borne aloft by beams of light pushing against the earth. Higher and higher she climbs. The morning mists fade away in the brilliant dawn. We are gone; like dreams in the night, we fade into the nothing we are. Our task is done now and we will rest. I turn to the ghost child and smile. We will play and then have tea.

The darkness has gone. I had deceived myself. I will not deceive myself again. I have worn many masks and will wear them no more.

What a wonder in the heavens; a new star brighter than the day. We poor earth bound creatures look up. The gates of hell have fallen and now we are free. The dark tower has fallen. The twelve have withered to dust and will not be reborn. Utas is dust and will not be reborn. The wind carries the dust where it will.

Lento nudges Luzora.
"Wake up," he whispers. All around them, there is a commotion. The people are crowded into the streets. Luzora follows Lento out from their hiding place and into the street. All around them is a soft light and gentle warmth. It is coming from above, like a gift from the heavens.
"What is happening?" asks Luzora as she looks up.
"Things are being set right," says Lento. "We are being set free."

Outside Riga, Zintoa and Eskanza sit watching in amazement as the Sun drifts from east to west.
"Come," says Zintoa, when the Sun drops below the horizon at last. Eskanza follows him back to his house. She has nowhere else to go, but it does not matter, she tells herself. She would follow him anywhere.

Glossary

Alaba: Daughter of Utas, she shines with a silvery glow but the light its fading and with it her health.

Borroka: The sergeant at Riga who takes the captured Alaba and Utas to the City of the Sun.

Cavall: The name Mukito gives to Zintoa's horse.

Erroi: A stranger who is travelling with Utas and then with Mukito.

Eskanza: The daughter of a rich merchant from Fadu. She is escaping from an arranged marriage she does not wish to make.

Fadu: A large town and a centre of mining and metal working. It is both very rich and very poor.

Fribolo: Eskanza's cousin, they are arranged to be married.

Gezuri: One of the priests of Vatu.

Greba: One of the priests of Vatu.

Gutiza: The Mayor of Riga, originally from the City of the Sun, he is exiled to Riga as a result of some past misdemeanour.

Hasera: Poor inhabitant of Riga, he is attacked and injured by capos after earning money from helping Mukito.

Hosta: Zintoa's younger sister.

Irruzura: One of the priests of Vatu.

Juana: Mistress of Gutiza, later mistress to Borroka.

Kilhanga: Stepfather to Mukito, a bandit killed by Erroi.

Kong: Chief of the priests of Vatu.

Kota: A distant town, as far from the City of the Sun as is possible to travel.

Lappura: One of the priests of Vatu.

Lento: Lame brother of Luzora, kills Pinxo.

Luzora: Sister of Lento, tries to protect him. Pinxo attempts to rape her.

Mukito: A teenage boy, his mother is dead and he is being brought up by Kilhanga, his stepfather. After Kilhanga is killed, he travels with Utas and then Erroi.

Palaia: A fish-faced civil servant.

Pinxo: An overseer, he tries to rape Luzora and is killed by Lento.

Pobre: Brother of Hasera, helps Mukito after Hasera is injured.

Riga: A poor farming town. Home of Zintoa and Borroka.

Tito: A soldier from Riga. He accompanies Zintoa and Borroka while they take Utas and Alaba to the City of the Sun. He is an older man and Borroka makes use of his wisdom and experience.

Utas: A travelling merchant and father of Alaba.

Vatu: The dark spirit who keeps the Sun in a box and opens it once a year.

Zauria: One of the priests of Vatu.

Zintoa: A soldier from Riga, he captures Utas and Alaba and accompanies them back to the City of the Sun as far as Fadu.

About the Author

David Rae lives in Scotland and grew up in a world where hordes of workers spill out of factories, a world where fog and smoke shroud all kinds of creatures, a world where ruined castles, factories and houses are haunted by ghosts, gangs and memories. He lives in a world where witches have been burned at the cross and martyrs have been hung on the Gallowgreen.

Since a child, he has tried to capture that world in words, poems, and stories. He has read every trashy novel, every children's book and every comic that came his way. Thank God for public libraries.

He studied Botany, Architecture, Mathematics, Computers, Geography, and Ecology. He worked in a candy factory (not as an Oompa-Loompa), as a scaffolder and ditch digger. He has worked as a draftsman and as an ecologist, as a statistician and as a policy maker. He is married and has four lovely children and now lovely grandchildren. And he continues to read and to write and marvel at the world he lives in.

Crowman is his first novel and the start of a dark fantasy trilogy.